About the Author

This is my first novel — though storytelling has long been a part of my life. I've written dramatic pieces for children, always with the hope of making truth tangible.

But this story... this one is different.

It's the fruit of years walking with God, reading and rereading His Word, it is living, comes alive on the pages, resonates in my heart. Each time, reading through Scripture brings something new, something deeper, something living. That hunger to understand, not just the stories, but the language, cadence, and weight behind each word, led me to begin learning Biblical Hebrew and Greek. Not as a scholar, but as a seeker.

I do not claim expertise. I am simply a worshipper, a student, a believer.

This book is the product of study, reflection, and the encouragement of many hearts and hands. I am deeply grateful first to God, who gave me the title in the night and the instruction to write the story from His viewpoint.

Though this is a work of fiction, its foundations lie in Scripture, steeped in prayer and crafted with deep reverence.

My hope is that through this story, readers will encounter Yehoshua not just as the Jesus they've heard about — but as the living, breathing, aching, rejoicing Son of God... who walked among us. And still does.

Dedication

My husband – Thank you.

To my sisters — Hazel, Pearline, and Valerie — and to friends and co-workers who prayed, encouraged, proofread, and supported me: thank you.

Special thanks to Hazel for her wisdom, leadership, and tireless support.

To Pearline and Joe, for their insight, encouragement, and keen proofreading.

To Valerie, for her faithful prayers and inspiration.

To my niece Christina, whose sharp eye and creativity shaped the final product — Her collaboration helped refine the front cover design, bringing beauty and clarity to this project.

And to Jackie, your encouragement, support, proofreading and laughter helped me immensely.

I also acknowledge the tools and platforms that supported my research — BibleHub, mainly NKJV, Google, ChatGPT by OpenAI, and especially the foundation of my Biblical Hebrew studies.

To all who walked this journey with me — in prayer, in spirit, in practical support — thank you.

Foreword

This book is not meant to replace Scripture — it is meant to draw you deeper into it.

You hold in your hands a story as old as time, and yet — perhaps, told here in a way you've never heard before. These are the words of Yehoshua, known to many as Jesus, told from His own point of view.

It is fiction, yes. But it is rooted in truth, the kind of truth that bleeds, that walks dusty roads, that breaks bread with both friends and enemies. The events follow the arc of the Gospels — birth, life, death, resurrection — but are woven through a lens of imagination shaped by Scripture. This is not a retelling to entertain. It is a cry to remember.

In these pages, you will meet not only Yehoshua, but Miryam, Kephas, Yochanan, and others — named here in their original Hebrew to bring you closer to the world in which they walked. You will enter the upper room, the garden, the tomb... and beyond. You will hear familiar words made unfamiliar again — personal, intimate, unsettling.

If you are a believer, I pray this draws you nearer to the One you love.
If you are searching, I pray you meet Him in a way that stirs your soul.
If you are sceptical — even angry — you are welcome too.
Yehoshua welcomed doubters, deniers, sinners, and saints.
He still does.

This is His story — written in blood, sealed in resurrection, told with love.

Let the journey begin.

Signed in Blood:
The Contract

Violetta E.L.

CONTENTS

KEY: Character Name

(For clarity, Hebrew/Greek names are used throughout this work)

Hebrew/Greek Name	Pronunciation	English Name	Meaning/Note
Adam (אָדָם)	Ah-DAHM	Adam	"Man, humankind, humanity, from the ground"
Adamah (אֲדָמָה)	Ah-dah-MAH	Adamah	"Ground, soil, earth" (feminine noun). Both Adam & Eve were called Adam until the fall.
Adonai (אֲדֹנָי)	Ah-do-NAI	Lord	"Lord/master"
Andrai (אַנְדְּרַי)	AHN-dray	Andrew	(Greek name kept with Hebrew form)
Avraham (אַבְרָהָם)	ahv-rah-HAHM	Abraham	"Father of many"
Bar-Abba (בַּר־אַבָּא)	bahr AH-bah	Barabbas	"Son of the father"
Bartimaios (Βαρτιμαῖος)	Bar-tee-MAI-os	Bartimaeus	"Son of the Honoured One"
Bar-Tolmai (בַּר־תַּלְמַי)	Bar TOHL-my	Bartholomew	"Son of Tolmai."
Chavvah (חַוָּה)	KHAH-vah	Eve	"To give life."
Chuza (חוּזָא)	KHU-zah	Chuza	He was steward of Herod Antipas. His wife Joanna hidden follower of Yehoshua.

Hebrew/Greek Name	Pronunciation	English Name	Meaning/Note
Dəvorah (דְּבוֹרָה)	Deh-vo-RAH	Deborah	"Bee" The connection to the bee suggests diligence, productivity, and order.
El'azar (אֶלְעָזָר)	El-ah-ZAHR (guttural 'ayin sound)	Lazarus	"God has helped."
Elisheva (אֱלִישֶׁבַע)	Eh-lee-SHEH-vah	Elizabeth	"God is an oath"
Eliyahu (אֵלִיָּהוּ)	Eh-lee-YAH-hoo	Elijah	"The Lord is my God"
Elohim (אֱלֹהִים)	Eh-loh-HEEM	God	"God plural form used for majesty or power"
Gavri'el (גַּבְרִיאֵל)	Gav-ree-EL	Gabriel	"Strong man"
Halfai/ Chalfai (חַלְפִּי)	khal-FAI	Alphaeus	"To change" or "to succeed."
Hallel—psalms Full Hallel (הַלֵּל-שָׁלֵם)	hah-LEL shah-LEM	Full Praise	Collection of Psalms 113-118, included in Jewish services on some holidays
Hannah (חַנָּה)	KHAH-nah (guttural "kh", like loch)	Anna	"Favour/Grace"
Hērōidēs (Ἡρῴδης)	heh-ROY-days	Herod	Greek "song of the hero" or "heroic"
Hevel (הֶבֶל)	HEH-vel	Abel	"Vapor," "Breath," or "Vanity"
Ketuvim (כְּתוּבִים)	Keh-too-VEEM	Ketuvim	Scripture – Writings

Hebrew/Greek Name	Pronunciation	English Name	Meaning/Note
Kleópas (Κλεόπας)	KLEE-oh-pahs	Cleopas	Greek. "Renowned father"
Levi (לֵוִי)	LAY-vee (some say Leh-VEE)	Levi (Matthew, the tax collector)	Already Hebrew. "Joined," "attached," or "joined in harmony"
Malʾakhi (מַלְאָכִי)	mahl-ah-KHEE	Malachi	"My messenger" or "My angel"
Marta (מַרְתָּא)	MAR-tah	Martha	Aramaic origin; Hebrew style. "The lady/mistress"
Matityahu (מַתִּתְיָהוּ)	Mah-tee-tyah-HOO	Matthew (Levi)	"Gift of Yahweh."
Matityahu (מַתִּתְיָהוּ)	Mah-tee-tyah-HOO	Matthias (after Judas)	Same as Matthew.
Mikha'el (מִיכָאֵל)	Mee-khah-EL	Michael	"Who is like El (God)"
Mikhah (מִיכָה)	MEE-khah	Micah	"Who is like Yah?"
Miryam (מִרְיָם)	MEER-yahm	Mary (Mother of Jesus)	"to be bitter" or "to be strong."
Miryam (מִרְיָם)	MEER-yahm	Mary (sister of Lazarus)	Context distinguishes.
Miryam ha-Magdalit (מִרְיָם-הַמַּגְדָּלִית)	MEER-yahm hah-mag-dah-LEET	Mary Magdalene	"Miriam of Magdala."
Mosheh (מֹשֶׁה)	Moh-SHEH	Moses	"To draw out"
Naftali (נַפְתָּלִי)	NAHF-tah-lee	Naphtali	"My struggle" or "Wrestling"
Netan'el (נְתַנְאֵל)	Neh-tahn-EL	Nathanael	"God has given."
Nevi'im (נְבִיאִים)	Neh-vee-EEM	Nevi'im	Scripture – Prophets
Nikódēmos (Νικόδημος)	nee-KO-deh-mos	Nicodemus	Greek. "Victory of the people"

Hebrew/Greek Name	Pronunciation	English Name	Meaning/Note
Noach (נֹחַ)	NOH-akh	Noah	"Rest" or "Comfort"
Paneb (Пⲁⲛєв)	PAN-eb	Paneb	Ancient Egyptian name "My Lord is there" or "The Lord is with me"
Paulos (Παῦλος / פָּאוּלוֹס)	PAW-los	Paul (Saul)	Greek origin. "Small / humble" In Hebrew bible, his name is kept as Sha'ul
Philippos (פיליפוֹס) (Greek: Φίλιππος)	FEE-lee-pohs	Philip	Greek origin. Friend of horses.
Qayyafah (קַיָּפָא)	Kai-ya-FAH	Caiaphas	"Basket Man, Cryptographer, Rock Man"
Rachel (רָחֵל)	Rah-khel	Rachel	"Ewe"
Rhódē (Ῥόδη)	ROH-day	Rhoda	Greek. "Rose/Rosebud"
Ruach HaKodesh (רוּחַ-הַקֹּדֶשׁ)	ROO-akh hah-KOH-desh	Holy Spirit	Spirit/breath The Holy (set apart)
Rut (רוּת)	Root	Ruth	"Friend/Companion"
Sarah (שָׂרָה)	SAH-rah	Sarah	"Princess/ noblewoman"
Sati (Cⲁⲧє)	SAT-ee	Sati	Ancient Egyptian name "She Who Shoots/pours"
Sha'ul (שָׁאוּל)	SHAH-ool	Saul (Paul)	"Prayed for" name change please see Paul

Hebrew/Greek Name	Pronunciation	English Name	Meaning/Note
Shimon (שִׁמְעוֹן)	Shee-MOHN	Simeon	The same as Simon
Shimon ha-Kana'i (שִׁמְעוֹן-הַקַּנָּאִי)	Shee-MOHN hah-kah-NAH-ee	Simon the Zealot	Shimon the Zealot. "He heard"
Shimon Kephas (שִׁמְעוֹן-כֵּיפָא)	Shee-MOHN KAY-fahs	Peter (Simon)	Shimon = "heard"; Kephas = "little rock."
Shlomit (שְׁלוֹמִית)	shlo-MEET	Salome	"Peace, wholeness, or completeness"
Shlomo (שְׁלֹמֹה)	shloh-MOH	Solomon	"Peaceful" or "His peace"
Shoshannah (שׁוֹשַׁנָּה)	Shoh-ah-NAH	Susannah	"Lily" or "rose."
Stephanos (סְטֶפָנוֹס) (Greek: Στέφανος)	STEH-fah-nohs	Stephen	Greek origin. "Crown/wreath"
Taddai (תַּדַּי)	tah-DAI	Thaddaeus	"heart-child" or "courageous."
T'oma (תּוֹמָא)	Toh-MAH	Thomas	"Twin" (Aramaic).
Torah (תּוֹרָה)	Toh-RAH	Torah	Scripture – Law 5 books Moshe
Tzeva'ot (צְבָאוֹת)	Tseh-vah-OHT	Hosts	"Hosts/armies"
Yaakov (יַעֲקֹב)	YAH-ah-kov (also: YAA-kov)	Jacob	Holder of the heel

Hebrew/Greek Name	Pronunciation	English Name	Meaning/Note
Yaakov (יַעֲקֹב)	YAH-ah-kov (also: YAA-kov)	James (Son of Zebedee)	Holder of the heel
Yechezqel (יְחֶזְקֵאל)	Ye-khez-KEL	Ezekiel	"God strengthens"
Yehoshua (יְהוֹשֻׁעַ)	Yeh-ho-SHOO-ah	Jesus	"Yahweh is salvation."
Yehudah Ish-Keriyot (יְהוּדָה-אִישׁ-קְרִיּוֹת)	Yeh-hoo-DAH EESH keh-ree-YOHT	Judas Iscariot	Yehudah = Judah; Ish-Keriyot = man of Kerioth.
Yeremiyahu (יִרְמְיָהוּ)	Yeer-meh-YAH-hoo	Jeremiah	"Yahweh will exalt" or "Yahweh has appointed"
Yishai (יִשַׁי)	yee-SHAI	Jesse	"Gift", "God exists", or "wealthy".
Yitzchak (יִצְחָק)	YEETZ-khak	Isaac	"He laughs" or "Laughter"
Yochanah (יוֹחָנָה)	Yo-KHAH-nah (feminine form)	Joanna	Feminine of Yochanan. Hidden follower of Yehoshua
Yochanan (יוֹחָנָן)	Yo-KHAH-nahn	John (Son of Zebedee)	"Yahweh is gracious."
Yochanan (יוֹחָנָן)	Yo-KHAH-nahn	John the Baptist	"Yahweh is gracious."
Yochanan Markos (יוֹחָנָן) (Greek: מַרְקוֹס) (Μᾶρκος)	MAHR-kos	Mark	Neither Hebrew or Greek, but Latin. "Warlike/ dedicated to Mars"
Yoel (יוֹאֵל)	Yo-EL	Joel	"YHWH is God"
Yosef (יוֹסֵף)	Yo-SEF	Joseph (Earthly father)	"He will Add"
Zakkai (זַכַּי)	zah-KAI	Zacchaeus	"Pure," "innocent," or "clean"

Hebrew/Greek Name	Pronunciation	English Name	Meaning/Note
Zavdai (זַבְדִּי)	ZAHV-dai (like "eye" at end)	Zebedee	"Gift of Yahweh" or "endowed by Yahweh."
Zevulun (זְבוּלוּן)	zeh-VOO-loon	Zebulun	"Dwelling" or "Exalted habitation"
Yonah (יוֹנָה)	Yo-NAH	Jonah	"Dove"

Chapter 1: The Descent

I knew this day was coming.

I Am, was never created, for I am the Creator. Timeless. Boundless. Eternal Spirit, unshaped by hands, unmeasured by stars. But today, I step away from splendour—perfect communion with Myself—for We are One: Av, the Father; Ruach HaKodesh, the Holy Spirit; and I, the Word (soon to be called the Son). Before time, We spoke together in unity. No distance. No delay. No veil. Joy without limit. Love without interruption. But now—I choose to descend. I will wrap Myself in a cloud of flesh. I will enter time, space, bone, and breath. Infinity taking on infancy. The uncontainable choosing to be contained. The Word becoming flesh.

I do not descend blindly. I know the weight of breath, the ache of bone, the sting of rejection, the silence of unanswered prayer. I know the cradle and I know the cross. Yet still, I move toward the womb. Not because I am compelled, but because I choose. Love compels. Mercy moves. Justice demands. Humanity, though dust-covered and defiant, is still Mine, etched with Our image, beloved still. And so, I go. Not as a storm, but as a seed.

Am I ready? For I know what is to come... Ready? Whether I am or not, I must go. I have no choice. If I do not, mankind will not survive. Why do I care so much for a stiff-necked people?

If only Adam...

His sin introduced sin. And yet, I gave them choice. It was My decision, for indeed, I Am. I knew. I knew what would come, and still, I chose to allow it. If only he had seen My heart, heard My tears. I spent time with them. Adam and Adamah walked with Me at a time of day that suited them. I poured Myself into their world. And still, they chose separation.

Still, it was the right decision.

So now, will they choose Me?

We have prepared them; so many prophecies, sent through The Prophets, My chosen ones. Will they discern which are for now and those for future?

I know the answer.

I sent My servants, and they struck many. They killed some. I know what they will do to the Word, to the Son. But they cannot do anything unless I allow it.

And still… I go.

Centuries ago? No. Eternities ago, before there were stars to measure time or breath to count it by, before time itself, I asked Myself a question.

We—Av, The Father; Ruach HaKodesh, the Spirit; and I, the Word—sat in the stillness that existed only in Us. We lacked nothing. We were joy unbroken, love unbound, glory without end. But love desires to give. And so, the question rose, not from need, but from desire:

"Shall We make him?"

Adam. Man.

To make him, we would need her—Adamah. She would be his counterpart, his echo, his equal and his other.

To create them, We would need a place for their feet to land—a world to hold them. So, We shaped light with thought, carved oceans with a whisper, painted the skies with the brushstroke of breath. We laid down the laws of gravity, the rules of rain, the music of atoms. All of it—every galaxy, every grain of sand—was the preparation of a cradle for two souls We would breathe into being.

But We knew.

We saw the future before the first nano-second passed. If We gave them choice, they would choose wrong. If We gave them freedom, they would turn it into chains. Yet, without freedom, there could be no love. Without love, no true relationship. Without relationship, no them.

So, We made them.

I remember the light in Adam's eyes when he first opened them. The awe. The innocence. He laughed before he spoke, and he sang before he knew what music was. Adamah smiled with the sky in her eyes. She danced in the garden's breath, admired the trees, loved life. We walked together, and I called them beloved.

I remember Adam naming the beasts. His joy at the lion, his surprise at the giraffe, his laughter at the small ones that leapt in grass. I remember Adamah's wonder when she first saw water reflect her face. I knew then what she would do in time to come, I saw the sorrow she would have to bear to replenish the earth.

Eden, the garden, a tinted mirror of My habitation, well, so to speak; as the heavens are My throne and the earth My footstool, I cannot be boxed. Nevertheless, I gave them a shadow of My splendour, gold, onyx, bdellium immeasurable, all types of precious metals and stones. Streams of water, vegetation for their food, animals of all kinds for their pleasure, and above all, I gave them Me.

But I also remember the silence after the fall. The sound of leaves under their feet as they hid. The tremble in Adam's voice when he said, "I was afraid." That was the first time I felt the sting of separation, I knew exactly when they would fall, when Adamah would become Chavvah, but even with that, they did not apologise, no repentance given, so I drove them out of Eden.

I felt the betrayal, the sadness of that fall. Understood what they never could...

That sin of rejection continued, even after I rescued them from Egypt, they chose not to commune with Me for themselves and the pattern repeated—what began in the garden, echoed in the wilderness!

They stood at the foot of Sinai, a people trembling, faces lifted to a mountain wrapped in cloud and thunder. The earth shook beneath them—not with violence, but with presence. Fire crowned the peak. Trumpets sounded, not played by human hands. The sky cracked with the weight of holiness. The invitation was clear: *Come closer.* Not just Mosheh. *All of you.* The covenant was not a contract imposed, but a communion offered.

And yet, they drew back.

Their knees buckled beneath the glory. Their hearts shrank before the voice. The mountain's smoke filled their lungs, but it was the voice that undid them. The voice that had split seas and summoned stars now offered *relationship*—face to face. But fear shouted louder than faith. "No," they said. "Let Him not speak to us, lest we die. You go, Mosheh. You speak with Him, and we will listen to you."

It was not reverence—it was resistance dressed as reverence. They wanted the benefits of covenant without the cost of intimacy. They preferred distance over direct communion, safety over surrender. They chose a mediator, not out of necessity —for I longed to speak with them—but out of dread. And from that moment, a veil was drawn—not just over the mountain, but over hearts. A veil that would remain until the sacrifice, My triumph on the cross then, on that day I will tear it in two.

If only they knew; had they chosen Me, I would have defeated their enemies, taken them through the wilderness in a heartbeat. But the sting of rejection continued...

I loved them.

I still do.

And when they fell, I knew... this moment—this descent into flesh—would follow.

Even then, I knew the tree that would be cut for My cross. I saw the thorns that would pierce My brow. I heard the cry of nails before the first hammer was forged, I saw the flow of My blood as it ran from My side. The horror that I would face in separation from Myself!

I see the spit. I feel the lash. I hear My name twisted into scorn. I taste the vinegar. I see the eyes of My mother as she watches her child die—and cannot stop it. I will be surrounded, yet utterly alone.

But still I chose to create them in My image...

And We spoke again.

"If We make them, We must redeem them."

"When they fall, One of Us must go."

"Who will go?"

I said, "I will." For indeed, I had already seen it.

Gavri'el wept with awe. Mikha'el stood in solemn silence, he asked

"Why? What is man?"

The angels did not understand the full cost, but they knew what glory was, and they felt the ache of its surrender.

Heaven held its breath.

Gavri'el turned his face. He could not bear the thought of blood. Not Yours. He thought. Mikha'el clenched his sword, not in readiness but in helplessness—he would fight for Me, but he could not shield Me from this. No angel could.

Around Me, the seraphim dim their fire. Cherubim lower their gaze. The living creatures, who never cease their cry, fall silent. Heaven does not understand death. It has never known defeat. And yet... it watches Love surrender to it willingly.

"Adonai" one called bowing low "Are you sure?"

I do not answer

Ruach Hakodesh, He looks at them as they huddle together. They step back bowing low.

"For mankind's sake, I must. If not, they will be no more"

"Will they understand?" one whispered.

"They will see," I replied. "But only through pain. Through loss. Through Me."

Another angel asked, "And what of Your glory?"

"It will be veiled," I answered. "Not lost. Hidden, like treasure in a field."

They bowed lower, not with full understanding, but with reverence. Even in their brilliance, this love was too vast, too intimate for them to fathom.

"I ask again" Mikha'el said stepping forward

"What is man, that you consider him so high?"

I do not answer; some things are best seen. So, with a swipe of My hand, I show them. They see, but do not fully understand.

I glance at the hosts gathered round—the multitudes who never sleep, the ones who watch the galaxies bloom. My gaze lingers on the place where time has no say, where I have always been. The golden streets, the thunderous praise, the throne surrounded by sapphire and flame; the angels with eyes within and without were still, I felt those eyes pierce Mine.

I pause—not from doubt, but from love. For even leaving this is a wound. Glory does not cling to Me. It releases Me with a holy hush.

I fleetingly look once more across eternity. And look away, toward Earth. The dust, the cold, the ache of time. And her—Miryam. A girl yet to be formed in her mother's womb. I saw her heart. Steady, quiet, brave. Her faith would carry Me. Her obedience would cradle Me. And him, Yosef, through his obedience, she would be protected, loved...

I saw the quiet faith of Sarah, the song of Hannah, the courage of Rut, the fire of Devorah. But none carried what she would. Miryam—hers would be a womb and a will both yielded. Not a throne, not a temple, but a teenage girl. Her courage will not roar, but whisper. And that whisper will change the world. Together, the ones that would nurture the child that I will become, raise the flesh that will be Me.

I will not look back, for go I must—to carry the weight of their sin, their iniquity. But even in My resolve, the ache begins.

I leave eternity behind, radiant and majestic, seated in authority, filled with divine glory. Limitless light, unbroken harmony, the song of angels resounding in the halls of heaven. Not with reluctance, but with reverence. Not with fear, but with a sorrow only love understands. For what is joy without the willing cost? I leave the throne not in defeat, but in decision. I, who dwell in everlasting praise, step into silence.

No more thunder beneath My feet. No living creatures crying, "Holy." No sea of glass or emerald rainbow arched above the throne. The harmonies of heaven grow faint behind Me. They do not fade—I simply step beyond them.

In a breath—or what will soon be breath—I descend to what?

To water that breaks. To a body that bleeds. To lungs that gasp for air. To a heartbeat that can stop. I will pass through the veil of flesh and take on the weight of it. The weight of hunger. The pull of gravity. The ache of grief. I will clothe Myself not in majesty, but in muscle and bone. My voice, once enough to shape worlds, will be reduced to a baby's cry.

Miryam will not be ready—but she will answer anyway.

Her "yes" will not be loud, but it will shake kingdoms. And Yosef—he will wrestle in silence, his honour tested. Yet he will believe the unbelievable, protect what he cannot understand, and love what heaven has entrusted to him.

The sound dims. The light softens. I step from always into once. From endless into now.

I feel the weight of time press against Me, the weight of limitation; the boundaries of space forming around Me like walls, oppressive and heavy. Glory gives way to obscurity, painlessness to pain. Limitlessness yields to confinement. Confined to time, day, night, week, month year. The Infinite becomes finite, an embryo. Bones, to bones. Sinews to flesh. Skin to cover, light to dark, glory to shame.

I, who once dwelled in every place at once, now stretch within a single form. I am confined to inches, to layers of skin and sinew. The One who once knew no boundary now presses against the walls of a womb. I sense the world narrowing—then deepening in complexity.

I descend toward dust, toward cold, toward waiting. Toward her—Miryam—whom I saw, steady as stone. She will not know yet the full cost of her yes, yet to experience the full warmth of her arms. But she will sing, and it will echo the praise I left behind. She will carry Me, and I will carry all.

And so, I yield—not power, but position. Not divinity, but visibility. The uncontainable chooses to be contained. The eternal folds Himself into time.

I, who commanded light to be, now wait in darkness.

The trees stretch toward light they cannot name. The rivers run with rhythm, waiting for footsteps that once walked Eden. Even the stars—they flicker with a hush, as if they too remember the voice that called them forth. Creation remembers, even if man forgets.

Am I ready?

Readiness is not the measure. Willingness is. And I am willing—fully, wholly, eternally. Yet I feel the tremble in the silence around Me. Not doubt. Not dread. But the holy pause before incarnation. I know what awaits: betrayal, bruising, thorns, thirst. I know the weight of wood across shoulders. I know the silence of tombs, the change in communion with God.

I see her—Miryam of Magdala, weeping in the garden. I see blind Bartimaios shouting through the crowd. I hear the breath of the adulterous woman waiting for the stone. I smell the tears on Shimon's shoulder. I see Yehudah Ish-Keriyot . I see Yochanan. I see the cross—and the dawn after it.
I feel their sorrow. I hear their pain. And I remember the prophets—countless ones—whose blood still speaks from the earth.

I see the rulers who cling to power, the beggars who cry to unseen skies. The child hiding under stone walls as war rages. The old man who dies alone, thinking no one remembers him. The woman betrayed by those meant to love her. Their wounds echo through the chambers of time. I cannot unsee them.

I see beyond the now—into a time still to come. A world of knowledge unrooted from wisdom. Where man's brilliance builds towers, but not truth. Where children perish before their names are spoken. Where war walks hand in hand with rumour, and peace is traded for profit. Where hearts grow cold, and light is mocked. I see the chaos, the cruelty, the confusion—and still, I go

For love compels Me. Not as a feeling, but as a covenant. I do not descend for the worthy. I descend because worth will be restored. I go for the ones who do not yet know to ask for Me. For the proud, the shamed, the violent, the weary, the oppressed. For those who mock, and for those who mourn. I go because no one else can.

Why do I care so deeply for a people so prone to wander?

Because they are Mine.

Not yet redeemed but already chosen. Not yet clean but already seen. From Adam's failure to the final cry, I have loved them. Always. And now, love must be wrapped in flesh, must walk dusty roads, must bleed.

So, I go.

The One who spoke light into being now curls within the shadows of the womb.

Darkness. Warmth. A slow, rhythmic thrum—her heartbeat, steady as creation itself. Sound reaches Me, muffled and soft, like whispers through water. The voices of the world I have made, distant and strange. I feel motion, the sway of her steps, the rise and fall of her breath. I am held, cradled in blood and bone. I smell nothing. I see nothing. But I am aware. Growing. Becoming. God, folded into flesh, learning as I grow, understanding the language of limitation, the language shrouded in time...

She doesn't know it yet, not fully, but her soul sings to Mine. I feel her wonder, her fear, her whispered prayers in the night. Her voice, though hushed, is already familiar. She speaks to Me as if I am hers—because I am. Her blood flows around Me, her heartbeat sustains Me, and yet I am the One who knit her together in her own mother's womb.

The paradox is complete: the Sustainer, now sustained; the I Am, now carried. Her love surrounds Me, fierce and unformed. She does not know My face, but she believes. And that belief warms Me more than the womb itself.

I will return to glory. But I will return with scars to redeem mankind.

The contract is already written. My blood, the ink. My body, the parchment. The seal will come—not with wax, but with thorns.

I descend. This is the beginning of the descent.

Still, I go.

Signed in blood.

Chapter 2: The Arrival

The world turns, unaware of what draws near.

Dust rises on the roads of Bethlehem, stirred by footsteps that carry more than they know. She is tired. I feel it in the tremble of her steps, the slow rhythm of her breath. He steadies her, uncertain and faithful. Yosef. My guardian by prophecy, not by blood. The silence between them speaks louder than their words—hope wrapped in mystery, love walking beside fear.

The jolt of the donkey's gait rocks Me gently, though her back aches with each step. Her hands cradle her belly often now, protective, reverent. She hums sometimes. Soft. Off-key. Beautiful. Yosef walks beside her, staff in hand, eyes scanning the road ahead. He's afraid. Not of the journey, but of what waits on the other side. I feel the strain in him—the weight of fatherhood he did not choose yet chooses every day.

The town draws near. The stars shift. Heaven watches. The time of the prophets ripens in every hoofbeat. Mikhah's words echo through the hills, though no one hears them now. "But you, Bethlehem Ephrathah, Though you are little among the thousands of Judah, Yet out of you shall come forth to Me The One to be Ruler in Israel, Whose goings forth are from of old, From everlasting."

They do not know what she carries. But I do. I Am what they have waited for. And the hour is close. How sad that they will reject Me. Nevertheless, I am here for those who will believe.

The donkey stops.

Murmurs fill the air—low, tired, frustrated. A door closes. Another turns them away. I sense her stress, her pain, the discomfort pulsing through every step. She is worried—where will she deliver? There is no place, no room, no welcome.

Her thoughts swirl. *"Were we wrong to come so close to my time? Should we have left the moment the proclamation was made?"* She sighs aloud. *"Is there any point to this wondering?"*

If only she would trust. If only she knew how perfectly timed it all is. Then this process would be easier on her. But I do not force rest. I only offer it.

She walks, stops, sits, walks again. Then stillness. She rests now, reclining in exhaustion, her hand over her womb, yes, I feel the weight of it. I hear her soft breaths and rhythmical heartbeat.

The town sleeps.

But heaven does not.

The silence deepens. The night prepares itself, unaware it will soon hold eternity in its arms. Yosef dozes against the wall. Miryam stirs. I wait.

Then it begins.

"Mum!" she cries.
"Agh!" The scream follows.
I hear it—though I'm unsure if it reaches Me through My divinity or these new, forming earthly ears.
Her cries stir Me from stillness.

Her breath quickens. I feel it—each sharp inhale, each gasp between cries. Her heartbeat races, no longer the gentle rhythm that lulled Me in silence, but a drumbeat of fear and love crashing together. Around Me, warmth shifts to urgency. Muscles tighten. A trembling begins in her spine, echoed in the very walls that hold Me. I brace—not in fear, but in knowing. This is the beginning of pain, and yet, the doorway to promise.

I press My legs on the walls of the womb and propel Myself towards the birth canal.

The pressure builds. The walls close in. Her body, which has carried Me with love and pain, now begins to push Me out. The womb that has held Me begins to expel Me.

Pain—not hers, now, but Mine. I am being crushed, pushed, forced into a world that is colder, louder, harsher. The passage narrows. Light flickers through closed lids. I am disoriented, compressed. My lungs clench, unready.

Comfort, where have you gone?

Sound erupts. Voices. Hands. Cloth. Chaos. Breath will not come yet. My chest heaves without air. The warmth is fading. The cold strikes.

Air—sharp and dry—touches skin never touched by wind.

And the Father? Ruach HaKodesh? Where are You?

Ah... You are here. Just different.

The cry rises—it is Mine.

Yosef, who had been pacing, stops. Then runs into the room.

"Ah, Yosef, wait..." Miryam's mother says, lifting a hand. "First, let me clean her."

Yosef glances down at Miryam, then quickly looks away. He

smiles—wide, astonished—and bends low to kiss her forehead. Gently, he places a hand on her shoulder, and Miryam's mother hands her the baby.

"Yosef! Out, out!" Grandma shrieks, shooing him with a cloth. "I'll call you back when she is decent!"

He laughs as he retreats, and Miryam smiles—pain and discomfort ebbing away, every earlier worry dissolving in the warmth of new life.

The world hears the first sound of the Word made flesh.

I see her now. Miryam. She looks different than before the descent—so small, yet so strong. Brown eyes wet with awe, skin glistening with effort. She takes Me into her arms, as if I am fragile.

I am.

Flesh. Breath. Blood. Bone.

Seen. Heard. Held.

Heaven rejoices. Earth sleeps. The inn is silent, but angels sing. A feeding trough becomes a throne, and swaddling clothes, a royal robe.

In nearby fields, shepherds stare at the sky still echoing with glory. Their hands still shake, their knees still bear the imprint of awe. They run—fumbling, breathless, wide-eyed—toward a promise wrapped in cloth. They kneel beside the animals, beside the straw, beside the miracle. They speak little. What can they say? Wonder fills the space between them.

Sheep bleat, as if adding their own hallelujah.

I Am, and now I cry a scream, mine-not hers. The contract is in motion. No turning back now.

Eight days.

The number is woven into the rhythm of covenant. Circumcision. The mark of the promise given to Avraham. The cutting away, the setting apart. I feel the pain—but deeper than flesh, I feel the gravity of it. This is not only the fulfilment of law, but the beginning of blood.

My name is spoken aloud for the first time by Yosef's lips. "Yehoshua," he says—voice hushed, trembling with something more than reverence.

And heaven leans close.

The name echoes softly through realms seen and unseen. It is not just a name—it is a promise. A thread between heaven and earth. Salvation spoken into flesh.

It settles into the air like a seal. The angels, though unseen, bow their heads. The Father smiles. The Spirit bears witness.

Yehoshua.
The One who will save.

The truth, the door, the way.
The Name given, now carried.

They wrap Me carefully. Miryam's hands are gentle, though still tremble slightly. Her fingers linger near My face longer than needed. She knows I am hers—but also not. The truth of it rests heavy in her eyes, even when she smiles. I feel her prayer: "Let Him stay mine... just a little longer."

Forty days pass. Now we go to the temple. The place where heaven and earth once touched—though they did not know how far it had drifted. The temple, a shadow of what once was. A promise folded in stone. It bears My Name yet does not recognise My face.

The steps are worn from pilgrim feet. The gates tall, bronze, echoing with prayers past. I am carried in—small, swaddled, human—and yet, this temple was built for Me.

The air smells of incense and lamb. Of dust and oil. I feel the press of generations—priests, prophets, widows, kings. All who longed for Me. Some who forgot Me. All of them part of the story.

Yosef's grip tightens as we near the court. He feels eyes on us—Hebrews from the south, some with long fringes, others with weary glances. A carpenter from Galilee doesn't blend in here. But he does not turn back. He knows why he came.

A priest takes the offering: two turtledoves. The price of poverty. Had they had more, they would've given it. But this was all they had. It is enough. For I am not here for silver or gold. I am here for obedience. For covenant. For hearts like theirs.

Then I see him. Shimon. Old. His eyes clouded by years, but his spirit clearer than most. He moves not by habit but by the Spirit. Today, he was told to come. He does not know why until he sees Me.

He stops. Breath catches in his chest. His lips, part, and a sound escape—part laugh, part sob. His hands reach out—not grasping, but reverent. Miryam looks to Yosef. Yosef nods. She places Me in Shimon's arms.

And then, I feel it.

All his waiting. All his prayers. All the whispered hopes of a dying man who only wanted to see salvation before he closed his eyes. And now he holds it. Not an idea. Not a symbol. Me.

"Now, Lord," he whispers, "You may let Your servant depart in peace, according to Your word…"

His tears wet My forehead.

"For my eyes have seen Your salvation…"

He looks into My eyes. Not searching—but found.

"…a Light to bring revelation to the Gentiles, and glory to Your people Israel."

He hands Me back, hands shaking. He turns to Miryam. His words grow heavy.

"This Child is destined for the fall and rising of many in Israel, and for a sign which will be spoken against—yes, and a sword will pierce your own soul also…"

She flinches—but does not look away.

Shimon departs, lighter than when he came.

But the moment is not finished.

Hannah. The prophetess. Wrinkled with time, radiant with hope. She sees Me and knows. She has lived here longer than most can remember—widowed young, yet never bitter. More than sixty years she has waited, —fasting, praying, waiting beneath these temple pillars. Her life, a sacrifice laid down in silence. She has seen kings come and go, priests rise and fall—but her eyes have searched only for One.

She sees Me—and she knows.

Walking with purpose now. Her eyes do not need confirmation. She has seen the shadow of My glory before. Now she sees the form.

She does not ask to hold Me. She simply falls to her knees and praises God—loudly. Others nearby look. Some shake their heads. Others listen, caught off guard by the fire in her voice.

"This is He!" she declares. "The One for whom we have waited! Redemption has come!"

Miryam clutches Me closer. I feel her heart pounding against Mine. Not fear—something else. A weight pressing in from every word spoken, wrapping itself around her soul like a prophecy she cannot unhear.

The priests nearby mutter. They see a young woman. A poor man. A baby. They do not see Me.

But Hannah sees.

Shimon saw.

And the temple now echoes with their testimony.

We leave not through the central gate, but quietly, by a side path. Yosef carries Me again. Miryam walks beside him, her fingers brushing My cheek now and then, as if to reassure herself that this is real.

As we descend the temple steps, I glance toward the inner court. One day, I will return. And when I do, I will overturn more than tables.

But for now, I sleep.

Not because I am weary, but because the moment is full.

The name has been spoken.

The blood has been shed.

The sacrifice has been seen.

The Light has been recognised.

And those who have eyes to see, have seen.

And so, begins the waiting. The growing. The learning of laughter, language, and tears. Though I hold eternity, I now count time by days, by footsteps, by her voice calling My name,

"Yehoshua."

Time passes. I grow.

My legs wobble beneath Me, but I walk. My lips form sounds that mimic theirs. Though I created language, in this flesh, I must learn as they do. My hands grasp hers—clinging to the familiar, the softness of her hair, the roughness of his hand.

We are still in Bethlehem when I first see stars that I once flung into the sky. I gaze upward in silence. Yosef chuckles, thinking it a child's wonder. It is wonder, yes. But also, memory.

One day, I see him mending a cartwheel. I reach for the tool in his hand. He lets Me hold it—briefly. "One day," he smiles.

And then, strangers arrive. Foreign, regal, reverent. They bring gifts: gold that glints like the crown I left behind, frankincense that rises like prayer, and myrrh—a bitter scent for a bitter end. Their eyes widen as they see Me. They kneel, kings before a child. My thoughts stretch between the divine that I Am and the earthly child I have become.

Their garments are fine, unfamiliar, embroidered with

symbols from distant lands. The scent of myrrh lingers long after they leave, a shadow of what is to come. I see the wonder in their eyes, and the sorrow too—as if, somehow, their spirits sense both majesty and mourning.

Yosef watches them carefully. He does not understand it all, but he trusts. He always trusts. He loves Me as though I were his own. His tender care has not gone unnoticed.

That night, the dream comes.

"Get up. Take the child and His mother. Flee to Egypt. Hērōidēs seeks the child's life."

I feel the urgency rise in Yosef before he speaks a word. He wakes Miryam, her family, with trembling hands. We leave under cover of darkness, each step heavier than the last— Me being moved from hand to hand.

We are fugitives now. Refugees.

The road to Egypt is long. The desert wind bites. The stars are cold sentinels overhead. I rest in their arms. Yosef walks ahead, never looking back. He speaks to the other men that accompany us. Angels bring up the rear, unseen. Hērōidēs' wrath burns behind us.

We camp, but never for long, checking, looking, praying. We are safe but I feel their anxiety, rushing the journey from Bethlehem to Egypt.

I, who once thundered on Sinai, now shiver beneath linen. I, who split the sea, now sleep beside it.

And then, the screams begin.

Rachel weeps for her children. Innocent lives taken by fear. Blood cries from the earth again. I hear them. I carry their cries in My bones. Judgement will come—but not yet.

In Egypt, I grow in silence. I laugh. I play. I speak My first words. I learn the sound of My mother's lullaby and the strength in Yosef's embrace.

Some days, mum and I sit under the fig tree behind our home and watch the street children run past, I am not yet 2 years old – almost. They invite Me to join them, Miryam is unsure, protective. Sometimes she allows and I do, little legs desperate to keep up with these bigger children. My laughter mingles with theirs. I am no different to their eyes. But the ground remembers Me. The trees know. The wind speaks softly when I pass. I sense the presence of angels and remember My divinity.

One evening, we go for a walk in the warm air and find an Egyptian boy crying by the river's edge. He has lost his sheep. Mum comforts him. I speak quietly, gently. He doesn't understand My words, but he understands My tone. I look up, his sheep runs towards us, bleating. He looks at Me with wide eyes. He tells his mother something. He didn't speak like us, but we looked similar, hence why I was sent to hide here.

I never forget who I Am and where I have come from. I read early: the Torah, the Nevi'im, the Ketuvim. The words I once breathed through prophets now rest on My lips as a child. I remember the command:

"And these words which I command you today shall be in your heart. You shall teach them diligently to your children and shall talk of them when you sit in your house, when you walk by the way, when you lie down, and when you rise up. You shall bind them as a sign on your hand, and they shall be as frontlets between your eyes. You shall write them on the doorposts of your house and on your gates."

"When you roam, they will lead you; when you sleep, they will keep you; and when you awake, they will speak with you."

I see Them. Speak to Them. The Two who, with Me, are One. Always One. Yet here, it feels... distant. Different. The veil of flesh clouds the clarity of eternity. I remember so much of life before the descent. And even now, I hear, I see, and I speak. But not as before. Angels minister to Me. My divine overcomes the flesh.

One morning, Miryam braids My hair as she hums a tune her mother taught her. Her hands are worn but gentle. Yosef carves near the window, shaping a doorframe. The scent of cedar mixes with morning porridge. I look between them— My protectors. Neither knew the full measure of what they carried. But they carried Me well.

My grandparents did not stay in Egypt, they left soon after we arrived. Sometimes I sense Miryam's longing for them. The wisdom of her father, the softness of her mother. I hold her face, with My soft young hands, rest My cheeks on hers. Hoping, praying that she will rest her worried brow.

A neighbour brings bread. I smile at her. She pauses, her eyes searching Mine. She says nothing, but I feel her wonder.

There are small miracles. A wound that heals too quickly. A fever broken with a whispered prayer. Nothing showy. Nothing loud. But Miryam sees. She tucks each moment into her heart, as if laying stones for a path not yet walked.

Sometimes I wonder what Yosef thinks. He has seen small

things—timely healings, odd silences, moments of wisdom that startle even him. He never says much. But his eyes hold questions he lays down every night like tools on a bench. He trusts the plan, though he does not know the steps. He trusts Me, though he does not fully understand why.

The sun rise slower here. Not like Bethlehem, where dawn stretched sharp and golden across hills. In Egypt, the light drapes the earth like honey—thick, warm, slow. In the morning, the women sweep the courtyards with palm brooms, humming songs passed from mother to daughter. Children chase goats between houses of mudbrick. The smell of lentils and spices drifts from clay ovens, and incense curls from doorways at sunset to honour the day's end. Life moves in rhythm here, familiar yet foreign.

Our neighbours were curious, but not unkind. Some spoke Aramaic, others only Egyptian. Their tongues curled around unfamiliar sounds, and Yosef's Hebrew carried a foreign rhythm in their ears.

Still, kindness needs no translation.

A woman from two doors down, Sati, came often—carrying dates in a clay bowl or warm flatbread folded in linen. She was older, with skin like weathered parchment and eyes lined with wisdom. Her laughter filled our small courtyard before Miryam even opened the door.

"I heard the boy again this morning," she said one day, grinning as she entered without waiting for an invitation. "Singing to the birds like a priest to the wind."

Miryam smiled, wiping her hands on her apron. "He sings everything. Even bread rising."

Sati chuckled. "He will be a priest then. Or a scribe. Or a

prophet."

Yosef, sanding down a piece of cedar he'd bartered for in the market, glanced up. "Or a carpenter," he offered.

"Ahh," Sati winked. "Yes, yes. But his eyes are older than your hands."

That made them pause.

They never speak of who I truly am. Not here. Not yet. But the questions hover in the dust between mortar and thatch.

That evening, as twilight cooled the stone walls, Yosef helped Sati's husband, Paneb, lift a fallen beam from their roof. The men grunted in silence as they worked, sweat darkening the collars of their tunics. When the task was done, Paneb placed a hand on Yosef's shoulder.

"You honour your God with your work," he said. "Not all Hebrews do. Not all Egyptians either."

"There's honour in labour," Yosef replied, simply.

Paneb nodded. "We are more alike than not."

And it was true. The Egyptians prayed to many gods, yes— but they revered the Nile as the Hebrews revered the Jordan. They marked their doorposts with symbols. They passed down stories in chants and firelight, just as Israel did. They mourned their dead with oil and linen, sang over harvests, and blessed their children at sunset.

When Miryam visited Sati's home, she found familiar things: herbs hanging from ceiling beams, flatbread on hot stones, a mother gently braiding her daughter's hair. The customs were different, but the heart was the same.

One afternoon, Sati watched Yehoshua play with her

grandson in the dust. She leaned in close to Miryam and whispered, "Your boy is different. Not strange—just... weighty. Like he carries more than bones."

Miryam said nothing. Just smiled softly and tucked a strand of hair behind her ear.

"We're glad you're here," Sati added. "You remind us that holiness can live among the ordinary."

For a time, Egypt was a shelter. A silence before the song. A place where I could laugh without danger, where Yosef could work with steady hands, and where Miryam could breathe between the prophecies.

They would leave soon—but not before Egypt shaped them too.

The danger fades, but we do not return—not yet.

Then My Father speaks through His angel.

"Those who sought the child's life are dead."

We say our goodbyes. This place of safety and friendship will soon become a distant memory.

Yosef stirs. We travel north, away from Judea to a quiet town named Nazareth.

Nazareth is quiet. I am quiet.

But My time will come.

The Word has become flesh.

One day, I find a common hoopoe that had fallen from a tall tree—or was it a cliff? It lay slumped and twisted. Had a cat, or some other creature, hunted it? In My stubby, tiny 3-year-old hands, I pick it up. Its head lolls. I look up toward the

heavens. I look back at it. It stirs, blinks, whistled its call—
and flies away.

I hear a sharp intake of breath. It is My mother, Miryam—
hand over mouth, eyes wide. She says nothing.

The bird circles once overhead, a blur of cinnamon and
black against the pale sky, then vanishes beyond the
rooftops.

Miryam doesn't speak of it. Not today. But later, I see her
wiping her face quietly as she kneads dough. Not in fear—
something else. Wonder. Memory. The weight of knowing
without understanding.

I look again to the heavens and silently apologise to the
Father.
"My time has not yet come."

One day, not too long after our arrival, I wake to whispered
tones; I slowly open My eyes to familiar faces; My mother
and grandmother sit in a corner of the room; I sense that
Miryam is discussing the bird incident. They notice I am
awake. Grandma picks Me up.

"Yehoshua, you have grown, so tall." She turns to Miryam

"He's too thin, doesn't he eat?"

My mind wonders to The Father, to before.

Their voice trails off.

I tuck the moment into My spirit, like a scroll sealed for later.
Not to be spoken of. Not yet. There is a path still to walk,
wounds still to feel, silence still to bear. But in that silence, I
remain. Watching. Waiting. Becoming.

And the Word will not stay silent forever.

Here, the world forgets Me.

But I do not forget them.

Not one.

Chapter 3: The Hidden Years

Nazareth. Humble. Unnoticed. A town without towers or thrones, without scrolls or scholars. Just dust, stone, and the echo of daily life. A patch of Galilean earth often bypassed, forgotten even by those who tread its paths. Yet here, I grow.

Tucked in the lower hills of Galilee, in the north of Israel—56 kilometres west of the Sea of Galilee—Nazareth rests in a shallow basin. A small, insignificant town. A scattering of farmers, tradesmen, and their families.

The cockerel is our alarm clock, its screeching rising from neighbouring farms long after we have already stirred. Persistent. Overzealous in its duty to wake the world.

Not once specifically mentioned in the sacred scrolls. No prophet ever names it. No king walks its paths. No priest offers sacrifice from its soil. And yet—this is where I am sent to grow.

I search the Scriptures, hungry for every word that I Myself once breathed. Bethlehem is there—yes. Zion, Jerusalem, even Egypt. But Nazareth? Absent.

Nevertheless, the gloom will not be upon her who is distressed, As when at first, He lightly esteemed the land of Zevulun and the land of Naftali, and afterward more heavily oppressed her, By the way of the sea, beyond the Jordan, In Galilee of the Gentiles. The people who walked in darkness Have seen a great light; Those who dwelt in the land of the shadow of death, upon them a light has shined.

And still, My Father chooses Nazareth of Galilee.

The prophets speak of a Branch, a Netzer—growing from Yishai's root. Humble. Hidden. Set apart. A whisper of what is to come. And Nazareth bears the sound of that name. It is not a place foretold—but it is a place prepared.

They say nothing good can come from here. But good is growing in their midst.

The sun rises gently here, not with trumpet blasts but with birdsong and the rustle of fig trees. The air smells of earth and firewood, of freshly baked bread and sweat. Men greet the dawn with hands already rough from labour. Women draw water from wells deeper than memory.

Here, My name is not questioned. I am simply Yehoshua, son of Yosef, of Miryam. A boy with dusty feet and calloused palms. A child among children. And yet, within Me, the fullness of the I Am dwells.

I rise before the sun. Yosef works wood, and I work beside him. My fingers learn the grain, strength of cedar, the yielding of olivewood. I listen as he explains how to shape, not just with tools but with patience.

"Not this way, do it like that." "Well done, son, you are learning well."

He speaks little, but he speaks with meaning, encourages. And he loves deeply.

"Yehoshua," he calls, "come, let me show you where and how to fell the trees that we use. Remember how I have told you which wood is best for which task?"

I, the Creator, now learn from the created.

I want to tell him how well he is doing. Sometimes he seems unsure, but inner strength always rises. We work hard, yet there is always food on the table—more than enough for our growing family. My grandparents are wealthy, but we've never needed their wealth, though they send gifts often. We never lack. Yosef's hands provide what we need. Many of our neighbours have known his generosity, too—blessings shaped by his labour.

I watch My mother, Miryam. She loves to hum while she grinds grain. Her voice is soft, steady. Her hands are strong, shaped by care and courage. Pregnant again. Yosef gleams each time, smile from ear to ear as her abdomen grows. Furrowed brow as her pains begins. Always pacing back and forth, until the cry, then running, laughing, speaking first loudly, then in hushed tones.

My mother is more than mother.

She rises before the sun, even before I do. Her steps are quiet but purposeful. I hear the whisper of fabric, the soft rustle of her veil, the grinding of grain. She begins the day with prayer, not for herself, but for us—for Yosef, for each child by name. She prays as she works. Her hands never idle, yet her heart is always turned upward.

She tends a small garden behind the house. Vines curl along the low stone wall, and herbs grow in the warmth. She gathers figs and presses oil. With careful hands she weaves, spinning wool into cloth, selling it to the merchant who passes through from Sepphoris, Galilee's capital. Her skill provides more than we need. I see the extra coin tucked carefully into the jar, always saved for others—for the widow down the hill, for the neighbour who lost his flock.

Miryam is strength in silence. She speaks little when tired, but when she does, her words weigh more than silver. She guards our home, not with swords or shouts, but with truth. Her presence alone turns away gossip and foolishness. Even the neighbours know— "If Miryam speaks well of someone, it must be so."

But be careful.

One look—a sideways glance—is all it takes to silence us. And if that fails, she'll lob the nearest object in the air with perfect aim to stop any behaviour she finds unworthy.

She looks well to the ways of our household. Nothing escapes her eyes. She knows when Yakov has hidden work beneath the mat, when Yehuda has stayed too long at the well, when Yosi has given away more than he should. She does not scold. She teaches. She draws out truth like water from the rock.

She laughs at the days to come, though they will be hard. She laughs not from carelessness, but from faith.

And Yosef? He praises her often. Not in flattery, but in honour. "Many daughters have done nobly," he says, "but you surpass them all."

She ponders much in her heart, as she always has. Even in the silence, her thoughts speak. She watches Me grow, day by day, and wonders when—if—the promise will unfold. She knows I am not like the others, though I laugh and cry as they do. Though I learn as they do. She sees it in My eyes sometimes—distance and closeness, all at once. I am her son. And yet, I Am.

She observes Me closely, not because she doubts, but because she wonders. Always wondering. She has not forgotten the angel. She has not forgotten Bethlehem, or Egypt. Nor have I.

I am not her only child.

In time, she bears more. Yakov comes first—Ya'akov, thoughtful and intense. Then Yosi—quiet, observant. Shimon, whose laughter fills a room. Yehuda, the dreamer with questions as wide as the hills. And sisters too—Miryam the younger, like our mother, and Shlomit the youngest. Their names are not recorded by man, but I know them well.

We share bread and bruises, chores and songs. They do not know who I am—not fully. To them, I am just the eldest, the helper, the one who lifts burdens and tells stories at dusk. They see My patience, but not the eternity behind it. My gentleness, but not the weight of glory restrained.

I love them. Fully. Freely.

One spring morning, before the sun could stretch fully across the rooftops, Yosef called us to gather our cloaks and packs. "We're going to the water," he said, his voice low but full of something rare — excitement!

We knew what he meant.

The Sea.

It wasn't far, but far enough that we'd need the whole day. Miryam packed dried figs, olives, and barley loaves with care, tucking them into a basket wrapped in linen. The younger ones chattered the whole way, voices rising with each step toward the glint of blue that shimmered between the hills. My brothers ran ahead and then back again, chasing shadows, chasing each other.

By midmorning, we stood on the shore.

Galilee stretched out before us, glittering and alive. Its waves whispered against the stones. I watched the younger ones kick off their sandals and run into the shallows, shrieking at the cold.

Yosef smiled.

He brought out the old net—coarse, mended many times— and showed us how to cast it. "Wait for the pull," he said. "Not too early. Not too late." He handed the rope to Ya'akov first, who threw it too soon. Then to Yosi, who waited too long. Then to Me. I held it for a moment, watching the patterns of the water. I listened—not to the waves, but to the silence behind them. Then cast.

A slow tug.

Small fish shimmered in the mesh.

Shimon and Yehuda clapped and laughed, racing to help gather the catch.

We ate by the rocks, salt in the air, bread in our hands. Yosef leaned back, arms folded behind his head, watching the sky. His eyes were quiet — rested. Miryam dipped a cloth in the water to cool the baby's brow. Shlomit fell asleep in her arms. For a few hours, the weight of the world lifted. We were simply a family. Laughing. Teaching. Catching. Learning.

Years later, I would call others from these shores. But on this day, I am just a son learning how to cast a net. Not to catch men. Not yet. Just fish—and joy.

We play in the olive groves, chase shadows through alleyways, splash in streams. I carve small toys from scraps of wood and tuck them into their sleeping hands. When one scrapes a knee, I am first to bind it. When one cries, I am near.

Nazareth gives Me laughter. It gives Me scars. It gives Me silence. It gives Me belonging—and misunderstanding.

I sit in the synagogue often. I listen to the scrolls being read aloud. The Torah. The Nevi'im. The Ketuvim. Words I once spoke through fire and wind now echo from earthly lips. I honour the rabbis, though I remember the moments when their words were born.

The villagers see Me grow but do not see. They notice My obedience, My questions, My silence. But they do not see the flame veiled in flesh. Not yet.

Still, at night, I speak with the Father. In dreams. In spirit. The veil makes the voice distant but never gone. Ruach hovers over Me in quiet moments. Heaven is near, even in the dust.

There are moments—subtle, quiet—when divinity presses outward. A fever that breaks with a touch. A storm that stills before it strikes. Miryam sees. Her eyes widen, but she says nothing. She treasures it all.

We travel south through the hills of Judah, the air warmer, the soil redder. The path winds through olive groves and across rocky ridges. Dust coats our sandals. The younger ones complain of sore feet, but Miryam encourages gently, always with a song or a story. I know where we are going. I feel it in My spirit before I see the house. Ein Karem, a village near Jerusalem in the hill country of Judea. Her heart beats differently when we are near Elisheva.

She opens the door before we knock, as if she's been waiting—not for us, but for something deeper. Her arms wrap around My mother, and for a moment they are not mothers of miracles, but simply women—friends—family, who have shared wonder and waiting. They whisper greetings, but their eyes say more. Zechariah lingers behind her, aged but steady. The silence that once fell upon him has not returned. His eyes meet Mine, and he nods with understanding. He and Yosef greet each other, they sit, talk, banter, full of laughter.

Then—Yochanan.

He bursts around the corner, limbs strong and wild from the hills. His eyes find Mine and pause, not in confusion, but in recognition. We run to meet, not with shouts, but with stillness. His hand clasps Mine like one remembering something lost. He smells of wind and river stone.

We speak little. We don't need to. Our play looks like other children's—climbing low fig trees, splashing in the stream behind the house, chasing light across the ground—but the air between us carries more. When we rest under the shade of an old terebinth tree, there is silence. Not awkward, but sacred. He leans his head back against the bark and breathes deeply. I do the same. The dust between our fingers seems to hum.

Our siblings gather in their own clusters, laughing, tossing pebbles, teasing. "They're strange," one of the younger girls' whispers. "They just sit there and don't say anything." Yakov rolls his eyes. "You two planning to save the world or something?" I smile. But I do not answer.

Later, we eat together under the vine canopy. Bread still warm from the hearth, goat cheese, olives, figs. The smell of lentils simmering in clay pots mixes with laughter.

Zechariah blesses the meal with slow reverence. The table is full, loud, alive. Yet Elisheva watches Yochanan and Me with a quiet intensity. She sees not just two boys. She sees prophecy made flesh.

The sun begins to fall. Shadows stretch across the courtyard. It's time to go. Yochanan runs to Me before we leave, presses something into My hand—a small, carved reed flute. "Keep it," he says. "So that you remember." I already do.

The road home feels longer. The younger ones are tired, dust-caked and dozing on each other's shoulders. Miryam walks beside Me, quiet now, her steps slower. Nazareth still waits for us, but part of Me lingers in those hills. In the stream. In the silence beneath the tree. In the eyes of a forerunner who already knows his call.

We arrive late. The house is dark and cool. The others collapse into sleep quickly, sandals discarded, cloaks curled beneath heads. I lie awake for a while, the flute still in My hand. The stars above are the same as they were in Judah. But the sky feels closer.

Today is not a day of rest. There is much to do to prepare for sabbath tomorrow, when we can rest from our travel and chores.

The sun begins its slow descent behind the hills, and Miryam lights the lamp. The house glows softly, shadows settling into the corners like quiet guests. The smell of fresh bread and lentils fills the air. Dust is washed from hands and feet, tools are laid down, and silence begins to grow— not empty, but full of expectancy.

She sings the blessing as she always does—low and steady,

like a heartbeat wrapped in melody. Her voice holds the same tone it did when I was a child in her arms, the same tone she used when she spoke to angels without trembling. The table is simple, but never lacking—wine, bread, olives, fruit, lentils, fish when we have it.

Yosef speaks the blessings—his voice warm and steady, more like prayer than speech. He blesses the wine, the bread, the day, the children. He blesses Me. I bow My head, though I feel the weight of eternity whispering beneath the words.

We recline as the Torah commands. We speak of the Exodus, of the wilderness, of promises made and kept. Sometimes Yakov asks questions. Sometimes I answer them. Sometimes I don't. The younger ones grow restless, but Miryam always finds a way to draw them back in with a smile or a story.

We eat. We laugh. We remember.

Later, Yosef reads from the scroll—sometimes aloud, sometimes in murmurs as the children begin to doze. I listen not as a student but as the Author. Still, I listen.

When the house quiets, I step outside beneath the stars. I remember the seventh day. I remember speaking it into being. I remember the breath of the Father over the chaos, the stillness after light, the rest that was holy not because it was earned, but because it was given.

And now I rest again. Not in glory, but in simplicity. Not on a throne, but at the table of a carpenter and a woman of song.

Years pass like river water—slow, steady, cutting deep.

Then comes the pilgrimage.

We travel to Jerusalem, My family and many others. The city overwhelms Me with sound and size. Stones stacked in splendour. Priests in white robes. Laughter, prayer, sacrifice. The Temple—a place I know yet have never stepped inside in this flesh. My heart stirs.

We celebrate the feast. We break bread and retell the story of deliverance. My eyes linger on the lamb. The symbolism is sharp. I feel the future drawing nearer.

The days end, and the caravan begins to leave. But I remain. My parents do not notice at first—they walk among friends and relatives, assuming I am with them.

I stay behind. Drawn.

In the Temple, I sit with the teachers. I listen to their questions, and then I answer. I ask questions of My own— deep ones. The kind that unsettles, not from arrogance, but from light.

They marvel. At My understanding. At My words. At My presence.

Three days pass.

Miryam finds Me. Her voice is tight with relief and rebuke. "Why have You done this to us? Your father and I have been anxiously searching for You."

I look into her eyes, full of love and confusion, and I answer gently:

"Why were you searching for Me? Did you not know I must be in My Father's house?"

A flicker of hurt. Maybe I should have asked them first. It didn't occur to Me that she wouldn't understand My need to learn-relearn. She does not fully understand. Not yet. But she treasures it. She always treasures the words.

I return with them to Nazareth. I obey. I grow.

I take up My tools again. I help Yosef rebuild a neighbour's roof. I teach Yosi how to measure and Yakov how to wait. I mend nets with Shimon and carry water with Miryam the younger. I share stories with Yehuda and sing songs with Shlomit.

They play often—laughter echoing through the groves and alleys. But I… I play less. The scrolls draw Me. The synagogue calls. I sit with the elders, absorbing, learning, asking questions not born of youth, but of memory. When My brothers grow careless in their games, or fight over trivial things, I step in—not harshly, but firmly. Sometimes with correction, sometimes with silence. It on occasion causes strain between us. Yakov, especially, watches Me with a puzzled eye. Not with hatred, but with resistance. They love Me, yes—but they do not understand Me. They want to know when and why I do not pursue a betroth, 13 years now, considered a man.

"The scriptures alone isn't life," Yakov teases, throwing pieces of wood at Me as I work.

I call for Dad. He is growing tired. I see it in his gait.

"Yakov! where is your honour for your older brother?" he scolds, with a smirk at the corner of his mouth.

"But Dad," he responds, "surely, he should be an example for us."

Yosef laughs.

"Yehoshua, he is right. Tell me again, what are you waiting

for? You have rejected all those that I have shown you.”

Mum rescues Me. “Agh, leave him. Let God be his guide.”

The kitchen is thick with the scent of rising bread and the sweet undertone of date syrup. Warm rolls from the clay oven, softening the air, casting shadows that flicker against the walls. Miryam stands at the low table, sleeves rolled, forearms dusted with flour. Her hair is bound in a scarf that’s slipped slightly, as it often does when she forgets herself in work.

Miryam the younger kneads beside her, hands smaller but learning. “Like this?” she asks, her dough still uneven.

“Not quite. Fold it once more, like tucking a baby,” her mother answers, pressing gently to show the motion. “The dough listens to your hands, if you’re gentle but firm.”

Shlomit, nearby, is focused on shaping small cakes, each one slightly more misshapen than the last. She frowns, sticks out her tongue in concentration, then tries again.

“Yours look like sandals!” Miryam giggles, pointing.

“At least mine don’t look like stones!” Shlomit fires back, but there’s no sting—only laughter.

In the hallway just beyond the room, I pause.

The light from the hearth flickers across the wall, their shadows moving like a dance I do not wish to disturb. There’s something sacred here—not because of miracles, but because of love. I lean silently against the archway, unseen for now, and simply watch.

There is flour on Shlomit’s cheek, a streak of honey on Miryam’s sleeve. Their chatter, their laughter—it rises like incense. I do not often feel removed from the moment, but here, for a breath, I feel like both Son and Stranger. It is good. It is enough.

A sudden nudge in My ribs.

Shimon grins, eyes sparkling. "Spying?" he whispers. "Or hiding?"

Before I can answer, he darts past Me into the kitchen, footsteps light as a fox.

"I'm starving!" he cries, dodging Miryam's outstretched hand. "Just one piece!"

"Shimon!" Miryam yells through a laugh as he snatches a warm heel of bread from the cooling rack.

Yakov, Yehuda and Yosi follow behind, and now the kitchen is full of noise. The girls shriek, defending their creations. Someone drops a bowl, and someone else catches it. It is chaos. It is joy.

I step into the room at last, hands raised as if in surrender.

Miryam eyes Me suspiciously. "You too?"

"I'm only here to restore order," I say, though the smirk betrays Me.

"Well, do it while sweeping the flour your brother just kicked over," she replies, tossing a cloth in My direction.

The kitchen erupts again.

Suddenly, the doorway darkens.

Yosef steps in.

Dust clings to his sleeves, his sandals scuff softly against the threshold. He takes in the scene—flour on the floor, dough clinging to fingers, Shimon still mid-bite, and Me standing with the cloth I have yet to use.

Silence.

Even Miryam freezes, a wooden spoon mid-air.

He surveys us slowly, eyes narrowing as if weighing judgment, lips pressed together.

Then he shakes his head.

And says, in that steady voice we all know, "At least tell me some of that bread survived."

The dam breaks.

Laughter erupts—unrestrained, bright. Miryam tosses the spoon at him; he catches it. Shimon doubles over. Even Yakov lets loose a grin. Yosef walks forward, slow and calm, reaching for a piece of bread before it's stolen again.
He takes a bite, nods, then gestures to Me. "Still watching, eh? Next time, sweep first, then spy." His lips twitch into a crooked smile.
Then, with mock solemnity: "I see we're feeding the whole village today... or just Shimon."
A beat of silence—then laughter bursts like a pot boiling over.
Miryam smirks, one brow arched. "They're behaviour is from you. You weren't exactly innocent either. My father used to say, 'If that carpenter compliments my fig cakes one more time, he's going to start paying for them.'"
Yosef raises both hands in surrender, grinning. "True. But at least I didn't trash the kitchen to get one."

The laughter swells again.

And in that small room, with warm bread and tired feet, the

kingdom of heaven touches the dust of Nazareth.

The laughter lingers, like the scent of warm bread—comforting, familiar. I watch them. My family. For this moment, we are only that. No prophecies. No burdens. Just love in motion, unspoken and full. We eat, we rest, we work, we laugh and play...

The world outside is loud—Romans' march, zealots whisper, prophets stir—but here, in Nazareth, there is peace. And purpose.

Years still to come. Silence still to hold. But in that silence, I am not dormant. I am forming. Preparing.

Nazareth remains a whisper on the edge of Israel. But from whispers, voices rise. From stillness, movement. From hiddenness, revelation.

The Word lives here. Waiting. Watching.

The days stretch long and familiar. The rhythm of life in Nazareth continues—measured by meals, prayers, and the creak of worn tools. I move among them as a brother, a son, a craftsman. The divine within Me does not press forward yet; it waits, cloaked in humanity, wrapped in routine. I am not hidden from the world—I am simply not yet revealed.

Seasons pass like whispered breaths. Time folds softly into itself, and life continues, almost unnoticed.

But there are signs.

Quiet ones.

Yosef tires more easily now. He holds his back longer after lifting. His hands, once firm and precise, tremble at dusk. I notice, though he says little. He smiles at Miryam as she brings water to the table, but behind the smile is weight, pain, weariness. Not worry—acceptance. He feels the approaching dusk in his bones. And I do too.

I pray to the Father, Should I heal him? Should I lengthen his life? Though we are grown, we are not yet ready. But He answers: "Let him go. It is his time."

There are fewer games now. More work. More weight. The household runs with practiced rhythm, but I can feel the strain beginning to stretch at its seams. My younger siblings now look to Me not only for guidance but for answers I cannot yet give. I carry burdens, yes—but not yet the mantle that awaits.

Some evenings, after the others are asleep, I sit beneath the olive tree beside our house. The breeze moves softly through the leaves, whispering reminders. I close My eyes and remember Eden. I remember silence unbroken by sorrow. I feel time gathering, like a wave drawing back, before the surge. Preparation is slow, but it is faithful.

He dies before My ministry begins, but not before he has shaped us all. Yosef—quiet in voice, mighty in spirit—leaves this world as he lived in it: with humility, obedience, and honour. By then, the house is full of grown sons and near-grown daughters. All have passed the age of reckoning. We have celebrated each one in our own way—the moment they take on the yoke of the Torah. And now, with Yosef's passing, the yoke of this household rests on My shoulders. I do not resent it. I carry it with reverence.

He does not suffer long. His final days are slow, like twilight. I watch his breath grow shallow, his voice retreat to memory. He tries to rise, even when his strength fails, ever the provider. I hold his hand when it stills. The others are there—each one quiet in their own way. Miryam, our mother, leans over him, whispering a psalm, not to calm him, but to anchor herself. When the moment comes, there is no thunder, no signs. Only peace. Only absence. I do not call him back. Not because I cannot—but because it is his time. I stand, not as the child who once followed him into the hills, but as the son who has learned from the father given to Me. A righteous man. Chosen not to speak My destiny, but to protect it. And protect it, he has.

It is not the first death we have known. We lost Miryam's parents—our grandparents—years ago. That was hard. There were others, cousins, family friends. But this… this is much harder. I feel My mother's pain like it is My own. I hear her sobs in the stillness of the night. The others cry too. all of them look at Me. I can hear their thoughts.

"Aren't You the one? Surely You could have done something…" But obedience to the will of the Godhead is greater than the comfort of one moment. Even this moment. I do not know how to explain it to them—especially to My mother. She believes, yes. But the others? They do not. Not fully. They do not know as she does. They do not carry the weight of angels' words. At least not yet.

The day after his burial, I rise before the light touches the threshold. The tools still rest where he last laid them— chisels dulled, saw wrapped in linen, the scent of cedar still clinging to the room. I lift the mallet and feel the weight. It is heavier. Not because of the wood, but because of the silence. I miss him, My earthly father. I feel an inner battle, pulling Me earthward, but a stronger pull towards My ever-approaching, destiny…

I work as he has shown Me—slowly, carefully, never forcing the grain. I hear his voice in memory more than in sound. Each strike of the hammer echoes like a heartbeat that has not yet fully left us.

Later, as the sun lowers behind the hills, I find Miryam sitting alone, her hands folded in her lap. Her face bears the calm of one who has known both joy and loss. I sit beside her. She does not look at Me right away, but when she does, her eyes are wet, not from fresh grief, but from a thousand memories trying to settle.

"Why" she asks. I look toward her, but do not respond.

"You could have…"

"It is not yet My time…" I interrupted slowly, word by word.

She sighs, a change of pace.

"You have worked harder since he's left…" her voice falters "He would be so proud of you," she says softly.

"I was proud of him," I answer. Thinking how well he did to protect, teach and see Me through to the threshold of My purpose. Knowing, that she still did not understand…

She rests her head against My shoulder. For a long time, we say nothing. The house is quiet, but in that stillness, I feel heaven watching. The carpenter is gone, but the foundation he has laid will not crumble.

The hour draws near.

That evening, the house is unusually quiet. The absence of his voice, his footsteps, his warmth—it leaves a hollow in the walls. We eat in near silence, each of us looking to one another, then down, toward the floor, as memories sweep over memories. We all are unsure of how to fill the space Yosef once held without effort. I catch Yakov watching Me across the table, as if waiting for Me to say something—anything. But I do not. I simply pass the bread.

Later that night, as the stars appear one by one in the darkening sky, I find Myself beside the younger ones. Shlomit leans her head on My arm. Miryam the younger, gazes, lost. Yosi dozes nearby. Shimon talks in his sleep. I speak softly—not a sermon, not a proclamation, just stories. Stories of our father. Of his humour. His quiet strength. His way of seeing what others missed. Their faces lighten. They smile through tears.

And in that moment, I feel the weight of heaven calling Me forward—and of home, holding Me still. I am not yet revealed, but the time is fast approaching. Already, I carry the weight of duty. But it cannot hold Me from what must come...

Chapter 4: Beloved Son

The Jordan stretches before Me, winding like time through the wilderness. Its waters shimmer in the morning light—ancient, slow, carrying the weight of prayers, repentance, and hidden hope. The air is thick with dust and anticipation. Crowds press forward along the riverbank, drawn not by spectacle but by the voice of one crying in the wilderness.

Yochanan.

I have not seen him in some time—since Yosef's death. His parents went first, after he had stepped into manhood and just as his ministry began. They were well beyond their years—aged, but strong to the end.

He is wild. Righteous. Unshaven. Robed in camel's hair. Burning with holy fire.
He baptises with urgency. With conviction. With expectation.

Yochanan's obedience echoes louder than any trumpet. He was born for this—for the turning of hearts, for the preparing of the way. I feel the weight of prophecy settling, not as a burden, but as a confirmation. This baptism is not just a beginning—it is the unveiling. The veil between heaven and earth grows thin. The journey of redemption has begun in full view. What was once hidden in shadow now steps into the light. From here, there is no turning back.

And then he sees Me.

He freezes—knee-deep in water, eyes locked on Mine. For a moment, time stills.

"Behold," he declares, voice trembling but strong, "the Lamb of God who takes away the sin of the world."

Murmurs spread like ripples on the surface of the water.

I step forward.

Yochanan trembles—not with fear, but with reverence. His hands, rough from desert living, clench into fists.

"I need to be baptised by You—and do You come to me!?"

I smile and step closer. The river laps at My feet.

"Let it be so now. It is fitting to fulfil all righteousness."

His hands open. He nods.

He lowers Me into the water—cool, heavy, grounding. I feel the weight of every sin, every sorrow, pressing against My flesh. And then, I rise.

The sky tears open—not with violence, but with a holiness too vast to be contained. A blinding radiance bursts forth like a thousand suns breaking through storm. Light cascades down in streams of gold and fire, saturating the river, the earth, the very breath of those watching.

Gasps rise from the crowd. Some fall to their knees, others shield their eyes, faces turned downward, undone by the weight of glory. Children cling to mothers. The boldest among them weep without knowing why. The air itself thickens—holy, electric, trembling with eternity.

And then—a Voice. Not a whisper, not a thunderclap, but something in between: ancient, all-consuming, echoing from realms unseen.

"This is My beloved Son, in whom I am well pleased."

It crashes through soul and sinew. The rocks seem to listen. Heaven leans in.

The Spirit descends, not merely fluttering like a dove, but enveloping Me—resting and remaining in a stillness louder than sound.

Time holds its breath.

And then—just as suddenly as it came, the moment lifts. The heavens roll back into stillness. The light recedes. The crowd stirs again, forever altered, though many will not yet understand why.

But the path is clear now.

The Son has been revealed.

The Spirit leads Me away—not to crowds, but to silence. To testing. To wilderness.

The heat of the wilderness wraps itself around Me. The stones burn My feet, but I hardly notice. For now, as in the beginning, I feel the communion of the Godhead. We are One again, as We were before the descent. We speak in eternity's tongue—about hidden things, mysteries that cannot be grasped by mortal minds.

Yet sometimes, humanity tugs at Me. I notice the windswept hills, the wadis like scars in the land, the dry riverbeds yawning through the wilderness. Jagged cliffs rise like teeth, and stony paths wind beneath skies the colour of brass. The wind lifts chalky limestone and dust into spinning whirlwinds, scattering it like ashes. These moments are fleeting—The Spirit draws Me back.

"The flesh must rest," He whispers.

So, I rest. Sometimes in shade, sometimes beneath stars.
Day and night blur, but I do not mind. My only desire is to
remain in Their presence. Communion is My sustenance.
I walk where Israel wandered.
I fast where Adam fell.

Forty days. Forty nights.
They pass in a breath—and yet My breath grows faint.
My body weakens, unnoticed until now. My vision blurs.
Thirst strikes like lightning. My tongue cleaves to the roof of
My mouth.
Sleep pulls at Me like a tide.

And then—he comes.
In a whirlwind of dust.
A surge of noise, of contradiction—light and shadow twisted
together.

I am strengthened. Not by flesh, but by Spirit.
He approaches with reason, with the same calculated
charm that poisoned Eden.

"Why are You here?" he asks, eyes glinting.
"Isn't this earth mine? Didn't your own give me the keys
when they let me in?"
I say nothing.

He circles. Then gestures to the stones.
"If You are the Son of God, command these stones to
become bread."

I don't look at the stones.
I look at him. A created thing. Cast out for pride and
rebellion.
My voice is calm, My gaze steady.

"It is written: Man shall not live by bread alone,

but by every word that proceeds from the mouth of God."

He flinches. Looks away.

Then—we are on the pinnacle of the Temple.
The wind whips around us. He leans in.

"Throw Yourself down. They'll catch You. It's written, isn't it?
Angels will lift You up, lest You strike Your foot against a stone."

Twisted truth.
I answer without hesitation.

"It is also written: You shall not test the Lord your God."

And then—we stand atop a high mountain.
All the kingdoms of the world shimmer before Me like jewels on a black cloth.

"All this I will give You," he says,
"if You bow down and worship me."

I turn to him. No anger. Just authority.

"Away with you, Satan.
For it is written: Worship the Lord your God,
and serve Him only."

He falters. Eyes narrowing.
He turns—head lowered—and in a flash, he is gone.

I return with the Spirit's strength upon Me.
Not in fire. Not in fury.
But in presence.

I walk back into Galilee—into villages worn by time, into homes lined with prayers and silence.
Not all recognise Me. But the land remembers.

Heaven whispers:
"Eat. Rest. Tomorrow, you begin to gather."

The river is quieter now. The dust has settled. But Yochanan remains—his voice hoarse, his eyes searching.

I return—not to be seen, but to be present. To stand where prophecy met water.

Then he sees Me.

His breath catches. His arm lifts. His voice, worn and cracked from days in the desert, rises again.

"Behold... the Lamb of God, who takes away the sin of the world."

The people still. Heads turn. A murmur moves like wind across reeds.

"This is He of whom I said, 'After me comes a man who ranks before me, because He was before me.'"

Some remember his words. Most do not understand. But a few—two young men near him—lean forward, their eyes sharp with wonder.

Yochanan continues, quieter now, but no less sure.

"I did not know Him at first, at least, I was unsure, for indeed, I knew Him... but the One who sent me to baptise said, 'The One on whom you see the Spirit descend and remain—He is the One who baptises with Ruach HaKodesh.' I have seen and testify this is the Son of God."

He does not look at Me when he says it.

He looks at them.

He does not move to follow Me. His role was never to walk

behind, but to go before. He stands in the place of transition, the hinge between old and new. And now, his hands release what his heart once held.

Andrai and Yochanan follow.

I do not turn immediately. I walk a little while, letting them consider the weight of their steps. When I stop, they freeze. I turn.

"What do you seek?"

They look at one another, hesitant. Not unsure of Me, but unsure of themselves. Finally, one speaks:

"Rabbi... where are You staying?"

It is a strange question. But not really. It is a way of asking, "Can we remain with You?"

I nod. "Come and see."

And they do.

We sit by a small fire. I speak of things ancient, but familiar. Their eyes search My face—not because they doubt, but because they remember. Somewhere in their spirit, they remember Eden.

Andrai leaves for a time. He returns with Shimon, his brother. The moment Shimon looks at Me, I see the man he is—and the man he will become.

"You are Shimon, son of Yonah," I say. "You shall be called Kephas—Little Rock."

He blinks, startled. Not because of the name—but because something in him already knew it. It was spoken in him before the foundation of the world.

The next day, I find another.

The sun leans lower in the sky, painting long shadows across Galilee. The air holds the stillness of something about to begin.

I walk a little ahead, the Sea not far behind Me, the hills before Me. Each step is known to the Father. Each path was traced in eternity. And then—I see him.

Philippos.

He does not see Me at first. He stands near a fig grove, examining the leaves with quiet focus. There's a patience about him—an internal world thoughtful and unhurried. He is not a man of crowds or loud declarations, but of steady questions and silent resolve.

He is of Bethsaida, like Andrai and Shimon—fishermen by trade, men shaped by the tides and the net. But Philippos? He gathers more than fish. He gathers words, ideas, longings. His heart is built for seeking.

I call him.

I do not explain, do not teach. I do not reason or persuade.

I simply say,
"Follow Me."

He looks up.

Our eyes meet—and he *knows*.

Not everything. But enough.

The silence around us feels sacred. The wind stirs the fig leaves like parchment being turned. In that moment, Philippos's life shifts. No trumpet sounds, no vision opens. Just one invitation—and an echo inside him that says, *This is the One.*

He does not ask for signs. He does not ask for proof. He simply goes.

Because when Truth speaks your name, your soul remembers how it was first spoken.

And now, awakened by purpose, Philippos turns to find another.

Philippos runs.

He does not hesitate. His legs carry urgency, but it is his heart that races faster. He knows where to go. Under the shade of a fig tree—always there, always thinking—is Bar-Talmai.

A man of conviction. Of scripture. Of silence and stubbornness. He is not quick to speak, nor easily swayed. His faith is deep but guarded. His hopes? Tucked away behind reason, layered under years of disappointment. He prays, but he questions.

And there he is, reclining beneath the wide fig branches, a scroll half-unrolled in his lap, eyes closed—perhaps mid-meditation, perhaps mid-doubt.

Philippos does not pause.

"We've found Him," he says, breathless. "The One Mosheh wrote about in the Law. The prophets spoke of Him. Yehoshua of Nazareth, the son of Yosef."

Bar-Talmai opens one eye.

A pause.

Then a scoff.

"Nazareth? Can anything good come out of Nazareth?"

His tone is not mocking—but honest. Raw. As if all the yearning inside him just hit another wall.

Philippos does not argue. He only says:

"Come and see."

And Bar-Talmai does.

He rises slowly, dusts off his robe. His mind resists but his feet move forward. He follows Philippos toward Me, his thoughts a tangle of curiosity and disbelief.

He sees Me first before I speak.

And I smile.

"Behold, an Israelite indeed, in whom is no deceit."

He halts, startled.

His face shifts—confusion, then awe.

"How do You know me?" he asks.

I look at him—not just *at* him, but *into* him.

I remember the fig tree. The quiet heart beneath it. The longing that worded itself in groans. I remember when he sat alone with the scrolls, when he asked the Father if He would ever come. I remember when he cried in silence, wondering if Heaven had forgotten him.

And so, I say,
"Before Philippos called you, when you were under the fig tree... I saw you."

The words strike deeper than he expects.

His breath catches. His doubt crumbles.

In one instant, the divine sees the hidden, and Bar-Talmai *knows*—this is no ordinary teacher.

His voice trembles now:

"Rabbi, You are the Son of God. You are the King of Israel."

But I see beyond his words. Beyond the revelation he can name. So, I answer:

"You believe because I told you I saw you under the fig tree. You will see greater things than these. Truly, truly, I say to you: you will see Heaven opened, and the angels of God ascending and descending upon the Son of Man."

He does not fully understand yet. None of them do. But the fig tree is behind him now—and the road ahead, lit with promise.

He walks it with Me.

The sun rises softly over Galilee. The mornings here are gentle—the hills catching light like cupped hands. In this quiet lull before ministry begins in full, we share simple days. Days of walking, of sitting, of speaking.

They begin to know Me.

Andrai, observant and eager, listens more than he speaks. He stays close, eyes scanning not just My face, but My hands, as if looking for confirmation that Heaven and Earth really meet in flesh.

Shimon—fiery and rough around the edges—wrestles openly. Not with belief, but with its implications. He wants to run, to act, to build something. Sometimes, he picks up stones and turns them over in his palms, like questions. Thoughts tumbling over questions.

"Will you not dispose the gentile rulers in our land and restore Israel under your rule"

I do not answer his thoughts though I hear them loud and clear.

Yochanan and Yaakov move like brothers do—shoulder to shoulder, often whispering thoughts between themselves, but always glancing at Me with eyes that carry both wonder and confusion.

Philippos—earnest, thoughtful—asks questions no one else dares to. And Bar-Talmai, quiet and intense, watches everything. He hasn't said much since the fig tree.

Then there is My family.

Miryam walks quietly beside us. She does not interfere, but she is never far. Her presence is both anchor and ache. She knows who I Am—more than the disciples do. Yet even she doesn't know what that will require. She touches My shoulder sometimes, gently. And when the others ask questions, she listens, not to answer, but to store things away—as she always has.

My brothers come and go. Curious, sceptical, protective. Yehuda, serious and sharp-eyed, often watches the disciples more than Me. Yaakov keeps mostly to himself, helping Yosef's cousins with the trade. They do not yet believe—but they are drawn. Not to glory, but perhaps to the quiet change in the air around Me.

Their lives continue, some marry, children come.

One evening, we gather under the olive trees outside the house. Bread is passed, oil shared, laughter flickers like the flame of a small lamp. I listen more than I speak. The disciples talk about the scriptures. Andrai repeats something Yochanan The Baptist once said. Bar-Talmai challenges it. Philippos adds another verse. Yochanan watches them, then glances at Me.

"You already know what we'll say before we say it, don't You?" he asks, half-laughing.

I smile. "And still, I want to hear it."

They go quiet for a moment; struck by something they cannot name. Something *close* and yet *immense*.

Later that night, Miryam finds Me near the well. She hands Me a cup, filled fresh.

"They're good men," she says.

I nod.

"They'll follow You anywhere. But they don't know where You're going."

I look at her. "Do you?"

She hesitates, then looks away. "I know enough to be afraid. And enough to trust."

The silence between us is soft, not heavy.

Then she says, "Remember the wedding in Cana?"

"I do."

"I am sure it will be ok to bring your friends, as long as they have wedding garments to wear."

I smile again.

The morning before we leave for Cana, I find Yaakov outside, repairing a beam along the wall. His hands move with confidence, but his eyes are far away.

"Will you be going to the wedding? After all they are family!" he asks without looking at Me.

"Yes."

"Yes," he echoes, with a smile that doesn't quite reach his eyes. "And your… friends are going too?"

I nod. "They've chosen to follow."

He sighs and sets the hammer down. "You were always different. But now—it's as if you're not even trying to hide it."

There's no anger in his voice. Just the ache of confusion, and a hint of disappointment.

"Will you come?" I ask.

"Yes," he says quickly. "of course."

"I'm sure most of your time will be spent with them and not with us" his eyes a little wet, filled with disappointment.

I say nothing.

It's hard for them, for a prophet is rarely accepted in his own home. And still – they do not understand.

Miryam watches from the doorway, a cloth in her hands. She says nothing, but I feel the quiet ache in her.

Yehuda passes behind her carrying a water jar. He offers a quick glance and a half-smile. "I hope your clothes are ready," he says with a wink, trying to break the tension.

I chuckle softly.

Cana of Galilee.

A wedding. A gathering of family, neighbours, and familiar faces.

Laughter floats on the warm Galilean air. The scent of roasted lamb mingles with sweet wine and dust. Children dart between tables. Men talk in low, hearty voices. Women adjust garlands, pass trays, keep watch over fires and joy.

I arrive not alone. Miryam, My mother, is already here—deep in the rhythm of preparation. My siblings too. This is no distant obligation; it is a family affair. We are not guests—we are bound to this day.

Miryam moves through the gathering with practiced grace, though I see the tension in her brow. She is concerned, not simply watching the festivities, but guarding them. This celebration is hers too.

The wine is running out.

A whisper travels through the kitchen like a flame through dry grass. Not enough. More guests than expected. Or perhaps the joy was too full, the cups too generous. It does not matter why—only that the jars are empty and the honour of the hosts teeters on the edge of shame.

She comes to Me.

"They have no more wine."

No plea. No demand. Just trust. She knows who I am. Not just the child she bore—but the One who once spoke galaxies into being. Her eyes search Mine. Her voice carries memory, common hoopoe, broken fever...

I say softly, "Woman, what does this have to do with Me? My hour has not yet come."

It is not a dismissal. It is a boundary — a veil not yet torn. The hour of full revealing — of signs undeniable and sacrifice unimaginable — is still ahead. But she does not argue. She trusts.
She turns to the servants. "Do whatever He tells you."
Then walks away.
I look — mouth slightly open.
They obey her before I speak a word.

Nearby stand six stone water jars, each large enough to hold the purification rites of many guests. Cold. Heavy. Empty. I glance toward them. The servants see and understand.

They move quickly hauling buckets from the well, pouring water into the jars until each is filled to the brim. They glance at Me, breathless. Waiting.

I say nothing. I do not raise My hand or whisper a command. I simply look.

And something shifts.

What was water becoming wine.

No sound, no flash, no trembling of earth. Just a quiet transformation.

I jester and whisper to the servants. They draw a sample and carry it to the master of the banquet. He tastes it—and his eyes widen.

He calls the groom with a laugh. "Everyone brings out the choice wine first," he says, "and then the cheaper wine after the guests have had their fill. But you—you have saved the best for last!"

The crowd laughs again, the tension forgotten. The music resumes, louder than before. Cups are refilled. Celebration deepens. No one questions where the wine came from.

But a few know.

The bridegroom stammers thanks, unaware of the miracle, unaware that eternity just brushed past his lips.

Only the servants know.
And My disciples.
They exchange glances—eyes wide, chests rising with quiet awe.

They begin to understand—not fully, but enough.

This is the first public sign. Quiet. Undeniable. Not for spectacle, but for those with eyes to see, something in them settles. Belief begins—not loud, not shouted, but steady. Seeded.

Later, the family and I sit quietly under the awning outside the house. The sun dips behind Cana's hills, casting long shadows. Music still floats from within, but the edge has softened. The feast is nearing its end.

Miryam leans over and tucks and strokes My hair. She says nothing about the wine. Not now. But her hand lingers on My shoulder a moment longer than usual. She remembers the angel's words, the shepherds' breathless retelling, Shimon's trembling prophecy. The years in Egypt. The questions she dared not ask.

She has always known.
But tonight, she sees.

The next day, we leave.
Not just I—but all of us: My disciples, My siblings, their spouses and children, and My mother. We travel together to Capernaum, a quiet town nestled near the Sea of Galilee.

Not far from Bethsaida. A fishing village, simple, unassuming—but important. The kind of place people overlook until it becomes impossible to ignore.

Capernaum will become a hub. A base. A home.

As we walk the dusty path between Cana and the lake, I hear them talking behind Me—Andrai and Kephas, whispering of the wedding. Bar-Talmai, quiet, thoughtful, the Cana native now seeing his village differently. Yochanan, still in awe, recalling the water and the moment.

They are beginning to see, but still not yet fully.
That is how belief grows—through signs and steps, through questions and quiet wonders.

As we near Capernaum, the fishing village nestled on the edge of the Galilean Sea. Blue water stretches wide, silver with morning light. The wind carries salt and the scent of fish in the air. Fishermen wave from boats, their nets heavy. Children play along the shore. Smoke rises from cookfires. Life here moves with the rhythm of the water, and soon, My words will ripple out from this place.

But for now, we rest.

We settle in a simple home, not small, has several rooms— one that had belonged to Miryam's parents, they had various homes, some rented, some as second homes.

Here, My siblings tease one another like before. Miryam kneads dough with My sisters. And I watch, quietly, knowing that soon, everything will change.

We do not stay long, only a few days. But the days are full.

I watch the shoreline at dusk, where fishermen cast their nets again and again. The rhythm of their labour reflects the hearts I've come to draw. Line by line. Net by net.

My brothers speak with the locals—some curious, some dismissive. The disciples listen to every word I say, even when I say nothing. There is a stir among them. A silent anticipation. Something has begun, though they cannot name it yet.

Here, no crowds gather. Not yet. The hour has not come, but it is near. Each step now carries the echo of the cross, though they do not see it. I hear it. I feel it. Even in the peace of Capernaum, purpose pulses just beneath the surface.

In the quiet, I commune with The Father.

The Spirit leads. The time draws near to go up to Jerusalem—for the Passover. What I do there will shake the hearts of many. But first, I walk the shoreline one more time, My feet brushing against the water, I sigh and enjoy the moment.

Soon, the words of the prophets will awaken.
The tables will turn.
The wind will carry truth across water.
But not today.

Here I relax and reflect.

The first sign has been given.
The water has turned to wine.
And the journey has begun.

The roads to Jerusalem are always crowded this time of year. Pilgrims from every corner of Judea and beyond. Dust clings to sandals and robes. Voices rise like incense, layered in languages and prayers.

We arrive through the Sheep Gate. The smell of animals, sweat, and expectation fills the air. Passover draws near.

The Temple rises—majestic, gleaming in the sunlight. Its courts pulse with life. But something is wrong.

The outer court, the Court of the Gentiles, is loud—not with praise, but with profit. Coin clinks. Animals cry. Merchants bark prices, scales are rigged, and holiness is for sale.

My eyes scan the scene. Tables piled with silver. Doves in cages. Lambs bleating. The sacred space meant for prayer has become a marketplace.

My chest tightens. Not with surprise, but with sorrow. Righteous anger burns low in My belly.

I step forward.

I pick up cords—discarded rope from the livestock pens—and twist them into a whip. Not crude violence. A prophetic act.

I drive them out. Not with fists, but with fury. With holy authority.

"Take these things away! Do not make My Father's house a house of trade!"

Coins scatter. Tables overturn. Animals bolt. Merchants scramble, calling after their goods. Eyes widen in shock. Some run. Others stare.

Zeal for My Father's house consumes Me.

The disciples remember the psalm: *"Zeal for Your house has eaten me up."*

They do not yet understand all they see—but something deep roots itself in them. This is not the soft-spoken child of

Nazareth. This is fire. This is judgment. This is the heart of God revealed.

Temple guards begin to murmur. Religious leaders question Me:

"What sign do You show us for doing these things?"

I look at them—not with defiance, but with divine knowing.

"Destroy this temple, and in three days I will raise it up."

They scoff. "It took forty-six years to build this temple, and will You raise it up in three days?"

But I was not speaking of stones and pillars. I was speaking of My body.

They do not yet see. But they will.

Later that night, as the city settles, I walk its narrow streets with My disciples. Whispers follow us—some of awe, some of fear. Already, the stirrings begin.

Some believe. Some recoil. Some remain curious.

But in the shadows, one approaches.

A man named Nikódēmos.

A teacher of Israel. A ruler. A seeker.

He waits until the crowds' sleep. Until voices die down. He finds Me alone. Lantern light flickers against stone.

"Rabbi," he begins, respectful, cautious, "we know You are a teacher come from God, for no one can do these signs unless God is with Him."

I look into his eyes. So much knowledge. So much hunger.

"Truly, truly I say to you, unless one is born again, he cannot see the kingdom of God."

He frowns. "How can a man be born when he is old?"

So, I speak of Spirit and water. Of wind and mystery. Of flesh and rebirth.

I speak of light in the darkness. Of the Son lifted up, as Mosheh lifted the serpent in the wilderness. I speak of the Father's love—not to condemn, but to save.

I see the conflict in his eyes. The heart pulling where the mind cannot yet follow.

He leaves, still questioning.

But he will return.

And now, I prepare to leave the city again.

But the seeds are planted.

The temple has been shaken. The teachers are stirring. The people are murmuring.

The Word has spoken.

And Jerusalem will never be the same.

After the hush of Nikodemus' departure and the city's hum faded behind us, we left Jerusalem. Not in haste, not in flight—just in obedience. We travelled into the countryside of Judea, where the land opened like a breath after tension, and the Jordan traced its slow path like a psalm whispered across the earth.

I did not go alone. My disciples came with Me—still new in their faith, still forming their understanding. And the people came, too. Hungry. Curious. Wounded. Word had spread quickly: I spoke with authority, but not like the others. I healed. I taught. I saw people, truly saw them. And I baptised—though not with My own hands. My disciples, under My direction, lowered them into the river's flow. Repentance still mattered. Washing still mattered. But the water was not the miracle. It was the turning of hearts.

Yochanan was still nearby, not far, baptising at Aenon near Salim. Water was abundant there, and so were the seekers. We did not compete. He rejoiced. For this was the season he had long prepared for. When his followers asked him about Me—why the crowds began to swell around My teaching—he smiled. His voice rang clear:

"A man can receive only what is given him from heaven. I am not the Christ, but I am sent ahead of Him... He must increase; I must decrease."

His joy in My rising was genuine. Not possessive. Not threatened. He was the friend of the Bridegroom, standing by, listening, full of joy at the Bridegroom's voice.

For a time, we baptised in tandem—two voices, two camps, but one purpose. One rhythm rising between riverbanks. The Kingdom was coming near, not just in message, but in movement. The ground itself seemed to remember. The Spirit lingered in the reeds. Eyes were lifted, lives re-centred.

No temple. No gold. Just water. Dirt. Hands. Tears.

It was a season of simplicity. Before the storms. Before the accusations and crowds and crosses. Here, in the in-between, we made disciples one by one. I called them by name. I watched them learn how to listen.

How to love.

How to follow.

For a while, we remained there and baptised.

And the Kingdom grew quietly like yeast in dough.

But then word reached the Pharisees.

They had heard that I was gaining and baptising more disciples than Yochanan—though it was not I who baptised, but My disciples. Still, the murmurs carried weight. Comparison breeds tension, and tension draws attention.

It was not yet My time.

So, I left Judea and began the journey back toward Galilee.

But I did not take the long way around.

I *had* to go through Samaria.

Not for speed. Not for convenience. But for purpose. For there, by a well, worn smooth by centuries of thirst, waited a woman whose life had been poured out and emptied. And I, the Living Water, would meet her there.

One conversation. One heart. One village.

But first—this road. These hills. These disciples, unaware of the moment we walked toward.

The ministry would deepen. The questions would sharpen.

But the Kingdom had begun.

And I was no longer alone in it.

Chapter 5: Living Water

The road winds through Samaria, a place avoided by many, but not by Me. Dust clings to My robe. The sun, a relentless witness overhead, presses heat into My shoulders. The disciples have gone ahead to find food. I remain behind. Not by accident. Not by delay. But by appointment.

The Samaritans were a people shaped by fracture and exile—descendants of Israelites who had remained in the land during the Assyrian conquest, intermarrying with foreign settlers brought in by their captors. Racially mixed, with both Jewish blood and pagan influence, they became a people with one foot in covenant and the other in compromise. They revered YHWH, clung to the Torah—the first five books of Mosheh —as sacred, and upheld the stories of Avraham, Yitzchak, and Yaakov. But their worship took place not in Jerusalem, but on Mount Gerazim, where they had built their own temple. This, to the Jews of Judea, was not only rebellion—it was heresy.

To the Jews, Samaritans were unclean, their theology tainted, their worship polluted. Centuries of tension had hardened into hostility. They were the "other"—not quite Gentile, but not welcome as brethren. Travellers would go miles out of their way to avoid Samaritan towns. Conversation was rare. Kindness, rarer still. And yet it was into this divide that I stepped. Into their village, to their well, to a woman who least expected to be seen.

And here, at Yaakov's well—where division once drew lines in the dust—I wait. Not for a crowd. Not for applause. For one soul.

I sit beside the well. It is old, ancient even, dug by Yaakov himself. Its stones hold stories—of thirst, of covenant, of waiting. I let My eyes rest on the horizon. Noon is not a time for water. Not for most. But I am not here for most.

Then I see her.

She walks with purpose, but not peace. She does not come with others. She carries no laughter with her. Only a jar, and something deeper. Shame, perhaps. Or sorrow. She comes when the sun is high and the world hides. But I do not look away. I wait. For this is why I came.

"Give Me a drink," I say.

She freezes. Her eyes search Mine. There is suspicion there, and confusion.

"You, a Jew, ask Me, a Samaritan woman, for a drink?"

Her voice is not hard, only guarded. Centuries of tension live between our peoples. Gender divides us. Culture separates us. Yet here we are. The walls, crumbling already.

"If you knew the gift of God," I reply, "and who it is that asks you for a drink, you would have asked Him, and He would have given you living water."

She studies Me. Her eyes linger on My hands—empty, with no jar.

"Sir, You have nothing to draw with, and the well is deep. Where can You get this living water? Are You greater than our father Yaakov, who gave us the well and drank from it himself?"

She speaks history. I offer eternity.

"Everyone who drinks this water will be thirsty again, but whoever drinks the water I give will never thirst. Indeed, the water I give will become a spring within them, welling up to eternal life."

Her expression shifts. The weight she carries seems to tilt. Longing now flickers behind her eyes.

"Sir, give Me this water so I won't get thirsty and have to keep coming here to draw."

"Go, call your husband," I say.

The air tightens. Her breath halts.

"I have no husband," she replies.

"You are right when you say that. You have had five, and the man you now have is not your husband. You have spoken truthfully."

Her face does not fall. Instead, her eyes widen. Not with shame, but with awe. I do not speak to expose her. I speak to reveal that she is seen—and still worthy of speaking with the Messiah.

"Sir, I see that You are a prophet. Our ancestors worshipped on this mountain, but you Jews say the place to worship is in Jerusalem."

A shift. From personal to theological. From pain to practice. Still, I do not deflect.

"Believe Me, woman, a time is coming when you will worship the Father neither on this mountain nor in Jerusalem. You Samaritans worship what you do not know; we worship what we do know, for salvation is from the Jews. But the time is coming—and now is—when the true worshippers will worship the Father in spirit and truth, for they are the kind the Father seeks. God is Spirit, and those who worship Him must worship in spirit and truth."

Silence. Then she whispers, "I know Messiah is coming. When He comes, He will explain everything to us."

I hold her gaze.

"I who speak to you, am He."

The words hang in the air like incense. A declaration not given to rulers or priests, but to her. A Samaritan. A woman. A seeker. Her jar slips from her hand, forgotten. Her thirst—quenched.

She runs.

She runs not from shame but with joy. She becomes the first evangelist, shouting into the streets, "Come, see a man who told me everything I ever did. Could this be the Messiah?"

Behind her, I sit.

The disciples return, baskets in hand, their clothes dusty from the road, eyes shadowed by sun and confusion. They see Me speaking with her—a woman, a Samaritan—and though their mouths remain closed, their eyes are loud with questions. But no one asks. Not now.

They offer Me food, eager to move past what they do not understand.

"Rabbi, eat," they urge.

But I am already full.

"I have food to eat that you know nothing about," I say.

Their confusion deepens. Murmurs ripple among them.

"Did someone bring Him something to eat?"

I do not speak to their stomachs, but to their souls.

"My food is to do the will of Him who sent Me—and to finish His work."

They grow quiet.

I rise and look toward the horizon, where the golden light clings to the fields. The wheat sways with the breeze, a living parable. I lift My hand to it.

"Don't you say, 'Four more months, and then the harvest'? I tell you—open your eyes. Look at the fields. They are ripe for harvest now."

They follow My gaze, but it is not crops I see—it is souls. I see the woman running back through the gates of the village, her voice ringing with urgency. I see doors opening. Faces turning. Feet moving.

A stirring begins.

She returns—not alone, but with a crowd trailing her like dust in the wind. Men and women, sceptical but curious, come to the well. And they listen.

At first, they believe because of her. Her passion. Her transformation. But then they hear Me. And the water they came for becomes secondary.

They draw living water instead.

Some wipe tears. Others ask questions. A few simply, stand still, overwhelmed by the presence of something they cannot yet name.

Two days we stay. And in those days, the walls built over centuries begin to crack. Not just between Jews and

Samaritans, but between heaven and earth, shame and grace.

Their faith grows.

Sick healed.

Word spoken.

"Not because of what you said," they tell her, "but now we have heard Him for ourselves. We know this man really is the Saviour of the world."

They say *Saviour.* And they say *world.* They see beyond tribe, beyond temple, beyond bloodlines. They see what even My own have not yet seen.

The well remains. The water still flows.

But the village is changed.

I came for one.

I found many.

And the harvest has begun.

The road from Samaria to Galilee feels shorter than it is. Joy walks with us. The harvest has begun—not just of grain, but of hearts. Yet I know what waits. The soil of My homeland is not always fertile for truth. Still, I return—not only to proclaim, but to plant. Galilee will hear what Samaria embraced.

From the soil of welcome to the stone of resistance, I step forward. Not with disappointment, but with resolve.

Before the scrolls are opened, before the tension of My hometown rises, I speak in villages along the way. Short messages. Simple words. Yet heavy with eternity.

"The time is fulfilled. The Kingdom of God is at hand. Repent. Believe the Good News."

These are not merely commands—they are invitations. A Kingdom unlike any they expected. Not military might. Not rebellion. But restoration. Renewal. Reconciliation. It begins not in thrones, but in hearts. And it is already here.

I return to Galilee—the hills, the olive groves, the smell of baking bread and earth after rain. I walk familiar paths, through towns where My laughter once echoed as a child, where Miryam bought lentils and Yosef crafted beams for homes that still stand. The people know My name—but not yet My purpose.

The hills are familiar, but the eyes that greet Me are not the same. Whispers follow Me—Yehoshua, son of Yosef. The carpenter. The quiet one who left.
But now I speak.

I enter the synagogue on the Sabbath, as was My custom. Scrolls are unrolled. The men shift in anticipation. Eyes glance My way. The synagogue is full. Sandals shuffled across the stone floor. The scent of old scrolls and warm cloaks thickens the air. Faces turn as I stand. Some tilt with curiosity, others with suspicion.

The attendant hands Me the scroll "The time is fulfilled. The Kingdom of God is at hand. Repent and believe the Good News."

A murmur ripples through the room.

Not revolution. Not revolt. But something deeper. An awakening.

This is not just a message—it is a summons. The Kingdom I

speak of is not built of stone or sword. It does not rise with banners and legions. It breaks in quietly, like morning light through shutters. It heals. It convicts. It calls.

I speak with authority—not borrowed from rabbis, not inherited by schooling, but from the Source. Because I Am.

The scroll is passed to Me again. This time, I turn to the writings of the prophet Yesha'yahu. I do not hesitate. I find the place. I know the words. I wrote them.

The Spirit of the Lord *is* upon Me,
Because He has anointed Me
To preach the gospel to *the* poor;
He has sent Me to heal the broken-hearted,
To proclaim liberty to *the* captives
And recovery of sight to *the* blind,
To set at liberty those who are oppressed;
To proclaim the acceptable year of the Lord."

The words I speak are not new. Not to them. But the voice that carries them—the weight in it, the fire underneath—this they do not expect.

I pause.
The words echo through the silence. Some close their eyes, reverent. Others wait. Curious. Cautious.

I roll up the scroll. I hand it back. And then, I say what has never been said like this before.
"Today, this Scripture is fulfilled in your hearing."

A breath is held across the room. A man's brow furrows. Worshippers look up.

Isn't this Yosef's son?
How can He speak this way?

Their amazement shifts. From wonder, to questioning, to tension.
I see it coming. I speak again. Truth wrapped in challenge. A prophet is never accepted in his own hometown.

I remind them of Eliyahu and the widow. Elisha and the leper. Outsiders who believed more than those within the fold.

Now the murmurs rise. Offence blooms where revelation tried to land.

They drive Me out. Fury, not faith, in their eyes. They lead Me to the edge of the cliff—Nazareth's rocky brow overlooking the valley.

But it is not My time.
I pass through them unseen.
Not with violence.
Not with fear.
But with purpose.

I walk alone.

The dust of Nazareth clings to My feet, the same soil I once played upon, now stirred by the heels of those who sought to throw Me from the cliff.

I pass familiar stone walls, fig trees I once climbed, homes whose doors once opened gladly at the sound of My mother's voice. But today, the doors are closed. Today, My name is no longer spoken with affection, but with suspicion.

I walk the path Yosef once took to gather wood, to carve beams, to build tables that may still stand in these very homes. He walked in silence often, but I wonder now—did he sense what would come?

I pause near the edge of a field where I once helped reap barley. The wind moves across it now, bending the stalks low. A child waves from the distance, unaware of the moment's weight.

They know Me, and yet they do not know Me.

I came with peace. I brought fulfilment, not fame. But their ears were closed by familiarity, their hearts shielded by expectation. A prophet in his own town is a mirror too clear. They would rather smash the reflection than change the face.

Still—I do not resent them.

My heart aches, not for the rejection, but for what they refused to see. For what they will miss. The Kingdom stood in their midst, and they tried to cast it over a cliff.

I turn from the rocky edge and keep walking. Dust rises behind Me. Silence walks beside Me. But so does the purpose.

The scroll has been read. The words have gone forth.

The seed has been planted, even in stony ground.

And I continue on.

Now, it must be lived.

I pass by the well where I once fetched water with My brothers. The fig tree where I read the Torah aloud for the first time. The shop that still bears the grooves Yosef carved into wood.

But now I speak.

The wind shifts over the hills of Galilee, stirring olive branches and catching the edges of cloaks and headscarves. The murmurs of daily life continue, children chase one another through dusty lanes, women grind grain, men barter in the markets. But heaven leans low today, closer than they know. Something eternal brushes against the temporal.

I walk through familiar streets, My sandals pressing into paths once wandered in youth.

I have returned to speak.

To begin.

And I do not wait for crowds or accolades. I step into a clearing where fishermen mend their nets, their hands raw from rope and salt. I pass shepherds leading bleating flocks to the shade. I stop near a group of men listening to a traveling rabbi speak of the law, their faces weary beneath the weight of interpretation layered upon interpretation. Their hearts long for something—but they know not what.

I lift My voice—not to echo tradition, but to announce a rupture in time.

"The time is fulfilled."

The words fall heavy, yet light. Like a bell tolling far off recognisable, but not yet understood.

All of history bends to this moment. The prophets longed to see it. Angels' peer into it. The law groans with the strain of its coming end. And now, the appointed hour arrives—not with armies, not with fire from heaven, but in sandals and silence. In Me.

"The Kingdom of God is at hand."

Not a theory. Not a dream. A Kingdom.

Not of men, not of swords, not of walls or thrones carved in gold. But a Kingdom built on justice that does not fail, mercy that does not run dry, and truth that pierces bone and spirit alike.

It is not far off. It does not wait for better weather or stronger kings. It is at hand. Within reach. Pressing into this present moment. Bursting into now.

They do not yet see it. But they feel it, like the first stir of wind before the rain.

I do not speak of Rome, or of Herod, though they expect Me to. This Kingdom is older than Caesar's crown and stronger than the gates of the Temple. It is the dream behind every exile's cry, the answer to every psalm of lament. It is the promise made to Avraham, the throne sworn to David, the longing of every prophet from Eliyahu to Malakhi.

Now—now it touches earth.

"Repent."

Turn. Not just from sin, but from smallness. From false expectations. From every lesser hope. From rituals without relationship. From striving without surrender. From hate and not love.

Turn from dead religion and come alive to God.

Turn from self-righteousness that cannot heal, from pride that cannot see. From the illusion of control, from the lies of the accuser, from the scars of shame that have masqueraded as identity.

Turn—and see.

For the Kingdom is not coming with banners and armies. It

will not be observed with signs that satisfy the curious. It is within you, around you, among you—if only you would look with eyes washed in Spirit.

"Believe the good news."

Believe—not just in theory. Not in concept. Believe as one who stakes their life upon it. Believe as one who leaves behind nets, fields, and comfort zones to walk into wonder.

The good news is not that judgment has arrived—but that mercy has. That the exile of the soul can end. That heaven has drawn near in sandals and skin. That God has come not to crush, but to restore, to fulfil. Purpose.

I do not shout. I do not wave My arms. I simply speak.

And those who have ears begin to listen.

A widow leans in from her threshold, her hands flour-stained, her eyes rimmed with years of unanswered prayers.

A boy pauses at the edge of the crowd, clutching the strap of his water jar, uncertain, but drawn.

A leper watches from afar, wondering if this Kingdom would dare include him.

They all feel it. The shift. The invitation. The nearness of something too good to be earned but too holy to ignore.

The Kingdom is at hand.

I Am that, Kingdom.

Where I walk, healing follows. Where I speak, darkness flees. Where I touch, purity does not recoil—it restores.

And yet, many will miss it.

They will look for crowns and miss the cross. They will

expect thunder and miss the whisper. They will want Me to conquer, and struggle to understand when I choose instead to kneel and serve.

But the Kingdom will grow.

It will begin like yeast hidden in flour. Like a mustard seed. Like light in the darkness.

It will transform fishermen into apostles. Tax collectors into evangelists. Outcasts into carriers of the divine.

This is no kingdom of empty religion.

It is Spirit and truth.

It is the reign of the Father through the Son by the Spirit.

It will confound the proud and lift the lowly.

And it has begun.

I speak again. Not louder, but deeper, My voice carries by the Spirit

"The Kingdom of God is at hand. Repent, and believe the good news."

And the ones who listen?

They will never be the same.

I return to Cana.

The hills feel familiar beneath My feet. The stones remember Me. The village stirs with morning voices—children chasing goats, women drawing water. It is here, in this quiet place, that the water once became wine. A whisper of glory still lingers in the walls of that wedding house. But today, the miracle will not be for celebration.

It will be for desperation.

A man comes.

He does not belong here—not truly. His cloak is finely woven, his accent sharpened by courtly habit. A man of status. Of authority. A servant of Herod, perhaps. His face is weathered—not by sun, but by worry. His steps are hurried. His dignity, thin.

He falls before Me.

He is not concerned with ceremony.

"Lord," he says, breathless, "please... my son is sick. Dying. Come. Come with me to Capernaum before he dies."

His voice cracks on the word *dies*. Not a request—an ache.

I hear the murmur behind him. Others watching. Waiting. Wanting signs, not salvation.

"Unless you people see signs and wonders," I say, not unkindly, "you will never believe."

The man does not flinch. He does not argue theology. He does not ask Me for proof. He only pleads.

"Sir. Come down... before my child dies."

And I see it. Faith—not fully formed, but real. Not in doctrine, but in desperation. His love for his son has stripped away all pretence. His need has made him ready. Ready not just for a miracle—but for Me.

"You may go," I tell him. "Your son lives."

No gesture. No touch. Only a word.

The man stares at Me—uncertain at first, as if weighing whether belief is possible without evidence. Then, slowly, he nods. And he turns.

He believes.

He walks away with nothing in his hands, only a promise in his heart.

The crowd stirs. Some disappointed I did not go with him. Some whispering already, wondering if the child will truly recover. But I do not follow him. I do not need to.

Because faith has already moved faster than feet.

Far off, in a house in Capernaum, a fever breaks.

At the seventh hour, the boy opens his eyes. His breathing evens. The colour returns to his cheeks. Servants shout. The mother weeps.

And the father? Still walking.

They meet him on the road, racing toward him with the news.

"Your son lives!"

He stops. Heart hammering.

"When?" he asks.

They answer. "Yesterday. The seventh hour. The fever left him."

He falls to his knees. Not from exhaustion.

From belief.

He had not seen the moment. But now he sees the One.

He returns home not with a miracle—but with revelation. Not only healed but changed.

And his whole household believes.

This was the second sign, in Cana.

Not water to wine, but word to life.

Faith that did not need to see to believe.

And again, Cana is marked—not just as a place of wonder, but as a witness.

The harvest continues.

The streets are loud today.

The shoreline of Galilee breathes beneath morning light, waves folding over themselves like prayers whispered in rhythm. The lake glistens—its calm deceptive, its depth ancient. Here, so much begins. Not in the courts of kings or the schools of rabbis, but on this water, where nets are cast, and calloused hands do holy work without yet knowing.

I walk along the shore.

The wind stirs gently, tugging at My robe. The scent of salt and fish lingers in the air. I hear them before I see them—the creak of wood, the thud of nets, the quiet exchange of men accustomed to labour.

Shimon. Andrai.

They work side by side, sweat already glistening on their brows despite the early hour. The lake is their livelihood. But today, it will become their altar.

"Follow Me," I say.

No long explanation. No persuasion. Just a call. But the words strike something eternal in them. Shimon turns first, his gaze locking with Mine. He does not understand everything, but something in him recognises the eternal Me. The breath of the prophets fills his lungs before he speaks.

They leave their nets.

They leave certainty.

They follow.

A little further along, two others—Yakov and Yochanan, sons of Zavdai. They are in the boat with their father, mending torn lines. The sea has been their story too, passed down in salt and wind.

"Follow Me," I say again.

Their father looks up, surprised. But he does not call them back. Something in the moment is sacred, undeniable. The boys look to him. He nods. A silent blessing.

They leave the boat. The nets. The familiarity.

The four walk with Me now. Four lives interrupted by eternity.

The shoreline fades as we move through Galilee—towns and hills and winding paths. Word spreads like fire in dry fields. People come—not for spectacle, but for something deeper. Their eyes tell stories before their mouths do: pain, desperation, hope not yet surrendered.

I teach in synagogues—simple, steady. Not with the weight of tradition, but with the breath of truth. I speak of the Kingdom. Not a kingdom of empires, but of hearts. Of healing. Of light breaking through shadow.

And they come.

From Galilee. From the Decapolis. From Judea, Jerusalem,

even beyond the Jordan.

They bring the sick. The broken.

A child with fevered skin, eyes glazed with pain. I touch her brow. The heat fades. She sits up, blinking, then smiles.

A man led in on a mat, limbs twisted, voice stilled by years of silence. I speak, and the cords of his tongue loosen. He laughs—louder than the crowd around him.

A woman bent by years of unseen weight. I place My hand upon her shoulder. Her spine straightens. Her face lifts to the sky for the first time in years.

Possessed ones scream as demons flee, clawing at the air as they go. The crowd shudders. But I do not. Light has no fear of darkness.

Blind eyes blink and widen. Lame feet find balance. Leprous skin becomes whole.

Tears fall freely—some from the healed, some from those who simply witness.

They press closer. Not all are healed in that moment, but all are seen. All are known.

The four at My side—Shimon, Andrai, Yakov, and Yochanan —watch with wide eyes. They do not yet grasp the fullness of what they have stepped into. But they see enough to keep following.

We sleep where we can—under stars, in borrowed homes, in quiet corners of busy towns. But even sleep is interrupted by knocks and cries in the night.

And still—we go.

From town to town. From synagogue to hillside.

I speak. I touch. I heal.

Not for fame. Not for power. But because the Kingdom is near. And when it comes, wholeness follows.

One morning, as the sun rises, I step away. The others sleep. But I climb a hill alone. The sky is a deep blue canopy above. The wind is cool. And I pray.

Not because I am weary—but because communion with the Father is the rhythm of My soul. From that place of stillness, strength flows.

When I return, they find Me again—another crowd, another need.

But I am ready.

Because this is why I came.

To call. To teach. To heal.

To show the world that the Kingdom is not a place to be reached, but a presence to be received, a fellowship requested long ago by that mountain, in that garden.

And here, on the shores of Galilee, the Kingdom has begun.

Chapter 6: The Break In

Here, I will dwell. Not in palaces, not in Jerusalem's courts, but among fishermen and tax collectors, among nets and calloused hands. Here, the Kingdom begins—not with coronation, but conversation. With small fires. With listening hearts.

I teach. Not like the scribes, who quote and defer. I do not offer borrowed insight. I speak as one who authored the words I read. As I speak, the atmosphere shifts. My voice does not rise, but the silence deepens. Hearts beat faster. Spirits stir.

Then suddenly, a cry cuts through the stillness.

A man stumbles forward. His face twisted, not with pain—but torment. Eyes wild, hands trembling.

"What do You want with us, Yehoshua of Nazareth? Have You come to destroy us? I know who You are—the Holy One of God!"

Gasps ripple through the room. Some draw back. Others stare.

I do not shout. I do not perform. I simply speak.

"Be silent. Come out of him."

The man convulses. A groan, deep and guttural, rises from within. His body shakes once, twice—and then stills. The presence that held him flees.

He collapses, breathing heavy. His eyes clear. His face— changed.

The crowd erupts. Murmurs and awe.

"What is this? A new teaching—and with authority! Even the unclean spirits obey Him!"

They do not understand fully, not yet. But their spirits know: something greater is among them.

The news spreads quickly, as wind through olive branches. From Capernaum to the hills beyond. But I do not linger for applause. The work is only beginning.

Shimon invites Me to his house.

I follow him through winding streets, the dust warm beneath My feet. His home is humble—stone walls, wooden beams, the scent of cooked barley still in the air. But something is wrong. A quiet urgency rests over the household.

Shimon's wife greets us, her brow furrowed. Her mother lies still in the corner, pale and trembling, gripped by fever.

They ask Me without words. Eyes pleading, hearts open.

I move to her side. Kneel. Her breath is shallow. Her forehead burns.

I take her hand.

At My touch, the fever flees. No flash. No struggle. Just peace.

She blinks. Then rises. Not slowly, not weakly, but with strength.

And then—she serves.

She pours water. Prepares bread. Laughter returns to the room. Healing is not just in the body, but in the rhythm of life restored.

Evening comes, but the day is not over.

At the edge of the city, a crowd forms. Word has spread. They bring the sick, the broken, the tormented. Mothers carry limp children. Friends support the lame. Eyes watch from behind cloaks, hesitant but desperate.

They gather at the door.

I step out. No stage. No ceremony. Just compassion.

I lay hands. I speak peace. One by one, they are healed.

Demons flee. Eyes clear. Backs straighten. Tears fall. Praise rises.

The stars appear above, but no one leaves. Hope is a light they have not felt in so long.

And yet—I do not heal to be seen. I do not cast out to gather fame. I do it because the Kingdom is nearby. Because wholeness is My nature. Because they are Mine.

Behind Me, Kephas watches, arms crossed, his eyes not just on the miracles—but on Me.

He does not yet know where this road will lead. But something in him—like the woman at the well—has already tasted the water that never runs dry.

By morning, I will retreat to pray.

But tonight, I walk among them.

And the Kingdom walks with Me.

He came while others stood back.
Where crowds had pressed close, they now recoiled. Where feet had shuffled forward, now they halted. One man walked alone.

I felt before I saw him, pushing forward, overcoming fear with each step.

His skin, whitish and cracked, carried not only sickness but shame. His eyes darted, head tilted towards the ground. His humiliation apparent. Garments torn in mourning, not just of body—but of life, of touch, of belonging. Eyes looked away. Hands lifted to stones. Whispers of "Unclean!" rose like dust. Embarrassed but determined. This must be a time of change for me, he thought, purposely, not looking at the crowd, as they moved out of the way.

But he came closer still.

He fell to his knees before Me. No pretence. No pride. Only pain wrapped in hope.

"If You are willing," he said, voice hoarse like wind through broken reeds, "You can make me clean."

He did not doubt My power. Only My heart.

And so, I showed him both.

I reached out My hand. I touched him.

Gasps spread like wildfire.

I did not flinch. I did not pull away. The skin others feared to see—I touched. The flesh others cursed I blessed.

"I am willing," I said. "Be clean."

And he was.

Not later. Not after seven days. In a breath, in a blink, his essence bloomed with life. The cracks disappeared. Colour returned. Brown skin luminous again. The sting of shame broke. His hands—trembling, scarred—became whole once more.

Joy quivered behind his eyes. Awe held him still. Tears flowed.

"Go," I said gently, "show yourself to the priest. Offer the gift Mosheh commanded—as a testimony to them."

But how could he keep silent?

How could one who had been dead to the world not shout, when life returned?

He ran. And he told them all.

The news spread like wind through fields. From village to village, the story rippled: "The leper was cleansed."

And because of this, I could no longer enter towns openly. The crowds surged, not for truth, but for wonder. Not for Kingdom, but for spectacle. So, I withdrew to lonely places.

But even there—they came.

Capernaum again. A house packed full.

Word had spread. They came from every direction— Pharisees from Judea, scribes from Jerusalem, farmers, fishermen, mothers holding children too sick to walk. The crowd pressed in. Shoulder to shoulder. Faces at windows. Feet spilling into the streets.

I was inside, seated, teaching.

But they did not come only for words. They came for hope. Some with hearts open, some with hearts hard—but all watching. Listening. Wondering.

Then the sound—above us.

Footsteps. A scraping. A pause. Then again.

Dust falls from the ceiling. A voice murmurs in protest.

Another shouts in confusion.

And then—light breaks through the roof.

The crowd gasps.

Four men—faces flushed with urgency—lower a mat through the broken clay and thatch. The ropes creak. The mat sways slightly.

On it, a man. Still. Helpless. Paralysed.

He does not speak. But I see his eyes. They do not plead for movement. They plead for mercy.

Their faith—theirs—is loud. Not in words, but in boldness.

I do not begin with healing.

"Son," I say, "your sins are forgiven."

The silence that follows is different now. Not awe. Suspicion.

I hear it before it's spoken: Who can forgive sins but God alone?

Their thoughts coil like snakes in the corners of the room. Their faces try to stay still, but their hearts scream.

So, I ask aloud, "Why do you think such things? Which is easier—to say, 'Your sins are forgiven,' or to say, 'Get up and walk'?"

A pause.

"But so that you may know that the Son of Man has authority on earth to forgive sins..."

I turn to the man. The still one. The listening one.

"Rise."

The word drops like thunder in silence.

"Take up your mat."

A second heartbeat.

"And walk."

He moves.

First a twitch. Then a shifting of his limbs. Then strength floods where only weakness had lived.

He sits up.

Gasps ripple through the house like waves breaking on shore. He stands. He bends. He rolls up his mat. And he walks—not limping, not unsure—as if he'd never been broken.

The room erupts. Awe, joy, fear. Some weep. Some stare. Some whisper prayers with trembling lips.

"We have seen extraordinary things today."

They came for healing. They left having touched the eternal.

The crowd eventually thins, drifting out with murmurs of amazement still trailing behind them like dust on sandals. The house quiets. The paralysed man walks home whole. Hope lingers in the air like incense.

From the back of the house, a voice—dry, unimpressed, familiar.

Kepha's wife.

She stands, hands on hips, brow raised.

She looks at the gaping hole in the roof, at the shards of thatch and broken beams still scattered on the floor.

Then at Me.

Then at him.

"But who," she asks flatly, "is going to fix my roof?"

Kephas shifts, suddenly remembering.

Yakov coughs, stifling a laugh.

Even Yochanan smiles.

I smile too.

The Kingdom has come—but the roof still needs mending.

Dust swirls with the shuffle of sandals, and the sharp ring of coins carries above the hum of trade. Capernaum wakes early—fishermen selling their catch, merchants unrolling bolts of dyed linen, children weaving between carts and beasts. Life moves quickly here, but not without notice.

I see him before he sees Me.

Levi.

They call him *matit'yahu*— "gift of God"—but few say it with affection. To the crowd, he is just a tax collector. A traitor. A collaborator. One who sits between the kingdom of Rome and the people of Israel and belongs to neither.

He knows what they call him. He hears the scorn behind every coin dropped on his table. He sees the way they avoid his eyes. He feels the weight of rejection, and the heavier weight of shame he cannot quite name.

Still, he stays. It's a living.

The booth is worn, but orderly. He keeps his records with precision, though there is little joy in his gaze. He does not lift his head when I approach—not at first. His fingers move over the wax tablet, counting, recording, surviving.

But then he feels My presence.

Stillness.

He looks up.

And I see it.

The ache. The longing. The quiet torment of someone who never intended to be so far from home. So far from hope.

I do not offer him a list of things to fix.

I do not ask him to explain his past.

I simply say two words.

"Follow Me."

He blinks.

The crowd quiets.

A woman clutches her child tighter. A merchant scoffs aloud. One of the synagogue rulers' stares in disbelief.

But I do not look away. I wait.

And then—

Levi stands.

He doesn't hesitate.

He doesn't ask where or how.

He simply rises. His fingers leave the wax tablet mid-count. His hand drops the stylus. The coins are left uncollected. The debts, unpaid.

He follows.

Not just in body—but in heart.

Later that evening, his house is full. Tables groan under the weight of roasted lamb, dates, figs, bread. Wine is poured. Laughter echoes off the stone walls. But it is not the laughter of the clean and respected. It is the laughter of sinners—those the righteous call unworthy.

They sit beside Me.

Levi has invited them all—those with no synagogue seats, no priestly blessing, no honour left to lose. And here, at this table, they are seen. Not as their labels. Not as outcasts. But as invited.

The Pharisees whisper outside.

They do not enter.

They speak to My disciples instead judging from a distance.

"Why does your Master eat with tax collectors and sinners?"

I hear them.

I answer.

"It is not the healthy who need a physician, but the sick. Go and learn what this means: 'I desire mercy, not sacrifice.' For I have not come to call the righteous, but sinners to repentance."

Levi hears it.

And something inside him breaks free.

He is no longer a record keeper of debts.

He has become a recorder of grace.

The house falls into hush. Levi lingers, heart thudding like distant thunder. The others move ahead, their sandals brushing dust from the threshold. But I see him glance back—just once—toward the booth he left behind. He will never return to it. Not as the man he was.

We walk. The road opens. The sea draws near. The wind carries the scent of salt and woodsmoke as I step into Capernaum. A town by the sea. Small, but not insignificant. The place chosen—not by chance, but by fulfilment. "Land of Zevulun, land of Naftali ... the people who sat in darkness have seen a great light."
And now, the light walks among them.

The city of Jerusalem hums with ancient breath—stones holding centuries of prayers, streets echoing with the murmurs of prophets and kings. I walk through its gates not with spectacle, but with purpose. My sandals press dust into the earth where Avraham once walked, where David once danced, where My Father's presence once filled the Temple like fire.

The people do not yet know what walks among them.

I pass the market stalls, filled with the smell of olives, bread, and incense. Children chase each other through alleyways. Merchants call out with hopeful tones. But I do not linger. My path is toward a place few speak of unless in whispers.

By the Sheep Gate lies the pool—Bethesda. Its name means "House of Mercy," but to many, it is a place of waiting. Five covered colonnades shelter the broken, the blind, the paralysed. They lie in the shadows, watching the water, hoping for its stir. Tradition says an angel touches it now and then, and the first to step in is healed. But most never move fast enough. Most have waited for years. Decades.

And among them is a man.

He has waited thirty-eight years. Longer than some have lived. His limbs have grown weak. His hope, weaker still. But he remains. Every day, someone helps him to his mat. Every day, he stares at water that never comes in time. And still, he waits.

I kneel beside him. He does not know Me.

"Do you want to be made well?"

His eyes flutter up, dulled by disappointment. "Sir, I have no one to help me into the pool when the water is stirred. While I am trying to get in, someone else goes down ahead of me."

I look past the pool. Past the superstition. Past the years of suffering.

"Rise. Take up your mat and walk."

There is no flare. No roar. Only unfolding. First, a flicker. Then a stir. Then strength floods into limbs long abandoned. He rises. Slowly, disbelieving. Then, steadier. He picks up his mat—the same one that cradled despair for nearly forty years. He walks.

And the Sabbath breathes its rhythm across Jerusalem.

But the watchers see.

Pharisees, robed in tradition, eyes sharp with scrutiny. They see not the healed man, but the mat under his arm.

"It is the Sabbath," they say. "The law forbids you to carry your mat."

He tries to explain. "The man who made me well said, 'Pick up your mat and walk.'"

But they are not interested in healing. Only rules.

Later, I find him in the temple—no longer lying but standing. Worshipping. I speak to him again. "See, you are well again. Stop sinning, or something worse may happen to you."

He nods, eyes wide with a different kind of fear. Not the fear of men, but of something deeper reverence.

He tells the leaders it was Me.

And so, the stirrings of conflict begin.

Another Sabbath. Another place.

A synagogue. Inside, the murmurs of Scripture being read, sandals sliding across stone, the shuffle of worn parchment. Eyes glance up as I enter. And there—a man with a withered hand. He does not speak. But the leaders watch. They whisper among themselves, hoping I will heal him, that they may accuse Me of breaking Sabbath law.

I stand.

"Come here," I say.

The man steps forward. I look around. Their eyes avoid Mine.

"Is it lawful on the Sabbath to do good or to do evil? To save life, or to kill?"

Silence.

Their hearts are hard. The law was meant to bring life, but they have twisted it into chains.

I stretch out My hand. "Stretch out yours."

And he does. Flesh restored. Bones straight. Strength returns. And still—no praise. No rejoicing.

Only plotting.

They leave, not in awe, but in anger. They conspire.

But I continue. For this is why I came. Not to appease tradition, but to fulfil the promise. Not to break the Sabbath, but to reveal its heart.

Mercy.

Healing.

Rest.

The hills were quiet that morning. The hush before movement. The stillness before commissioning.

I walked through the early light, feet pressing into dew-covered grass, the sky soft with promise. Around Me, the scent of olive trees and wild thyme lifted on the breeze. I had spent the night in prayer—alone, yet never truly alone. Heaven spoke. The Father confirmed. The time had come.

Many followed Me now. From cities, villages, deserts, seas. Some came for healing, others for hope. A few came for Me. But from the many, I would choose twelve.

Not because they were the wisest. Not because they were the strongest. But because they would follow. Because they would carry the message when My feet no longer walked their roads.

The crowd gathered early. Faces expectant. The murmurs stilled as I stepped forward. One by one, I called them.

"Shimon." He looked up. Rough hands, weathered by salt and sun. Eyes restless, passionate, burning. I had renamed him already. Kephas. The stone or little rock. Though his spirit trembled like waves, I saw what would anchor.

"Andrai." Quiet strength. A seeker, even before he found Me. He had brought his brother once. He would bring many more.

"Ya'akov son of Zavdai." He stepped forward with his brother, thunder in their veins. A voice that would someday echo in Jerusalem, bold and sure.

"Yochanan." His eyes gentler than his brother's, but no less fierce in truth. The beloved. The one who would stay longest and write of love that casts out fear.

"Philippos." He had questions. He always did. But he followed quickly, earnestly. A heart hungry for understanding.

"Bar-Talmai." Also called Netan'el. Guileless. Pure-hearted. A man of Scripture and solitude. Under the fig tree, I saw him before he saw Me.

"Matityahu." The tax collector. Reviled by many, but seen by Me. He left coins for the Kingdom.

"Toma." Doubter, they would call him. But honest. Loyal unto death. The wound in My hands would one day heal the wound in his heart.

"Ya'akov son of Chalfai." Quiet. Faithful. Less known by men, but not by Me.

"Taddai." Called Lebbaeus, too. Zealous in ways unseen. He would speak boldly when the time was right.

"Shimon the Zealot." Once ready to take Rome by sword. Now ready to take hearts by truth.

"Yehudah of Kerioth." He came when I called. I gave him authority, even knowing his part. Cried knowing he would choose greed over love. Even then, I loved him.

Twelve.

Not perfect. But chosen.

I gave them authority—to cast out demons, to heal disease. To preach that the Kingdom of God had drawn near. But more than power, I gave them purpose. I gave them me.

"You will not be like the rulers of this world," I told them. "You will serve. You will carry the weight of this message not in scrolls but in scars. You will be My witnesses. And when I am gone, you will not be alone. The Spirit will come. He will teach you. Remind you. Strengthen you."

They looked at each other—fishermen, sceptics, nationalists, outcasts. No thrones awaited them. No palaces. Only dusty roads and persecution.

And yet, they nodded.

They stood together. Twelve stones set for a new foundation. One would fall, but another would rise. The message would endure.

I turned My face toward the next village. They followed. The world would never be the same.

The mountain behind us. The mission before us. And with each step, the Kingdom advanced.

Chapter 7: The Kingdom in Motion

The crowds have grown.

Word travels faster than sandals can carry. From village to village, lips pass on stories: a man who heals with a touch, who speaks with authority, who casts out demons with a single word. Some come seeking miracles. Some come curious. Others come hungry for truth, for the Messiah. And still more, for hope.

They follow Me, not just for signs, but for something deeper—something their souls recognise though their minds cannot name.

I climb the slope of a Galilean hill, overlooking the Sea, green and flowering in the spring light. The breeze carries the scent of wild thyme and the distant cry of fishermen returning from early catch. Behind Me, My disciples follow. And behind them, the crowd gathers—mothers with children, men with weary eyes, old ones leaning on staffs, all drawn to the mountain.

I sit. They sit. The hush falls.

And I begin.

Not with law, but with blessing. Not with thunder, but with promise.

"Blessed are the poor in spirit, for theirs is the kingdom of heaven." My voice carries, everything is heard.

Gasps catch in some throats. This is not what they expected. Not strength, not power, not those who conquer.

But the broken. The humble. The desperate. These are the ones Heaven welcomes.

"Blessed are those who mourn, for they shall be comforted."

Their sorrows are not wasted. Their grief is seen. I do not ignore pain—I meet it.

"Blessed are the meek, for they shall inherit the earth."

Not the violent. Not the oppressors. But the gentle ones. The ones who yield, who do not demand, those that shake off pride, who trust.

"Blessed are those who hunger and thirst for righteousness, for they shall be filled."

Those who ache for justice, who long to see wrongs made right—I see them.

I continue.

Mercy. Purity. Peace making. These are not sidelines in the Kingdom; they are the very heart of it.

And then I say what they never expected:

"Blessed are you when men revile you and persecute you and say all manner of evil against you falsely, for My sake. Rejoice and be exceedingly glad, for great, is your reward in heaven."

Some shift uncomfortably. Others lean in. It is upside-down. Or perhaps, right side up—only the world has been standing on its head for far too long.

"You are the salt of the earth." "You are the light of the world."

Not the powerful. Not the learned. But you—the ordinary.

The overlooked, the downtrodden. The ones who have gathered here, hearts open like fields ready for rain.

I tell them not to hide their light, not to bury their salt. I have not come to abolish the Law or the Prophets, but to fulfil them—to show what they always pointed to.

Righteousness must go deeper than surface. Beyond scribes and Pharisees. It must reach the heart.

"You have heard it said... but I say to you..."

I speak of anger as murder. Of lust as adultery. Of oaths, of vengeance, of loving enemies.

Each word falls like seed.

Some hearts are stony. Some are shallow. But some—some will take root.

The Kingdom of Heaven is not far. It is here. In Me. And now, in them.

I see their faces—awed, puzzled, stirred.

And I continue.

I speak of secret giving, of quiet prayer, of trust that doesn't parade.

"Do not store up treasures on earth..." "Consider the lilies..." "Seek first the Kingdom of God..."

Worry must bow. Judgment must pause. Forgiveness must flow.

I teach them how to live. Not just what to believe. The narrow way. The fruitful tree. The house built on rock.

And when I finish, silence holds the hilltop. A silence filled with weight. With glory.

They came for a sermon. They leave with a summons.

The mountain will remain. The words will echo. And the Kingdom will grow.

I descend from the mountain, leaving footprints in the path where heaven met earth. The faces of those who listened still linger in My thoughts—some radiant with understanding, others furrowed with questions. But all were stirred. The Word has been sown, and though the soil varies, some seed will take root. I walk now not away from the sermon, but into its outworking—into lives that need more than words. Into hearts that ache not for truth alone, but for touch, for healing, for hope made flesh.

The breeze carries the scent of dust and olive trees as I enter Capernaum once more. Whispers travel faster than footsteps. Crowds stir, gathering not in riot, but in desperate hope.

Then—he comes. Not a Jew. A Roman. A centurion, soldier of empire, cloaked not just in authority but in an unexpected humility. He does not come himself at first but sends elders of the synagogue—the very men many fear, now plead on his behalf.

"He is worthy," they say urgently. "He loves our nation. He built our synagogue. Please, come."

I walk toward his house, the dust rising beneath My feet. Before I reach the door, he comes, breathless.

"Lord, do not trouble Yourself," he says. "I am not worthy to have You come under my roof. That is why I did not even consider myself worthy to come to You. But say the word, and my servant will be healed. For I too am a man under authority, with soldiers under me. I say to one, 'Go,' and he goes; to another, 'Come,' and he comes. And to my servant, 'Do this,' and he does it."

I stop.

I turn to the crowd that presses behind Me, their faces questioning, waiting.

"I tell you," I say, My voice carrying across the road, "not even in Israel have I found such great faith."

Faith—born not of lineage, nor of covenant birthright, but of recognition. He sees the authority of heaven clothed in human skin—and believes.

I lift My eyes to heaven. No need to enter the home. No need for signs or spectacle. I send the word.

The servant, near death moments before, rises whole.

And still, I walk.

The day unfolds beneath My steps, each moment heavy with unseen purpose.

We move south toward a small town cradled in the hills—Nain. A village worn by time, its streets narrow, its homes leaning into each other like old friends weary of bearing their burdens alone.

As we near the gates, another crowd approaches—sombre, slow. A funeral procession.

The widow leads them, her face drawn tight by grief. Her only son—her last hope, her last comfort—laid lifeless on a bier. The weeping is deep, tearing not only at the heart of a mother but at the fragile edges of a community bound by sorrow.

I see her.

The ache of her spirit thunders louder than the mourners' wails. She is not just losing a son. She is losing her protection, her standing, her very survival. In her world, a widow without a son walks into a future of vulnerability and forgottenness.

Compassion rises within Me—not pity, but a fierce, holy tenderness.

I step forward.

The procession halts, confusion rippling through the crowd.

"Do not weep," I say.

Some recoil—how dare a stranger speak such words at a moment like this?

But I know.

I touch the bier. The bearers freeze, their hands trembling under the sudden stillness.

"Young man," I call, voice cutting through veil of death, "I say to you, arise!"

For a moment, time seems to hesitate.

Then—movement.

Eyes once dulled by death blink wide.

The boy sits up, breath rushing back into once-stilled lungs. His first words stumble over dry lips, and the crowd gasps, recoiling in terror and awe.

I help him down and place him into his mother's arms. Her sobs change—grief melts into trembling, breathless joy.

The crowd murmurs, shouts, falls to their knees.

"A great prophet has risen among us!" they cry.

"God has visited His people!"

The story spreads like fire on dry grass, leaping from village to village, carried by tongues astonished by what they have seen.

But I do not stay to bask in wonder or fame.

I came for the broken, the mourning, the dead.

And there are many yet to raise.

The Kingdom is moving—not in palaces, but in processions halted by compassion, in centurions' faith, in widows' joy reborn.

And it is only beginning.

The mourners have dispersed. The woman of Nain—once bowed under the weight of grief—now holds her son, weeping again, but this time with wonder. The crowd's awe spills down the hillside like the wind, some running ahead to tell the tale, others lingering, unable to part from the presence that touched the untouchable.

But not all are rejoicing.

A question comes to Me, carried not on the wind, but in the footsteps of messengers. Dusty from travel, they approach quietly, uncertain, reverent. They speak not their own words, but another's—a man behind stone walls, his voice growing hoarse with waiting.

"Yochanan, the Baptist" they say, "has sent us to ask: Are You the One who is to come, or should we look for another?"

I pause. Not in hesitation, but in compassion. For even the

boldest prophets, when hemmed in by iron bars and silence, begin to wonder if the wind they once felt was real. He, who leapt in the womb, now doubts in the dark. He, who once cried, "Behold the Lamb," now whispers, "Was I wrong?"

I do not scold the question. I do not rebuke the messenger.

Instead, I turn—and answer not with words, but with deeds.

Blind eyes open. Lame legs rise. Lepers feel again. Ears once sealed ring with laughter. The dead sit up and speak. And the poor? They receive the good news as royalty.

"Go," I tell them. "Tell Yochanan what you have seen and heard: the blind sees, the lame walk, the lepers are cleansed, the deaf hear, the dead are raised, and the gospel is preached to the poor. And blessed is the one who is not offended by Me."

They leave with wonder in their eyes. I turn to the crowd.

"What did you go out into the wilderness to see? A reed shaken by the wind? A man in fine clothes? No—Yochanan is a prophet. More than a prophet. Among those born of women, none is greater than he."

The people listen, some with tears. Some with heads bowed in silent agreement. Others, arms folded, lips tight. The Pharisees and experts of the law refuse to be moved, refusing even now to be baptised by repentance.

"To what shall I compare this generation?" I ask. "They are like children calling out in the marketplace: 'We played the flute for you, and you did not dance. We sang a dirge, and you did not mourn.'"

They wanted a lion and were given a lamb. They expected

thunder and received Meekness robed in strength. They neither rejoiced with the healed nor wept with the weary. But My voice does not chase applause. It calls the broken.

I lift My gaze. The crowd draws close, leaning in.

"Come to Me," I say, "all you who are weary and burdened, and I will give you rest."

A hush falls.

"Take My yoke upon you, and learn from Me. For I am gentle and humble in heart, and you will find rest for your souls."

The dust settles beneath their feet, but something rises in their hearts.

"For My yoke is easy, and My burden is light."

And those crushed under law, those bent beneath shame, those tired of carrying what they were never meant to bear... begin to believe rest is possible.

That the door is open, for I AM the way.

That the Kingdom has arms—and they are stretched wide.

The words settle over them like the cool shade of a fig tree in the heat of the day. "My yoke is easy. My burden is light." Yet they do not drift away like soft sayings—they remain, weighty, wrapping themselves around hearts worn thin by religion, law, and expectation.

I walk on, but quietly. The crowd begins to thin. Some remain at a distance, eyes lowered, not ready. Others linger, not out of duty, but hope. I feel it in the air—softening, searching, the shift of souls beginning to trust that maybe, just maybe, I am not like the others.

I stop outside the house of a Pharisee. Shimon. He has

invited Me to dine. Not in devotion—but in curiosity. Perhaps to test Me. Perhaps to prove what he already believes. His heart is tidy, guarded, proud. But I do not come only for open hearts. I come for all.

Inside, the table is low, the oil lamp flickers. Reclining guests speak in low tones, the scent of food mingling with incense and something unspoken in the room. I feel eyes on Me—but not all eyes are equal.

And then she enters.

Not from the door, but from the shadows.

A woman.

No title. No name spoken aloud. Only her story follows her like a trailing robe of shame. The murmurs begin before her feet cross the threshold. "Sinner." The word slithers through the air like smoke.

But she does not turn back. The desire for change drives her forward.

Clutched in her hands—an alabaster jar. Her tears have already begun to flow.

She kneels behind Me, her sobs silent but deep. The kind that come not from fear, but release. She lets her tears fall upon My feet, washing what Shimon would not even offer water for. Her hair becomes the towel. Her kisses, the offering. And then the perfume—broken, poured, irretrievable.

The room recoils.

Shimon's silence is louder than his thoughts.

"If this man were truly a prophet…"

I lift My gaze to him, but My voice does not rise.

"Shimon," I say. "I have something to say to you."

He nods, reserved.

"There were two debtors. One owed five hundred denarii, the other fifty. Neither could repay. The lender forgave them both. Who will love him more?"

Shimon answers, carefully, "I suppose the one who was forgiven more."

"You have judged rightly."

I turn to the woman—but still speak to him.

"Do you see her? I entered your house. You gave Me no water for My feet. But she has washed them with her tears. You gave Me no kiss. But she has not stopped kissing them. You did not anoint My head with oil. But she has poured perfume upon My feet. Therefore, I tell you, her many sins are forgiven—for she loved much."

The silence swells.

"But he who is forgiven little, loves little."

Then, to her—only to her—I speak with softness the law cannot understand:

"Your sins are forgiven."

Gasps. Eyes widen. Hearts stumble over the grace in My words.

"Your faith has saved you. Go in peace."

She does not speak. She does not need to.

Peace follows her as she leaves. But behind her anger –

hatred grows.

Forgiveness lingers like the perfume she poured.

And still, the Kingdom grows.

The room still breathes with the scent of her worship.
Whispers rise behind closed doors, but so does wonder.
For every scoff, a soul stirred.
For every glare, a heart softened.
Not all rejoice — but some begin to follow.
And so, I continue.

The road winds again. I walk from town to town, not alone
but with those who once only followed from a distance.
Now, they walk with Me. Some men and women. The
Twelve, yes—but also those whose lives have been
rewritten.

She walks among them—Miryam of Magdala.

Once bound by torment, now free. Seven spirits once tore at
her peace, but they are gone now. She carries no titles,
holds no office. Yet her devotion is deep, unwavering. She
does not seek the spotlight, but I see her. Always near,
always steady.

Her past is behind her—but not forgotten. Not by others.
Some still whisper. Some still wonder. But I know her name.
I know her story. And I call her daughter.

She gives from her own means. So do others—Yochanah,
wife of Chuza, steward to Herod; Hannah; women of wealth,
women of wounds. They do not fund an empire. They fuel a
mission. And the Kingdom advances with every step they
take.

The world may not record their sermons. But I do. In heaven, their names echo.

Miryam walks near, her eyes alert, her silence saying more than words ever could. And where she walks, freedom follows.

The crowd presses in, hungry for healing. A man is brought to Me—blind, mute, possessed. His eyes are clouded with torment, his tongue bound by darkness. But I do not hesitate.

I cast the spirit out.

His eyes clear. His voice rises. He speaks for the first time in years. The crowd erupts—astonished, electrified.

"Could this be the Son of David?"

The words ripple. Faith awakens. Hope stirs.

Still, some remain unmoved.

Pharisees push forward; their robes stirred by more than wind. They feel the ground shifting beneath them—and they grasp for control.

"It is by Beelzebul, the prince of demons, that He casts out demons," they say.

Their words are careful. Calculated. Cowardly.

I turn to them—not in fury, but fire.

"If Satan drives out Satan, he is divided against himself. How then can his kingdom stand?"

They shift, uneasy.

"And if I drive out demons by Beelzebul, by whom do your people drive them out? Let them be your judges."

They cannot answer.

"But if I drive out demons by the Spirit of God, then the Kingdom of God has come upon you."

The air thickens.

"Or again—how can anyone enter a strong man's house and carry off his possessions, unless, he first binds the strong man?"

I do not raise My voice.

But the words pierce.

"I tell you the truth: every sin and blasphemy will be forgiven men. But the one who blasphemes against the Ruach HaKodesh —this will not be forgiven."

Their eyes narrow.

"Whoever is not with Me is against Me. And whoever does not gather with Me, scatters."

A line is drawn.

Not with chalk, but with truth.

They wanted healing, but not repentance. They wanted signs with no surrender. They wanted Me—on their terms.

But the Kingdom will not be bent to man's agenda.

And now, some walk away.

Some still follow.

But none can say they do not understand the choice before them.

The light is here.

They have seen it.

And still—some choose the dark, how sad.

The crowd is thicker now. Faces I do not know press forward. Some come for healing. Others for truth. But some come for neither. They come to test, to trap. To silence.

The murmurs reach Me before the words do.

"Teacher, we want to see a sign from You."

As if the blind seeing, the mute speaking, the dead rising was not enough. As if the sign they sought was not already standing in front of them, clothed in flesh and truth.

"A wicked and adulterous generation asks for a sign," I say.

They blink. The words sting.

"But none will be given it except the sign of the prophet Yonah."

I pause. Some lean in.

"For as Yonah was three days and nights in the belly of the great fish, so will the Son of Man be three days and nights in the heart of the earth."

They do not understand yet. But one day, they will.

"The men of Nineveh will rise at the judgment with this generation and condemn it. For they repented at the preaching of Yonah. And now—One greater than Yonah is here."

I see their faces twist.

"The Queen of the South will rise at the judgment with this generation and condemn it. She came from the ends of the earth to hear the wisdom of Shlomo. And now—One greater than Shlomo is here."

Their silence is heavy.

But they are not ready to repent.

Not yet.

Not when repentance costs them control.

I enter the synagogue. They sit in seats of honour, their robes pristine, their phylacteries wide. They teach the law but do not love it. They weigh down the people with burdens they themselves do not carry.

I do not flatter.

"Woe to you, teachers of the law and Pharisees—hypocrites! You shut the door of the Kingdom in people's faces. You yourselves do not enter, nor will you let those who would enter go in."

Their faces harden. Still, I continue.

"You travel over land and sea to win a single convert, and when you have succeeded, you make them twice as much a child of hell as you are."

Gasps ripple. Some rise to leave. But others stay—anchored by a truth they didn't expect to find.

"You clean the outside of the cup, but inside you are full of greed and self-indulgence."

I speak not in wrath, but in lament.

"Woe to you. You are like whitewashed tombs—beautiful on the outside, but full of dead men's bones."

They seek honour. But they do not know the One whom honour comes from. They seek Torah but ignore the One who gave it breath.

Later, by the shore, the crowd follows. But I no longer speak plainly. The divide has widened. Ears hear, but hearts do not.

I speak in parables.

"Listen: A Sower went out to sow his seed..."

The story is simple. A farmer scattering seed. Some fall on the path—snatched away. Some on rocky soil—sprouting quickly but withering for lack of root. Some among thorns—choked. But some—some fall on good soil. And it bears fruit. Thirty, sixty, a hundredfold.

"He who has ears, let him hear."

The disciples look at Me, puzzled.

"Why do You speak to them in parables?"

"Because the secrets of the Kingdom have been given to you," I say, "but not to them. They see but do not perceive. They hear but do not understand. For their hearts have grown dull."

Parables are not riddles to be solved. They are mirrors, revealing hearts.

I tell them another.

"The Kingdom of Heaven is like a mustard seed... like yeast hidden in dough... like treasure buried in a field... like a merchant searching for one pearl of great value."

Each story is simple but layered. Truth tucked beneath story. Invitation veiled in imagery.

I tell them about the fig tree—barren, fruitless, cursed by its own pretence of growth.

I tell them about lamps—meant not to be hidden but set on a stand to give light.

And some begin to see.

Not many. But some.

They see that the Kingdom does not come in thunder, but in truth. That it does not grow by violence, but by seed. That the greatest are not those who sit in high places, but those who humble themselves like children.

The parables draw lines.

The proud become angrier.

The broken hold their breath.

Some say, "He has a demon."

Others whisper, "No one speaks like this."

And still I teach.

Still, I sow.

Because even if only one seed takes root in the heart of good soil—it will bear fruit enough for generations.

The evening comes, and with it, stillness. The crowds have gone. The sun lowers, painting the lake in strokes of orange and purple. I step into the boat with My disciples. The water laps against the sides as we push away from the shore.

"Let us go to the other side," I say.

They do not question. They are tired, but content. The day was full. Healings. Teachings. Parables. The Kingdom whispered in every word.

I go to the lower part of the boat and sleep.

But they do not yet understand the storm within the calm, nor the power that sleeps in the stern.

We sail. The wind is gentle. The stars blink overhead.

Then it begins.

A wind stirs. Then roars. Waves rise like walls. The sky folds in on itself. The sea tosses, violent and dark. The boat shudders. Water pours in. lightening lights up the skies, thunderclaps.

They panic.

"Master! Teacher! Don't You care that we are perishing?"

I rise.

Rain lashes My face. Thunder rolls. Fear clings to their skin. I do not rush. I do not shout.

"Peace. Be still."

And creation obeys.

The wind forgets its fury. The sea rests like a cradle. Silence stretches wide. Skies deep blue.

They stare at Me. Eyes wide. Mouths open.

"Who is this, that even the wind and waves obey Him?"

They know Me, yet they do not. They follow Me but cannot fathom My fullness.

The boat glides to shore on the other side. The region of the Gerasenes. A land of tombs and silence and chains.

Before their feet touch soil, he comes.

A man, naked and scarred, screaming from the tombs. Eyes wild. Voice torn. Possessed.

He runs to Me and falls.

"What have You to do with me, Yehoshua, Son of the Most-High God? I beg You, do not torment me."

He speaks, yet not alone. A legion writhes within him.

I do not flinch.

"Come out of him, unclean spirit."

The demons plead.

"Send us into the pigs."

I allow it.

They go.

And the herd—two thousand strong—rages toward the cliff and dives. The water churns with their death.

The herdsmen flee.

The townspeople come. They find the man—clothed, seated, sane. And they are afraid.

They ask Me to leave.

They fear power they cannot control. Mercy they cannot explain.

The man clings to Me. "Let me go with You."

But I shake My head.

"Go home to your friends and tell them how much the Lord has done for you. How He has had mercy on you."

He watches the boat drift away.

And begins to proclaim.

And the Kingdom spreads—even in Decapolis.

The sea behind Me is still.

But the storm continues in hearts not yet ready for peace.

The path winds back toward Nazareth—My boyhood home. The hills do not forget Me. They echo the laughter of My youth, the ring of Yosef's hammer, the gentle rhythm of Miryam's voice calling Me in from play. The streets remain narrow, the rooftops low, the familiar dust of childhood still clings to the air.

But I am not returning as the boy they once knew.

I enter quietly. Some turn their heads. Others whisper. A few smile out of familiarity, though they cannot hide the questions in their eyes.

They say, "Isn't this the carpenter's son? He blasphemed in the synagogue

They say, "We know His brothers—Yaakov, Yosef, Shimon, and Yehuda. His sisters still live among us."

They look for familiarity—and because of it, they cannot see what stands before them.

I return to the synagogue, the place where I first read the scroll, where words once met fury. This time, I say little. I teach, yes—but they marvel only briefly before suspicion rises again. No mighty miracles follow. Not here. Not because I lack power—but because they lack faith.

Only a few receive healing. Only a few come near.

A prophet is not without honour—except in his own town.

So, I leave Nazareth, not with bitterness, but with clarity. Their rejection sharpens My mission. I will not linger where hearts are closed. The Kingdom is moving forward.

I gather the Twelve.

They stand before Me—fishermen, tax collector, zealot, brothers in blood and spirit. Rough hands. Honest eyes. Unlikely vessels for divine commission. Yet it is through them that My message will multiply.

I call them by name, each one:

Shimon, whom I named Kephas—Kephas—the little rock. Andrai, his brother, steadfast and true. Yaakov and Yochanan, sons of thunder, passion burning in their veins. Philippos and Bar-Talmai, earnest seekers of truth. Mattityahu, once seated at a tax booth, now seated at My feet. Toma, the twin, who wrestles with doubt but will stand firm in the end. Yaakov son of Halfai, and Taddai, faithful though quiet. Shimon the Zealot, fire for his people. And Yehudah from K'riot, whose footsteps already carry a shadow.

I give them authority—over unclean spirits, to cast them out, and to heal every disease and affliction. Not to build kingdoms for themselves. Not to carry swords. But to go as I came—lowly, bold, full of truth and mercy.

I instruct them:

"Go not among the Gentiles or into any Samaritan town just yet. Go instead to the lost sheep of Israel. Preach this message: 'The Kingdom of Heaven has come near.'

Heal the sick. Raise the dead. Cleanse the lepers. Drive out demons. Freely you have received—freely give."

They look at Me, eyes wide, hearts stirred.

"Take no gold, silver, or copper. No bag for the journey. No extra tunic or sandals. The worker is worthy of his keep. Stay with those who welcome you. Shake the dust from your feet when they do not."

I speak of danger—not to stir fear, but readiness. Sheep among wolves. They will be hated. Persecuted. Some will fall. But they will not be alone.

"I send you as My voice, My hands, My witness. What is whispered in darkness, proclaim in the light. What is spoken in secret, shout from the rooftops."

They nod, not fully understanding. But faith does not require full understanding—only obedience.

I place My hand upon each one.

"You will do greater things. Not because you are greater, but because I will go—and the Spirit will come."

I send them out.

Two by two, down dusty roads, into homes both humble and hostile. Into cities where sandals are removed at the door, and villages where stones may be lifted instead. They go, not with prestige, but with purpose.

And as they disappear beyond the horizon, I watch.

The Kingdom moves—not just in Me now, but through them.

The sun dips low as Matityahu and Philippos walk the narrow path between fields of barley and olive trees. One is quiet, the other full of questions. Neither carries coin nor staff. Only the authority Yehoshua placed within them, and the dust of Nazareth still clinging to their robes.

Philippos glances sideways. "Do you remember how surprised we all were when He chose you?"

Matityahu smiles faintly. "More surprised than I was when He looked past my booth and said, 'Follow Me.' I was used to people speaking to me only when they had no choice."

Philippos nods. "You still write down everything He says."

"Someone has to," Matityahu replies. "It all feels... eternal."

They approach a small village. Smoke curls from clay ovens. Goats bleat lazily in the heat. A child runs past them, stops, stares, and then vanishes behind a doorway.

Philippos whispers, "What if they don't receive us?"

Matityahu doesn't answer. Not with words. He knocks at the first door.

A woman opens it, suspicious at first, wiping flour from her hands.

"Peace be to this house," Matityahu says gently.

She hesitates. Her eyes soften. "Come," she says. "If you're hungry, we have bread and figs."

Inside, they speak of the Kingdom—not with lofty words, but with parables and peace. The woman's husband, crippled from an old injury, leans against the doorway. Matityahu asks gently to pray for him.

Hands are laid. A whisper of Yehoshua's name. A cry. Then stillness.

The man straightens—shaky, unbelieving.

The house erupts in tears and laughter. A neighbour runs to

see. Then another. Soon, the small home overflows.

"Who are you?" someone asks.

"We are His," Philippos replies. "Yehoshua, the Messiah sent us."

They return, full of wonder.

The sun has barely risen when the news reaches Me.

He is dead.

Yochanan. The forerunner. The voice in the wilderness. Silenced—not by time or age, but by pride and fear. His head now lies apart from the body that once trembled with fire and truth. A banquet of kings ended in the blood of a prophet. A jest, a dance, a vow — and a righteous man removed like an inconvenience.

They think it is over. That silencing a voice will silence the movement.

But they forget: I Am the Word.

Still, I do not speak immediately. Not to the crowd. Not to the disciples. The pain sits within Me like a storm waiting to break. My cousin. My messenger. My friend.

The disciples of Yochanan come to Me, their faces lined with grief. They tell Me everything.

Miryam is nearby. She says nothing, but her eyes watch Mine closely.

I withdraw. Quietly. Across the lake. Into the wilderness again. Not to be alone—but to commune. To breathe. To feel. To speak to the Father in the silence that only grief can birth.

The disciples follow. So do the crowds.

Even in sorrow, the people come.

They are desperate. Hungry. Some carry children. Some carry disease. All carry need. And though My heart aches for My friend, it swells with compassion for them.

Because I see them.

Not just their illness, or their weariness—but the lostness. They are like sheep without a shepherd.

And so, I do what He would have done. What I must do.

I stay.

I teach.

I heal.

Yochanan's voice may be gone from the earth, but the message is not.

Repent. The Kingdom of Heaven is still at hand.

And it will not be stopped.

Not by swords.

Not by priests.

Not by kings.

Not even by death.

Evening falls. The light fades, but the crowd does not.

Thousands now. Men, women, children. They have followed us around the lake, step for step, word for word. And they remain. Not because of signs alone—but something deeper. Hunger, yes—but not just of stomach.

Still, hunger presses in.

The disciples' approach, worried.

"Send them away," they say. "Let them go to the villages and buy food."

I look out at the multitude.

"They do not need to go away. You give them something to eat."

They stare at Me, startled. Their brows crease. Their pouches are light. The nearby towns could not feed this many.

A little boy comes forward, sent by his mum, "Sir, I have five loaves and two fish,"

Good. That will be more than enough. I smile and thank him.

I tell the people to sit on the grass. I take the loaves. I lift My eyes. I bless. I break.

And I give.

The baskets pass from hand to hand. And they do not empty.

Mouths open in laughter and disbelief. Children clap. Old men blink away tears. Women gasp at the overflowing fragments gathered after. Twelve baskets. One for each of those who doubted. They give it to the little boy. He gleams with delight!

Not just bread. Not just fish.

Abundance.

Not just provision.

Revelation.

Here is the Kingdom: where little becomes much, where hunger meets grace, where bread breaks and eyes open.

They want to make Me king.

I retreat.

Night falls.

The disciples board the boat. I remain behind. Alone with the Father. The hills cradle My prayers. I speak—not out of ritual, but out of longing, longing for home, for fellowship. The weight of the day, the pain of Yochanan's death, the pressing expectations of the people—all of it, I bring into silence.

Below, the sea begins to churn.

Waves rise. The wind howls. The boat tosses in darkness, far from land. They strain at the oars. They are fishermen, but this storm is different. This storm tests more than their skill—it tests their sight.

Then I come to them.

Not in a boat. Not from behind.

But walking. On the water.

Terror grips them. They cry out. A ghost, they think.

But I speak.

"Take courage. It is I. Do not be afraid."

The sea still rages, but the sound of My voice cuts through wind and wave.

Kephas calls out, "If it's You, Lord, tell me to come to You on the water."

"come"

He steps. His foot touches water—and holds.

Faith, like the sea beneath him, rises.

But then the wind. The waves. His eyes shift.

He sinks.

"Lord, save me!"

I reach.

I pull him up. "O you of little faith, why did you doubt?"

Together, we step into the boat.

The wind ceases.

The sea lies down like a calmed child.

They fall to their knees.

"Truly, You are the Son of God."

In that moment—faith blooms.

In the bread, they saw My power.

In the water, they see My nature.

And though the crowds still chase signs,

Though the opposition quietly sharpens,

Though the cross looms in the shadows beyond Galilee's edge—

Tonight, there is worship.

Tonight, there is belief.

Chapter 8: The Turning Point

The road leads back to Capernaum. Familiar streets, familiar faces—yet the murmurs now follow Me more than My steps. Crowds press in, not merely to see, but to demand, to question. Their hearts want miracles; few seek the truth.

I step into the synagogue. Dust stirs from the worn stones, and the sun, slicing through narrow windows, scatters it like gold spun in the air. They gather, pressed close, expectant. Some hunger for bread that fills the belly. Few hunger for bread that fills the soul. I stand among them—not with thunder, nor spectacle—but with the hush of eternity settling over the room.

"I am the Bread of Life," I say.

Murmurs. Furrowed brows.

"He who comes to Me will never go hungry. He who believes in Me will never thirst."

Some lean in, hearts kindled by a fire they do not yet understand. Others recoil, offended at the mystery they cannot control.

They ask for signs, though signs have walked among them. They ask for proofs, though Heaven itself leans into their midst.

I speak plainly:
"You seek Me not because you saw signs, but because you ate of the loaves and were filled. Do not labour for food that perishes, but for the food that endures to eternal life."

The Word is sharper than any sword. It pierces through their hunger for comfort, cutting toward a hunger they have long forgotten. Many turn away. The Bread offered is too costly to consume.

Still, the Kingdom advances.

Whispers among the Pharisees grow louder. They mutter warnings about leaven—about corruption that seeps silently into faith, puffing it up, hollowing it out. I caution My disciples:
"Beware the leaven of the Pharisees."

Not yeast of bread, but yeast of pride. Of hollow religion. Of hardened hearts.

The road carries Me onward, through villages and fields kissed by the Galilean sun. Dust clings to My robe. Faces watch Me pass—some with hope, some with disdain.

In Bethsaida, a blind man stumbles toward Me, led by trembling hands. His world has been shadows and whispers. His faith is raw, desperate. I take him by the hand, leading him outside the village. Away from the noise. Away from the unbelief that chokes miracles.

I touch his eyes once. He sees—barely.
Men like trees, walking.

Again, I touch him.
Clarity breaks like dawn. Sight rushes in, pure and brilliant. He blinks against the brightness. He falls to his knees, overwhelmed.

I send him home, saying, "Do not even enter the village."
Not because the miracle is secret—but because the faithless demand for signs will not sustain the soul.

And then—we walk north. Toward Caesarea Philippi. A place of idols and monuments to false kings. A place where the air is thick with the weight of misplaced worship.

There, among the cliffs and temples built to gods who cannot save, I ask the question that will shake the world:

"Who do you say I am?"

We walk north. The cliffs of Caesarea Philippi rise ahead, jagged against the sky, their altars and temples littering the hillside like broken promises. Statues stand where living faith should. Shrines carved into rock whisper the names of gods who neither hear, nor answer.

It is here, in the shadow of counterfeit kings, that I ask them the question that matters most.

"Who do people say that I am?"

The disciples' glance at one another. They have heard the whispers on the roads, the murmuring in the synagogues. One by one they answer.

"Some say Yochanan the Baptist."
"Others say Eliyahu."
"Or Yeremiyahu, or one of the prophets."

Their words tumble like loose stones—close, but not enough.
I look at them—at their faces lined by dust and hope—and ask again, softer now:

"But who do *you* say that I am?"

A silence settles, heavy and sacred.

Then Kephas steps forward—brash, bold, the fisherman with calloused hands and an uncluttered heart.

He meets My gaze without flinching.
The words fall from his lips—not born of flesh but carried from the throne of the Father.
"You are the Messiah. The Son of the Living God."
The wind stills, holding its breath. Even the dust at our feet seems to lean in, listening.
"Blessed are you, Shimon son of Yonah," I say, My voice wrapped in joy, "for flesh and blood has not revealed this to you, but My Father who is in heaven."
I look at him—not only the fisherman, not only the man—but the stone he is becoming.
"You are Kephas," I say—the little rock, the foundation set by the Father's hand. They hear the wordplay. They feel the weight of it, though they do not yet grasp its fullness.
"And upon this Rock—upon Me, the I AM—I will build My assembly, My gathering, My Church.
And the gates of Hades—"
I lift My hand slightly, gesturing to the dark place looming nearby, that ancient mouth swallowing the lost—
"—the gates of Hades will not overcome it."
Here, in the shadow of fear and false gods, I plant the seed of an unshakable Kingdom. The declaration is made not atop a palace or in the Temple—but here, amid idols and dead gods, here in the place of the gates of hades. Light born in darkness. Kingdom declared where counterfeit thrones crumble.

Kephas lowered his eyes, as if the truth he had spoken was too heavy to carry all at once. The others shifted uneasily, glancing at the mouth of the cave, at the shrines carved by desperate hands.
Here, in the shadow of false gods, truth had been spoken.
But shadows do not yield easily.

Their hearts burned with revelation—but fear and misunderstanding would soon follow.
The road from here would not be paved with crowns, but with thorns.
Still, I did not turn back.
The rock had been named. The war had been declared.
And the gates of hell would not prevail.

I give them strict orders not to tell anyone yet. It is not time. There is a road yet to walk, a cross yet to bear. They do not understand it fully. Not yet.

The conversation shifts. I speak openly now about what must come.
About Jerusalem. About betrayal. About suffering. About death. And life after death.

Kephas, so newly bold, rebukes Me. "Never, Lord! This shall never happen to You!"

I turn to him—not in anger, but with deep sorrow.

"Get behind Me, Satan! You are a stumbling block to Me. You do not have in mind the concerns of God, but merely human concerns."

The way of the Kingdom is not paved with swords or crowns. It is paved with sacrifice. They must learn this. All of them.

"If anyone would come after Me, let him deny himself, take up his cross, and follow Me."

The path ahead is narrow. Steep. But it leads to glory.

Shimon, lowers his gaze, flushed with shame. Still, he does not fully understand. But I walk on.

The sun lowers over Caesarea Philippi, painting the cliffs in gold and shadow. I lead them down the mountain trail. The air grows cooler. The chatter of idols fades behind us. We turn our faces toward Capernaum once more.

Toward the next feast.
Toward Jerusalem.
Toward the cross.

The road will grow darker.
But the Kingdom will shine all the brighter.

The road back to Capernaum is quiet. Each footstep kicks up small clouds of dust that hang in the cooling air.
The disciples walk behind Me, still turning over My words in their minds—their dreams of glory grinding against the reality of sacrifice.

In Capernaum, the familiar sea stretches out before us, shimmering under the late sun. Fishermen call to one another, and the smell of roasting fish drifts through the alleys. The village seems unchanged.

I move quietly among the streets, healing those who come.
A child with a crooked spine stands straight at My touch.
An old man, blind since youth, blinks against the sudden brightness of day.
A woman with fever finds her strength again and sings softly as she carries her pitcher home.

Yet not all welcome Me with open arms. The Pharisees murmur. They question. They accuse in whispers, sharpening their hearts against Me.

It is near time for the great Feast—the Feast of Tabernacles. All Israel will soon stream toward Jerusalem, carrying branches of palm and willow, remembering the wilderness years, remembering how God made His dwelling among them.

My brothers urge Me.

"If You are doing these things," they say, "show Yourself to the world."
"Go up to the feast," they insist. "Make Yourself known."

They speak with more sarcasm than faith. They do not yet believe.

I answer them quietly.
"My time is not yet here. For you, any time will do. The world cannot hate you, but it hates Me because I testify that its works are evil."

I will go, but not yet. Not as they wish.
Not with banners or fanfare.
Not with the sword.
But in My Father's timing. In His way.

For now, I remain a little longer in Galilee, gathering strength in stillness.
The fishermen mend their nets.
The olive trees bow under their own fruit.
The sea breathes against the shore, waiting.

And soon—I will ascend to Jerusalem once again.
Not to reign.
Not yet.
But to declare.

The Kingdom draws nearer.

The time approaches when the temporary shelters of men will fall—and God Himself will tabernacle among them in a way they have not dared to dream.

And when I walk into the courts of the Temple,
Heaven will lean low again.

The roads to Jerusalem pulse with life.
Pilgrims stream from every corner of Israel—men with
bundles slung across their shoulders, women carrying
baskets, children clinging to their fathers' robes.

The air hums with expectation.

Palm branches rustle in the wind.
Booths of woven branches and cloth spring up along the
roadsides, reminders of the wilderness wanderings. Songs
rise—some joyful, some ancient and aching.

I walk among them unnoticed at first. No heralds, no
trumpets.
I ascend quietly, My steps blending into the thousands.
The time of hiddenness draws to a close—but not all at
once.

Midway through the feast, I step into the Temple courts.
The marble stones, worn by centuries of feet, seem to
whisper beneath Me.
The porticoes brim with worshippers, merchants, teachers.
I lift My voice—not with anger, but with authority that stirs
the dust and the heart alike.

"My teaching is not My own," I say.
"It comes from Him who sent Me.
Anyone who chooses to do the will of God will find out
whether My teaching comes from God or whether I speak on
My own."

Heads turn.
Scholars' frown.

The ordinary people lean closer, hunger flickering in their eyes.

"Has not Mosheh given you the law?" I ask, My voice cutting through the din.
"Yet none of you keep the law. Why are you trying to kill Me?"

Murmurs rise.
"You are demon-possessed," some say.
"Who is trying to kill You?"

They know.
Their leaders know.
And I know.

I speak not to accuse, but to reveal.

I remind them of the healing at Bethesda.
Of the man who rose and walked because life itself commanded it.

"I did one miracle," I say, "and you are all amazed. Yet you circumcise a boy on the Sabbath... why are you angry with Me for healing a whole man on the Sabbath?"

Do not judge by appearances. Judge with right judgment.

A division stirs the crowd like a storm gathering in the distance.
Some whisper, "Could this be the Messiah?"
Others scoff, "But we know where this man is from! When Messiah comes, no one will know where He is from."

They misunderstand. They stumble over knowledge and miss revelation.

I call again.

"You know Me, and you know where I am from.

I have not come on My own authority, but He who sent Me is true. You do not know Him, but I know Him, because I am from Him, and He sent Me."

Now fury sharpens into action.
They try to seize Me.
Hands move toward My robe.
Guards are sent.

But no one lays a hand on Me.

Because My hour has not yet come.

Among the crowd, faith flickers.

"When the Messiah comes," some reason, "will He perform more signs than this man?"

The seeds are being sown.
Some fall on rocky ground. Some are stolen by the birds.
But some—some find good soil.

And the Kingdom spreads.

Even here, under hostile stares and temple banners snapping in the breeze—
Even here, where plotting hearts gnash against unseen grace—
The Light shines.

The Feast will end.
The booths will come down.
The crowds will return home.

But I remain.
And soon, I will offer a different invitation—
One that will echo across generations yet to come.

The final day of the Feast dawns bright and heavy with expectation.

The great day.
The culmination.

Priests gather at the southern steps of the Temple, descending in solemn procession toward the Pool of Siloam. Silver trumpets gleam. The people sing the Hallel—psalms of joy and longing—as water is drawn into a golden pitcher.

The water procession begins its ascent back to the Temple.

Crowds press together. Shoulders brush shoulders. The fragrance of sacrifices, crushed myrtle, and dust fills the air.

They chant the words of Isaiah:
"With joy you will draw water from the wells of salvation."

Water—life—blessing.

The priests approach the altar. The golden pitcher tilts. Water and wine are poured out, mingling together, splashing over the stones.

And at that moment, with the Temple thrumming under thousands of feet, I step forward.

I lift My voice—not a whisper, not hidden—but clear, strong, a cry cutting through the chanting, through the ceremonies, through the centuries:

"If anyone is thirsty, let him come to Me and drink."

Silence falls as if the world itself holds its breath.

"Whoever believes in Me," I say, "as Scripture has said, streams of living water will flow from within him."

The priests freeze, the water still dripping from the altar stones.

The crowds blink, some stunned, some furious, some pierced by a longing they cannot name.

Living water. Not drawn from a pool.
Not carried in pitchers of gold.
But flowing from within—from Spirit, from heart, from the innermost being of those who believe.

I speak not of ceremonies.
I speak of what is to come.
Of the Spirit yet to be poured out when My work is finished.

Some whisper among themselves, "Surely this man is the Prophet."
Others say, "He is the Messiah."

Still others, bound by lineage and assumption, argue, "How can the Messiah come from Galilee?"

Division.

Some move toward Me—hands open in wonder.
Some move toward Me—hands clenched in fists.

But still—no one lays a hand on Me.

Because the Living Water cannot be seized.
It can only be received.

The guards, sent to arrest Me, return empty-handed.

"Why didn't you bring Him?" the chief priests' demand.

"No one ever spoke the way this man does," they reply.

The rulers snarl, accusing them of deception, of ignorance.

But one among them— Nikódēmos —speaks quietly:

"Does our law condemn a man without first hearing him, to find out what He is doing?"

Mockery follows him. Scorn.

But the question lingers.

And in the quiet places of the heart, where no crowd can follow, the Spirit stirs.

I watch them.
I see the thirst behind the debates.
The aching hunger behind the arguments.

They have celebrated the Feast.
They have poured water onto stone.

But the true well stands before them, arms open.

Few recognise it.

For now.

The Feast ends. The crowds disperse, carrying their arguments and amazement like embers smouldering beneath cloaks.

But I remain still, My eyes set not on the departing festival lights, nor on the emptying courts of the Temple.

I set My eyes toward Jerusalem—not the city of the feast, but the city of sacrifice.

I know what waits there.
I know the road.
And still, I choose it.

I gather My disciples, the dust of the city still clinging to their sandals. They look at Me—some weary, some wondering, some with a fire kindling in their hearts they cannot explain.

The time for quiet ministry among the hills and waters is drawing to a close. The time for healing and teaching crowds under open skies is giving way to something deeper. Harder. Final.

I do not promise them safety.
I do not promise them comfort.

I promise them truth.

"We must go to Jerusalem," I tell them.

The words weigh heavy in the air.

There, the Son of Man will be handed over. Rejected. Condemned. Killed.

But after three days—He will rise.

They do not understand yet.
How could they?

Their minds are still filled with dreams of crowns, not crosses.

Still, they follow. Not fully knowing. But loving enough to move their feet.

I turn My face toward the rising sun. Toward the city that will mock Me, scorn Me, pierce Me.

I turn My face toward Jerusalem—and I do not flinch.

For love drives Me forward.

For joy set before Me, I endure what lies ahead.

Every step now is chosen.
Every word now is measured.

The Kingdom has come—but not as they expected.

It will come through a narrow gate. Through pierced hands.
Through an empty tomb.

And so, we begin the journey.

Through villages dusty with routine.
Through valleys echoing with the songs of old psalms.
Through the hearts of those ready—and those who will
betray.

Each step is a thread woven into the great tapestry of
redemption.

Each breath a countdown to glory.

The path is set.
The hour draws near.

And I, the Lamb, walk forward.

For the world.

For those yet to come.

For the ones who will believe.

For the joy of their salvation.

The road stretches ahead, dry and sun-baked.
But the work cannot wait.

The Kingdom must be proclaimed—not only by My voice,
but by theirs.

I gather them—seventy of My followers. Ordinary men.
Rough hands. Weathered faces. Faith flickering in some,
blazing in others.
I gather them not because they are strong, but because they
are willing.

The harvest is great.

The labourers are few.

I look into their faces, one by one. Fishermen. Shepherds. Craftsmen. Mothers' sons and fathers' hopes. I see both fear and fire in their eyes.

"The harvest is plentiful," I tell them, "but the workers are few. Pray therefore the Lord of the harvest to send out workers into His harvest."

The air stills. They listen.

"Go your way. I send you out as lambs among wolves."

No illusions.

No false promises.

The road ahead will not be smooth, nor the reception always kind. But the message—the Kingdom—is worth every risk.

"Carry no money bag, no knapsack, no sandals; greet no one on the way."

Their eyebrows lift slightly. This is no leisurely mission. This is urgent. Swift. Eternal.

"Whatever house you enter, first say, 'Peace be to this house.' If a son of peace is there, your peace will rest upon it; if not, it will return to you. Stay in that same house, eating and drinking what they provide. For the labourer is worthy of his wages."

They nod. Some hesitantly. Others with quiet resolve.

I continue, My voice firm but full of love.

"Heal the sick who are there and tell them, 'The Kingdom of God has come near to you.'
But if they do not receive you, go into their streets and say,

'Even the dust of your town that clings to our feet we wipe off against you. Nevertheless, know this—the Kingdom of God has come near!'"

Some will welcome.
Some will curse.
Some will listen.
Some will turn away.

But the seed must be scattered.

The Word must be spoken.

The light must shine, even into places that will not receive it.

I send them out two by two—so that when one grows weary, the other will lift him. So that when one doubts, the other will pray. So that love, not loneliness, will be the banner over their mission.

Their sandals kick up the dust of destiny.

Their hearts beat a little faster.

Their names are not recorded in the courts of Rome, but they are written in the halls of heaven.

The Kingdom marches forward—not with swords, but with sandals.

Not with threats, but with peace.

Not with armies, but with the anointing of the Spirit.

I watch them scatter across the hills and valleys, toward towns large and small.

My heart swells—not with pride, but with hope.

They will taste both joy and rejection.

They will know both laughter and tears.

But through their obedience, the world will be prepared.

Prepared for My arrival.

Prepared for the cross.

Prepared for the resurrection.

Prepared for the coming of the Spirit.

They go, bearing the message like treasure in earthen vessels.

And the Kingdom moves closer.

The dust had hardly settled from the sandals of the seventy when I continued walking. Town by town, the Kingdom pressed forward.

Outside a small village along the border of Samaria and Galilee, ten men stood apart from the path. Their clothing was ragged; their bodies bore the marks of disease—leprosy, the silent exile. They lifted their voices together when they saw Me, not daring to approach.

"Yehoshua, Master, have mercy on us!"

I stopped. The disciples shifted uncomfortably behind Me; the custom was to keep distance. But I did not step back. I spoke with clarity, without gesture.

"Go. Show yourselves to the priests."

The command confused them at first. The Law demanded a healed leper present himself to the priest as proof of cleansing. Yet their skin still bore the scars. Still, they obeyed.

And as they went—obedience before evidence—their skin

cleared. The sores vanished. Fingers straightened. Their steps grew lighter.

Only one returned.

A Samaritan.

He fell at My feet, voice broken with praise, face buried in dust. His gratitude rose like incense.

"Were not ten cleansed?" I asked the watching crowd. "Where are the other nine? Was no one found to return and give glory to God except this foreigner?"

I lifted the man to his feet. His eyes shone with wonder.

"Rise and go. Your faith has made you well."

The days moved on, and I taught again in the temple courts, where the stones remembered Shlomo and David, but the hearts had grown harder than the mortar.

I spoke of the Kingdom. Of mercy greater than sacrifice. Of hearts that mattered more than ceremonies.
Some listened with longing. Others with sharpened stares.

A lawyer, seeking to trap Me, raised his voice over the murmurs.

"Teacher, what must I do to inherit eternal life?"

I turned the question back.

"What is written in the Law? How do you read it?"

He recited: "Love the Lord your God with all your heart and with all your soul and with all your strength and with all your mind—and love your neighbour as yourself."

"You have answered correctly," I said. "Do this, and you will live."

But he, wanting to justify himself, pressed further.

"And who is my neighbour?"

The crowd leaned in, intrigued, waiting to hear my reply.

I told them of a man traveling the treacherous road from Jerusalem to Jericho, who fell into the hands of robbers. Beaten, stripped, left half-dead.

A priest passed by—crossing to the other side.
A Levite came—saw—and walked away.

But a Samaritan...
The word alone stung the ears of many listening.

A Samaritan stopped. Bandaged wounds. Poured oil and wine. Lifted the broken man onto his own animal. Paid for his care with his own silver. Promised to return.

"Which of these three," I asked, "was a neighbour to the man who fell among thieves?"

The lawyer lowered his gaze.

"The one who showed mercy."

"Go," I said quietly, "and do likewise."

Word of the 70 began to return, carried on eager footsteps and radiant faces. They gathered, dust-caked and breathless, reporting miracles, wonders, the impossible become tangible.

"Lord, even the demons submit to us in Your Name!"

I smiled, joy rippling through My spirit.

"I saw Satan fall like lightning from heaven. Behold, I have given you authority to tread on serpents and scorpions and over all the power of the enemy, and nothing shall hurt you."

Their eyes gleamed. Their hands shook with excitement.

"But," I said, voice steadying their elation, "do not rejoice that the spirits submit to you. Rejoice that your names are written in heaven."

They paused.

They understood.

In that hour, I rejoiced in the Spirit, My heart lifting to the Father:

"I praise You, Father, Lord of heaven and earth, that You have hidden these things from the wise and understanding and revealed them to little children. Yes, Father, for such was Your good pleasure."

The Kingdom had come.
And it had found unlikely soil in which to grow.

But not all soil is the same.
Some hearts carried the seed of the Kingdom gladly.
Others—though called—began to harden in secret.

Among the twelve, Yehudah Ish-Keriyot carried the purse.
A position of trust, yet trust is a fragile thing in the hands of one who measures worth in silver.
What began as a subtle temptation had become a quiet habit.
Each clink of coin was a whisper, a promise: *You deserve more.*
So coins meant for bread, for shelter, for the poor were reduced.
And like a vine left untended, small compromises had

begun to wind their way around his heart.

Seeds of betrayal do not bloom overnight—but they had begun to sprout.

The road stretched onward, quieter now. The seventy had gone back to their towns. The crowds thinned. Even the disciples, though still near, spoke in softer tones. We made our way toward a village near Jerusalem—Bethany—where friendship, not fame, would welcome us. A house waited there, and with it, two sisters whose hearts, though different in rhythm, would each reveal something precious about the Kingdom.

The sun tilts low as we approach Bethany. Dust hangs in the still air. Olive trees lean over narrow paths like old friends listening for footsteps.

Word has gone ahead. A knock on a door, a whisper passed from mouth to ear: He is near.

Miryam opens the door before we even reach it. Her face is flushed, her hands still white with flour. She wipes them on her apron, her smile stretching wide.

"Come in, Master. Come in."

Her sister, Marta, is close behind. Practical. Focused. Already calculating how many loaves will be needed, how much water to draw, how many mats to lay down. Hospitality to her is not duty—it is devotion. Love, worked out through labour.

Inside, the house is simple, but warm. It smells of bread, olives, and fresh herbs crushed underfoot.

I sit. The disciples, too, finding corners, leaning tired bodies against the cool walls.

Marta rushes about. Gathering bowls. Kneading dough. Stirring stew. She hums under her breath—a song of welcome, though her brow furrows in concentration.

But Miryam? She does not move to the kitchen. She does not count or measure. She sinks to the floor, to My feet, as if drawn by gravity stronger than obligation.

She listens.

The room fades for her. The clatter of jars, the rustle of cloaks, the scrape of sandals. All of it falls away. Her eyes hold Me. Her heart leans close.

And Marta notices.

She passes by once, twice, three times, waiting, hoping that her sister will rise and help. But Miryam stays.

At last, Marta bursts.

"Master, don't You care that my sister has left me to serve alone? Tell her to help me!"

Her voice cracks under the weight of more than chores. It is the cry of one who wrestles with duty and the need to hear.

I turn to her—not with rebuke, but with love.

"Marta, Marta," I say, her name spoken like a song, "you are anxious and troubled about many things. But one thing is necessary. Miryam has chosen the better part, and it will not be taken away from her."

A silence settles. Heavy, but healing.

Marta stands still, her hands full of bread and worry. Slowly, she breathes. Slowly, she understands.

I have not come to be fed, but to feed. I have not come to be served, but to serve.

And it is not that Marta's labour is unworthy—but that her heart must first sit where Miryam sits. At My feet. In love. In listening.

The stew will feed the body. But My words? They will feed the soul.

Miryam remains, still and small, by My side. Her heart wide open.

The evening stretches long into laughter and learning. Oil lamps flicker against the walls. Stories pass between us like warm bread. Hope rises like leavened dough.

And in Bethany, in a house simple but sacred, the Kingdom grows—quiet as seed, sure as sunrise.

Later, after the house has quieted and the last bowls have been cleared, the disciples draw near again. The lamps burn low. The day's dust clings to their feet. Something stirs within them—not just wonder at My words, but a longing deeper still. They have seen Me slip away at dawn, heard the whispers of prayer on My breath, glimpsed the peace that flows from unseen wells. And now, one among them finds the courage to voice what all their hearts are asking:

"Master," he says softly, "teach us to pray."

I nod, sensing their hunger for something eternal. I lead them outside, where the night breathes cool against our skin. Stars stretch like stitched promises across the heavens. We sit among the stones, the earth firm beneath us.

"When you pray," I begin, "say this:"

I let the words fall gently, not rushed, each syllable woven with life.

"Our Father—Avinu—who is in heaven,
hallowed be Your Name."

They listen; breath held tight between ribs. Some close their eyes. Others watch My face, as if the prayer might be caught not just by ear, but by heart.

"Your Kingdom come.
Your will be done, on earth as it is in heaven."

The wind stirs, lifting cloaks and hair, as if the very air leans closer.

"Give us this day our daily bread."

I see hunger flicker—not just for food, but for faith. For trust in the unseen hand that provides.

"And forgive us our sins,
as we forgive those who sin against us."

A silence heavier than stones settles over us. Forgiveness—both given and received—is weighty. Necessary. It tears down the walls pride has built.

"And lead us not into temptation,
but deliver us from evil." I glance towards Yehudah Ish-Keriyot , hoping, praying...

The words form a shelter around them, a path and a protection. A prayer simple enough for a child, yet deep enough to anchor the soul.

I lower My hands, the prayer complete. But they are not just words to recite—they are a doorway into relationship. An invitation not to strive, but to trust. To ask. To seek. To knock. And to believe that the door will be opened.

I see it in their faces—the glimmer of understanding. The beginning of a new way of walking with the Father.

Prayer is not a ritual. It is a conversation. A breath between heaven and earth.

But still. The purse hung heavy at Yehudah Ish-Keriyot ' side.
I saw—though no one else noticed—how his hand lingered a moment too long when the coins were counted.
A few shekels, slipped unseen into his own pouch.
I did not call him out.
Not yet.
Mercy must be given space to breathe, even when the heart begins to harden.

The stars burn quietly above us, listening, as My disciples sit still in wonder.
A small beginning—but the Kingdom often starts that way.

Small seeds.
Deep roots.
Eternal harvest.

The days shorten.
The nights sharpen.
And the city of David calls again.

Word spreads through the towns and villages: the Feast of Dedication approaches. Hanukkah—festival of lights. A celebration not commanded by Torah but held dear in every heart that remembers deliverance. The cleansing of the Temple. The faith of a few who stood against many.

We rise early one morning, wrapping cloaks tighter against the chill. The disciples gather what little we carry. No one asks where we go. They already know. To Jerusalem. Again.

As we walk, I teach still—parables along the road, lessons tucked between the fig trees and the pathways trodden by generations before us. Yet there is an urgency now, a weight in the air heavier than before. Each step toward Jerusalem is a step closer to the hour appointed from the beginning.

The Temple gleams in the distance, white and gold under the winter sun. Crowds swell, filling the courts with laughter, prayer, the clinking of coins, the smoke of offerings. Candles will soon be lit, menorahs standing proudly in windows and doorways.

Light against darkness.
Hope against despair.

And in their midst, I walk.
The True Light, unrecognised.
Yet soon, no longer hidden.

Chapter 9: Toward the Tomb

The Jordan greets Me once more.

Not as it did before—when Yochanan stood waist-deep in its currents, and the heavens split open with a Voice of pleasure.
Now the river runs quieter, its waters cooler in the winter air, winding like a ribbon of memory through the wilderness.

I cross over.

Here, beyond the crowds and the courts of the Temple, among the reeds and stones, there is peace.
The noise of accusation fades. The pressure of hostile eyes loosens its grip.
Only those who hunger for truth follow.

Many come.
Not the self-assured. Not the proud.
But the bruised, the curious, the desperate.
Their feet are dusty, their faces open.

They whisper among themselves, recalling Yochanan's words.

"Yochanan never performed a sign," they say. "But everything he spoke about this man was true."

Their hearts open where others closed theirs.

They listen—not to catch, not to trap, but to believe.
And believe they do.

Here, near the place where the Kingdom first touched earth at My baptism, belief blooms quietly.

No Temple stones overhead. No Sanhedrin council glaring.
Only open skies, open hearts, and open hands.

I speak to them by the river.
I do not shout.
I do not rebuke.

I tell them of the Father's heart.
Of the Spirit's call.
Of the Kingdom still pressing nearer.

Many believe.

No miracles demanded.
No signs required.
Just truth meeting trust.

The waters of the Jordan sigh against the banks.
The breeze stirs the reeds.
And heaven leans close.

The harvest grows—even in the wilderness.

As the crowds grew larger, Yehudah Ish-Keriyot moved
among them, sharp-eyed.
Some came offering gifts—small coins, tokens of
gratitude—and Yehudah received them with practiced ease.
Not all found their way into the treasury.
His fingers tightened around a few extra coins here, a little
silver there, pockets lined not with the needs of the poor,
but with quiet greed. Not the first, not the last time.

No one questioned him.

They trusted too easily.

But while his hands clutched silver in secret, another kind of urgency was already on the wind.

The message reaches Me beyond the Jordan. Breathless runners. Dust on their tunics. Panic in their eyes.

"Lord," they gasp, "the one You love is sick. El'azar ."

I know.
I knew before they spoke.
I feel it—like a tremor in the fabric of this broken world.
Miryam's prayers. Marta's worry. El'azar 's shallow breaths.

Still, I wait.

Two days pass.
The disciples shift nervously.
They whisper among themselves.

"Should we not go? Surely, He will heal him?"
"Why does He linger?"

They do not understand.
Even My heart aches with the waiting.
But greater glory must bloom from greater pain.

On the third day, I speak:

"Let us go back to Judea."

Their faces fall.

"Rabbi," Toma says, hesitant, "just a short time ago they tried to stone You—and now You want to go back?"

I meet his eyes, steady and sure.

"Are there not twelve hours in the day? Anyone who walks in the day will not stumble, for they see by this world's light. It is when a person walks at night that they stumble, for they have no light."

They do not understand. Not yet.

"Our friend El'azar has fallen asleep," I tell them, "but I go to wake him."

Still, they do not see.

"Lord, if he sleeps, he will recover," they reason.

I sigh.

"El'azar is dead," I say plainly. "And for your sake I am glad I was not there, so that you may believe. But let us go to him."

We walk the winding roads back toward Bethany.
The air grows heavier with each step.
News travels faster than feet—by the time we near the village, mourners fill the streets.
Women wail. Men stand silent, heads bowed.
The scent of death lingers in the air, sharp and sour.

Marta runs to meet us before we even reach the gates.

Her face is streaked with dust and tears, her hands trembling.
But her voice strong.

"Lord," she cries, "if You had been here, my brother would not have died!"

Her grief is not accusation. It is desperation.

"But even now," she says, hope flickering, "I know that whatever You ask of God, God will give You."

I meet her gaze.

"Your brother will rise again," I say.

She nods, mechanically.

"I know he will rise again at the resurrection at the last day."

But I shake My head gently.

"I," I say, stepping closer, "am the resurrection and the life.
The one who believes in Me, even though they die, yet shall
they live.
And whoever lives by believing in Me will never die.
Do you believe this?"

Tears spring afresh to her eyes.

"Yes, Lord," she whispers, "I believe that You are the
Messiah, the Son of God, who is to come into the world."

She turns and runs back to the house.

Moments later, Miryam comes.
The sight of her breaks Me.
She falls at My feet, sobbing.

"Lord," she weeps, "if You had been here, my brother would
not have died."

The crowd follows her—wailing, mourning, some watching
with wary curiosity.

I see their grief.
I feel it in My bones.
The brokenness of this fallen world presses heavy on My
spirit.

I weep.

Tears I do not stop.
Tears for El'azar .
Tears for Miryam and Marta.
Tears for the death that has reigned so long over those I
love.

"See how He loved him," some whisper.

But others scoff.

"Could not He who opened the eyes of the blind man have kept this man from dying?"

Their words do not wound Me.
But they reveal how small their sight remains.

I move toward the tomb.

It is a cave, a stone laid across its mouth.
The scent of decay already seeps out.

"Take away the stone," I command.

Marta gasps.

"Lord," she says, "by now there will be a bad odour, for he has been there four days."

I turn to her.

"Did I not tell you that if you believe, you will see the glory of God?"

Trembling hands roll back the stone.

The stench of death rushes out, making many, step back.

I lift My eyes to heaven.

"Father," I say aloud, "I thank You that You have heard Me. I know that You always hear Me, but I say this for the sake of those standing here, that they may believe that You sent Me."

Then I call out.

"El'azar – come forth!"

The words slice through death itself.

The crowd gasps.

From the shadow of the tomb, something stirs.
Shuffling.
Ragged breathing.

Thump,

Thump,

Thump.

One last jump, and then—he emerges.

Still wrapped in grave clothes, legs bound, linen clinging to flesh that should have rotted but now breathes anew.

The people reel backward, some screaming, some weeping, some fearful.

"Unbind him," I say quietly, "and let him go."

They rush forward, trembling hands freeing him.

El'azar blinks against the sunlight, bewildered but alive.

Miryam falls to her knees, sobbing again—but this time with joy.
Marta clutches her chest, laughing through her tears.

They stare at their brother, then fall into his arms, weeping and laughing as they hold on to the living proof of hope.

Faith fills the courtyard like floodwaters.

Yet not all believe.

Some run to Jerusalem.
They whisper to the priests.
To Qayyafah.

They plot.

For the raising of one man has sealed the death of another.

But for this moment—this breathless, radiant moment—
death has been conquered.
The grave has lost its sting.

The Kingdom presses on — steady, unstoppable.

The streets of Jerusalem buzz, but not with celebration.
Whispers coil through the alleys like smoke from unseen
fires. Some say I am a prophet. Others call Me a
blasphemer. The leaders plot in dark corners, their prayers
turning to strategies, their fear sharpening into resolve.

In the chambers of the high priests, a council is convened.
Words rise and clash—concern, suspicion, fury.
"What are we accomplishing?" they say. "This man is
performing many signs. If we let Him go on like this,
everyone will believe in Him, and the Romans will come and
take away both our Temple and our nation."

Their fear is not misplaced. They sense it, though they do
not name it: a Kingdom not of this world, drawing near.

Then Qayyafah, high priest that year, speaks with a chilling
clarity: "You do not realise that it is better for you that one
man dies for the people than that the whole nation perish."

He thinks he speaks from cunning.
He does not know he speaks a prophecy older than he is.
Not from wisdom, but from fear, the plan is sealed.
They will seek to kill Me—not openly, not yet—but soon.

And so, for a time, I withdraw.

I gather My disciples, and we leave Jerusalem behind—its

stone walls glowing in the sunset, its heart darkened by pride and fear.
We move northward, to the edge of the wilderness, to a quiet town near the desert's breath.

Ephraim.

It is a place few think about—a threshold between life and desolation, between ambition and surrender. A town on the cusp of emptiness. Here, there are no crowds pressing at My heels. Here, the storms of Jerusalem are distant thunder.

The air is cooler here. Dry winds whisper over barren rocks. Olive groves stretch gnarled hands to the sky. The pace slows. The breath deepens.

Here, I teach My disciples.
Not with the urgency of the public squares.
Not with the pressing of multitudes.
But with the depth of quiet days and long nights beneath endless stars.

Here, I remind them what is coming.

I tell them again: the Son of Man must suffer many things.
Must be rejected. Must die.
And rise.

They hear, but they do not yet understand. Their faces fall, their steps falter.
They want victory. Triumph. Thrones.
They do not yet grasp that the path to life winds first through death.

But I am patient.

During one such teaching, I hear Yehudah Ish-Keriyot – his

thoughts...

At first, he justified it.
A small fee for my service. A reward for my loyalty. No harm done.
The thoughts came easily, draped in the false dignity of necessity.
Yet each coin stolen thickened the veil over his heart.
What once would have stung his conscience now barely brushed it.
If the others knew what true sacrifice cost, they would understand, he reasoned.
But it was not sacrifice he sought.
It was gain.

I say nothing, knowing what must come, praying for him, so that he does not become the vessel in the devils' hands.

Each evening, we sit by the fire.
The flames dance in their wide eyes.
I speak of seeds falling into the ground. Of vineyards and harvests. Of gates narrow and burdens light.
I speak of My Father's love.
I prepare them, word by word, moment by moment, for a storm they cannot yet see.

In the mornings, I rise before the sun.
I slip into the hush of the desert, where only the Spirit speaks.
There, I pour out the weight of what is coming.
There, I feel the ache of coming separation—the betrayal, the thorns, the nails.

And still, I say yes.

The town of Ephraim becomes a sanctuary, a silent altar.

A place of breathing, of bracing, of believing.

Even now, the tides move.
Pilgrims gather in Jerusalem for the Passover. The city swells with expectation and unrest. The Sanhedrin sharpen their plans like knives.
The cross draws nearer.

But not yet.

For a little while longer, there is Ephraim.
A quiet before the roar.

The stillness of Ephraim is broken at last.
The time draws near.
I set My face toward Jerusalem.

The disciples sense it.
A new gravity rests upon us as we move southward, through the winding valleys of Judea.
The air is cooler now. Spring stirs in the olive groves.
But the path ahead is heavy.

Along the way, the crowds find Me again—lame, blind, poor, broken. They do not come with fanfare; they come with need. And I welcome them.

One Sabbath, as I teach in a synagogue, I see her.
A woman, bent low.
Her back is twisted, her body bowed by an affliction that has held her captive for eighteen long years.

She does not approach Me.
She has learned to stay in the shadows, to move small and unnoticed.

But I notice her.

I call her forward.

Gasps ripple through the synagogue—scandalised by My summons, pitied by her sight.
She hobbles into the open, each step a portrait of pain. Her eyes to the floor, she cannot see my face only my feet.

I place My hands upon her shoulders.

"Woman," I say gently, "you are freed from your infirmity."

At once, her spine straightens.
Her eyes lift to meet Mine.
The weight of nearly two decades falls away like dust shaken from a cloak.

She stands upright.
And she praises God—loudly, freely, without restraint.

The synagogue leader, rigid in rule-keeping, protests.
"There are six days for work. Come and be healed on those days, not on the Sabbath!"

But I answer—not in anger, but in truth:

"Hypocrites! Does not each of you on the Sabbath untie his ox or donkey and lead it to water?
Should not this woman, a daughter of Avraham, whom Satan has kept bound for eighteen years, be set free on the Sabbath day?"

They are silenced.
And the people rejoice.

But the lines are drawn sharper now.
The leaders watch, nursing their fury in secret.

We continue toward Jerusalem, weaving through villages and fields.

One evening, as we dine at a ruler's house, I notice how the guests jockey for places of honour.

I speak.

"When you are invited to a wedding feast, do not sit in the place of honour, lest someone more distinguished be invited, and you are asked to move in shame.
Rather, sit in the lowest place. For everyone who exalts himself will be humbled, and he who humbles himself will be exalted."

The room shifts. The lesson cuts deeper than decorum.
It is a call to live upside down in a world obsessed with status.

Another voice, braver or more naïve, calls out:

"Blessed is the one who will eat at the feast in the Kingdom of God!"

I answer with a parable.

A man prepared a great banquet and invited many guests.
But when the feast was ready, the guests made excuses.
One had bought a field. Another had new oxen to test.
Another had just married.

The master, enraged, said: "Go out quickly into the streets and bring in the poor, the crippled, the blind, and the lame."

And still, there was room.

The invitation is wide.
But the cost is real.

I turn to the crowds following us—crowds eager for miracles, slow to grasp the road ahead.

"If anyone comes to Me and does not hate his own father,

mother, wife, children, brothers, and sisters—yes, even his
own life—he cannot be My disciple.
Whoever does not carry his own cross and follow Me cannot
be My disciple."

They stumble over the words.

I speak again.

"No one builds a tower without first sitting down and
calculating the cost.
No king marches to war without considering whether he can
face the opposing army.
So too, any of you who does not give up everything he has
cannot be My disciple."

The Kingdom is free—but not cheap.

It demands all.

I see their faces—some sobered, some unsure, some
beginning to turn away.

The way is narrow.
But it leads to life.

We do not linger. Grace has spoken, but the journey
continues. There are still hearts to stir. Still eyes to open. So
I walk on.

The road winds downward now—through rocky cliffs and dry
ravines—toward Jericho, the city of palms.
The scent of dates hangs heavy in the air. The River Jordan
glitters in the distance, winding its silver way through the
desert.

Crowds thicken along the roadside.
Word spreads: *He is coming. The Teacher. The Healer. The*

One who raises the dead.

I hear them even before I see them—two blind men sitting by the way, crying out above the din.

"Son of David, have mercy on us!"

The crowd tries to silence them.
Their cries seem out of place, an interruption, a nuisance.

But they cry louder still, "Son of David, have mercy on us!"

So, I stop.

I call them forward.

"What do you want Me to do for you?" I ask.

They do not hesitate.

"Lord, we want our sight."

Pity wells up from deep within Me—holy, powerful.

"Receive your sight," I say. "Your faith has healed you."

And just like that—their eyes open.

They blink against the sun, weeping and laughing all at once.
They follow Me, their first steps of sight taken in pursuit of
Light Himself.

The gates of Jericho loom ahead.

The crowd presses tighter, dust rising in the dry air.

And there—perched in the branches of a sycamore tree—I
see him.

Zakkai.

A tax collector.
A traitor in the eyes of many.

Small in stature, yet willing to climb like a boy just to catch a glimpse of Me.

I smile.

I call up to him:

"Zakkai, hurry and come down, for today I must stay at your house."

Gasps ripple through the crowd.
Whispers hiss like serpents.

He's gone to be the guest of a sinner!

But Zakkai scrambles down the tree, his face alight with wonder and shame and hope all mingled together.

In his home, crowded with suspicious faces and disapproving glares, he stands and declares:

"Behold, Lord, half of my possessions I give to the poor, and if I have cheated anyone, I will repay them fourfold."

Salvation floods the room like sunlight.

I say aloud for all to hear:

"Today salvation has come to this house. For the Son of Man came to seek and to save the lost."

Not the proud.
Not the self-righteous.
The lost.

As we prepare to leave Jericho, the air shifts again.
The road ahead rises sharply, winding its way up to Jerusalem.

I pause, gazing toward the holy city, still hidden by hills and valleys.

The cross waits there.

The city of peace where blood will be spilled.

The Lamb must be offered.

But not yet.

For now, the road still stretches before us—dusty, bright, and heavy with prophecy.

The road crests one last hill, and there it lies before us—Bethany.
A village tucked between olive groves and dusty fields, two miles from Jerusalem, yet a world away from its noise and plotting.

I feel the tension in the air.
The disciples feel it too, though they do not yet understand it.

Word has already reached the chief priests and Pharisees.

The raising of El'azar has stirred the hornet's nest.

Whispers of arrest and death hang over Jerusalem like a gathering storm.

But of course, I knew this would come. It was a setup — a divine delay, knowing that postponement would lead to death, and death to life.

But here, for a moment, there is peace.

Miryam, Marta, and El'azar greets Me with tearful eyes and joyful smiles.
They have prepared a meal—a simple table, heavy with bread and figs, lamb and wine.

The laughter of old friends fills the house, mingled with stolen glances of wonder.

El'azar speaks easily, his voice rich with life.
Yet I hear a deeper echo—the sound of tombs breaking open, of death losing its grip.

Marta serves with brisk affection, bustling about with trays and pitchers.
Miryam sits at My feet, as she always does, her eyes wide, her heart open.

Then she moves.

Without a word, she takes a jar of pure nard—perfume costly enough to feed a village for a year.
She breaks it.

The scent floods the house, thick and sweet, clinging to every corner.

She pours it on My feet, the oil flowing like rivers of grief and worship.
She dries them with her hair, the strands catching the light like rivers of onyx and fire.

The room stills.

The murmurs start—Yehudah Ish-Keriyot , scowling, whispering about waste.

But I defend her.

"Leave her alone," I say. "She has done this for the day of My burial."

Burial?

The word settles heavily over them, though they do not yet grasp it fully.

The poor will always be among them.

But I—
I will not.

Not for long.

That night, under the strained breath of the olive trees, Yehudah Ish-Keriyot's mind churned with restless thoughts.

What a waste — nard, for burial?

Why do I even bother? He doesn't understand the need to save. He speaks of wealth and investment yet allows her to pour out a year's wages on His feet — as if the poor don't matter. It's reckless.

His eyes flicker — not with reverence, but with calculation.
There must be a way to profit more…
The priests are desperate. They offer silver for information.
And He always escapes them, somehow.
If I lead them to Him, what harm is there? He will slip away again—as always—and I will have the silver in my hand.
Greed dressed itself as reason.
Betrayal cloaked itself in logic.
And with each whispered thought, the coin purse grew heavier around his heart.

The scent of the perfume clings to Me as we leave Bethany and turn toward Jerusalem.

It will cling to Me still when they seize Me.
When they mock Me.
When they pierce Me.

The anointing of death already begun.

I step into the twilight, the sky burning with the last light of day.
Ahead, Jerusalem waits.
Cloaked in prophecy.
Dripping with destiny.

I do not turn aside.

I set My face like flint.

The road narrows.
The hour draws near.

The King approaches His city.

But He does not come as they expect.

Not yet.

Chapter 10: The Final Week

The road winds downward from the Mount of Olives, dusty and narrow, cutting a path toward Jerusalem.
The city sprawls before Me—golden in the morning light, crowned with the Temple, alive with the hum of Passover pilgrims.

I pause at the crest of the hill.

The disciples gather around, their faces lit with anticipation.
They whisper to one another, their hearts surging with hope.
Finally, they think. Finally, He will reveal Himself.
Finally He will take His rightful throne.

But they do not yet understand the throne I seek.

I send two of them ahead.

"Go into the village opposite you," I say, "and immediately you will find a donkey tied, and a colt with her. Untie them and bring them to Me. If anyone says anything to you, say, 'The Lord has need of them,' and they will let you go."

They go.
Faithful. Obedient. Unknowing.

It is the fulfilment of ancient words:

"Say to the daughter of Zion,
Behold, your King comes to you,
Gentle and riding on a donkey,
And on a colt, the foal of a donkey."

Not a war horse.
Not a chariot.

A donkey.

The symbol not of conquest, but of peace.

They return, leading the animals by ropes.
Cloaks are spread across the mothers back, whilst a couple on the colt.
I mount, surprisingly, it stands still. Never been ridden, until now. My feet almost dragging the ground, the picture of humility.

The road ahead swells with people—pilgrims and farmers, traders and fishermen, women with baskets of bread and children waving palm branches.

Whispers spread faster than the breeze.

"It's Him. The Prophet from Nazareth. The miracle-worker."

Crowds gather.

They lay their cloaks on the road before Me, a carpet of honour.
Palm branches are cut from the trees, waving in the air like banners of expectation.

And then, the cry rises—first a murmur, then a roar:

"Hosanna to the Son of David!
Blessed, is He who comes in the name of the Lord!
Hosanna in the highest!"

Their voices shake the stones.
The earth itself seems to bow with anticipation.

Some climb the trees, shouting.
Others fall to their knees, tears streaming down their faces.

Children run before Me, scattering flowers, laughing without understanding, caught up in the joy that only heaven fully knows.

I ride on.

Closer.

Closer to the place where altars smoke and prayers rise like incense.

Closer to the place where lambs are led to slaughter.

The crowd sees triumph.

I see sacrifice.

They want a crown.

I carry a cross.

The cheers fade behind Me as I dismount near the Temple's southern entrance.
The outer courts swell with people—throngs pressed shoulder to shoulder, a tide of pilgrims come to offer sacrifice for Passover.

But the smell hits Me first.

Not the scent of incense rising in prayer—
Not the aroma of roasted lambs offered in devotion—
But the stench of greed. Of exploitation.

The Court of the Gentiles, meant to be a house of prayer for all nations, has become a marketplace.
Moneychangers bark out rates. Merchants haggle over the price of doves.
Coins clatter into greedy hands. Animals bleat, cages rattle.
The air is thick with dust and deception.

My heart burns.

I stride forward, My pace quickening, My Spirit rising like a storm.

I weave together cords into a whip—swift, purposeful.

Then I move.

Tables crash to the ground, coins scatter across the stones,
rolling and ringing like accusations.
Birdcages split open doves burst upward into the bright,
startled sky.
The merchants shout in outrage.
The moneychangers scramble for their silver.
But no one dares to touch Me.

I do not shout.
My voice is not shrill.

It thunders.

"It is written:
'My house shall be called a house of prayer.'
But you—
you have made it a den of thieves!"

My words crack across the stones louder than any whip.
No one answers.
No one can.

I drive them out—the sellers, the buyers, the cheaters.

The blind stumble into the open space, sensing the shift.
The lame limp toward Me, drawn by hope.

I welcome them.

Here, now, the Temple breathes again.

I lay My hands on the broken, and they rise healed.
Sight is restored. Crippled legs straighten.
Worn faces lift in wonder.
And the songs of children rise in the newly cleansed
courtyard, pure and unashamed.

"Hosanna to the Son of David!" they cry again.

The chief priests and scribes stand at a distance, watching,
their robes stiff with outrage, their hearts clenched like fists.

"Do You hear what they are saying?" they demand.

I meet their gaze, unwavering.

"Yes," I answer. *"Have you never read,
'Out of the mouth of babes and nursing infants You have
perfected praise'?"*

They say nothing.

But already, they plot.

I turn away.

I leave the Temple not in fear, but in sadness.

The stones are heavy with promises forgotten.
The walls long to rejoice, but they are not ready.

Not yet.

I retreat to Bethany, to the home of My friends.
The sun dips low behind the hills.
The crowds disperse into the night, still buzzing with the
day's upheaval.
The city sleeps uneasily.

Tomorrow will bring more teaching, more confrontation.
But for now, silence wraps itself around Me like a thin cloak.

And the Passover draws near.

The next morning, the city stirs under a heavy sky.
The Temple courts buzz again—pharisees whisper, scribes
watch, Sadducees confer in tight, frowning circles.

But I do not hide.

I walk openly into the courtyard, where stone pillars rise like ancient sentinels.
The crowds find Me quickly, drawn by hunger—hunger not for bread this time, but for truth.

I teach.

Not with riddles. Not with flattery.

But with fire.

The parable of the two sons—one who says he will obey but does not, and another who rebels but repents.
The parable of the tenants—wicked men who kill the son sent to them by the master.

Each word slices through the facade of religion.
Each story plants seeds in willing hearts—and thorns in the hearts of My enemies.

"The stone the builders rejected has become the cornerstone," I declare.
"Everyone who falls on that stone will be broken to pieces."

The chief priests grit their teeth.
They know I speak of them.

But the people listen.
And that terrifies them more than any miracle.

They come with their traps:

"Is it lawful to pay taxes to Caesar?"
"Whose wife will she be in the resurrection?"
"What is the greatest commandment?"

Each question a snare, each word laced with poison.

But I do not stumble.

"Give to Caesar what is Caesar's, and to God what is God's."
"In the resurrection, they are like angels in heaven."
"The greatest commandment is this: Love the Lord your God with all your heart, soul, and mind. And the second is like it: Love your neighbour as yourself."

Their mouths close.
Their plots darken.

I turn to the people and speak plainly now—no longer veiling the warnings.

"Woe to you, scribes and Pharisees, hypocrites!"
"You shut the door of the Kingdom of Heaven in people's faces."
"You clean the outside of the cup, but inside you are full of greed and self-indulgence."
"You are like whitewashed tombs—beautiful on the outside, but full of dead men's bones within."

The Temple shudders with murmurs.
Mothers clutch their children tighter.
Men shift uneasily.

But still, some lean closer.

Still, some dare to believe.

I look over the city—the city that kills its prophets and stones those sent to her.

I weep.

"Jerusalem, Jerusalem, you who kill the prophets and stone those sent to you!

How often I have longed to gather your children together, as a hen gathers her chicks under her wings—but you were not willing."

I turn from the Temple, tears still dripping.

"Behold, your house is left to you desolate."

The sun sinks heavy toward the Mount of Olives.
Shadows stretch long across the valley.
We leave the Temple behind, its grandeur hollow, now in the dying light.

Night wraps itself over Jerusalem.

The Passover draws near.

I gather the Twelve in the upper room—a space prepared by unseen hands, guided by My Word.

The table is set.
The lamb roasted.
The wine poured.
The unleavened bread laid in baskets.

The disciples come, laughing nervously, unaware how the world will tilt by morning.

I kneel before them, one by one, basin and towel in hand.

Their protests falter under My gaze.

I wash their feet—the feet that will soon flee, stumble, deny.
I wash away dust, knowing blood will follow.

I rise, wash My hands.

We recline at the table.

I break the bread.

"Take, eat. This is My body, given for you."

I lift the cup.

"Drink from it, all of you. This is My blood of the covenant, poured out for many for the forgiveness of sins."

The words are simple.
But heaven and earth tilt under their weight.

The lamb on the table is not the true sacrifice.

I Am.

The night hums with unseen currents.
The betrayer's hand dips with Mine into the dish.
His eyes flicker—fear? Defiance? It does not matter.

"What you are about to do, do quickly."

He rises and slips into the darkness, reasoning with himself.

The door swung closed behind him with a hollow thud.
The room's soft light faded, swallowed by a darkness thicker than night itself.

Does He know? Is He aware I go to the high priest?

Yehudah Ish-Keriyot pulled his cloak tighter, he felt fear, looked around, an unease gripped him. He wanted to turn back, but his feet would not let him. The cold penetrated his garments to his skin; this cold was not natural it gripped his bones; fear could not be warded off by cloth.
The streets twisted ahead of him, familiar yet foreign, the torches guttering low as if shrinking from what now walked among them. He felt the crowd; no one was there.
His feet moved quickly, but the faster he walked, the more the crowd pressed in.
The silver coins clinked softly in the pouch at his side—a

cruel lullaby, he gripped the pouch.

"This is the right thing to do"

"Stop concerning yourself" he said.

In the alleys between homes, shadows shifted.
Not the innocent shadows of torchlight and stone.
These shadows *watched.*

Invisible voices whispered along the cracks of the street.
Soft, seductive—then sharp, commanding.

"Now, Yehudah Ish-Keriyot . Now."

"No, he said out loud, this is wrong"

"it is right, continue on your way"

"This is wisdom."
"This is strength."
"Take what you are owed, give the rest to the poor."

He pressed his hand tighter over the pouch, as if to silence
the accusing clink of coins.
The skin on the back of his neck prickled.
Though no man followed him, he was not alone.
Darkness clung to him like a second cloak, whispering
promises, feeding the growing, gnawing hunger inside his
soul.

You deserve more.
Don't let this chance slip away.

A whirlwind of dust.
A surge of noise — contradiction, shadows, dust.
Laughter.
Fear.
He turns to go back — but it's too late. He was already here.

Why retreat now? The threshold is already crossed.

The courtyard of the high priest loomed ahead, lit by torches that flickered against cold stone.
The guards lingered near the gates, laughing harshly, their hands on sword hilts.

Yehudah Ish-Keriyot hesitated again—but only for a moment.

The voice of greed, of self-justification, of rage at promises unfulfilled...
they stitched themselves together inside him until he could no longer tell them apart from his own thoughts.

"He will escape."
"You know He always escapes."
"You will have the silver, and He will walk free."
"No harm done."
"And if not... was it not written?"

He stepped into the courtyard.
The guards look up. Recognition flashed across their faces.
They sneered—but they let him pass.

Thirty pieces of silver.
Not enough to buy peace.
But enough to damn him.

The deal was struck in a few hushed words, sealed by a nod, by the cold clatter of coins against a table.

Somewhere, far above, the heavens shuddered.
Somewhere, unseen, angels wept.

But Yehudah Ish-Keriyot —thinking he has outsmarted the Sanhedrin smiled.

And the darkness smiled with him.

The room grows heavy. The Eleven sat in uneasy silence,
their eyes lowered, their hands restless on the table.
The last notes of the psalm still trembled in the air, fragile as
spider silk.
I looked at them—beloved, bewildered, burdened—and
knew: soon the storm would break.
But for now, we sat together, holding a final breath before
the world would shatter.

I speak of the vine and the branches, of love and suffering,
of the Spirit who will come after.

*"In this world you will have trouble.
But take heart. I have overcome the world."*

Their faces—so young, so fearful.
Yet soon, they will carry the fire across nations and
kingdoms.

I lead them in song—the ancient psalms of ascent.
The melody is thin but full of hope.

We linger a moment longer, the weight of unseen sorrow
pressing down like a second roof above us.
No one speaks. No one needs to.
Then, with a breath shared between heaven and earth, we
rise.

Into the night.

Toward Gethsemane.

Toward the waiting cup.

Toward the cross.

Chapter 11: The Garden

The night clings close around us as we leave the upper room.
Jerusalem murmurs in her sleep, unaware that her heart will soon break.
Our feet find the worn path down the hill, through the narrow alleys thick with the smell of oil lamps and baking bread.
The stones are slick with dew.
The air is heavy—pregnant with things unseen.
The city gates loom ahead, yawning open like a mouth.
Beyond them, the road bends toward the Kidron Valley, and beyond that—the olive-shrouded slopes of Gethsemane.
We walk in silence.
The Eleven close behind Me, their steps slow, uncertain.
Only the distant bleat of a lamb from some unseen courtyard breaks the hush.
Above, the moon hangs pale and bruised, like a warning.
The stars blink cold and distant, as if they cannot bear to watch what will unfold.
Dust and pebbles cling to My sandals, but I do not stop.
Face set like flint.
And I go.
Knowing, what is already unfolding.
I feel it.
The weight of it.
Every sin.
Every sorrow.
Every betrayal.
It is heavier than life itself!
The cup waits.

I must drink it, otherwise, what was the point of leaving My throne?
All the questions have been asked.
But I do not fear.
Knowing that the garden is the place of My surrender – not My defeat!
I sense My Father, His presence so strong.
Ruach Hakodesh leads Me on.
The angels walk to My left and to My right; I sense them pulling up the rear.
I continue on.
We pass a few people hoping for their deliverance. I feel their eyes boring through My spine. But the time for healing, for now, has passed. For I must go; for the time to pray is now!
The trees of Gethsemane sway in the midnight wind, their twisted branches like arms outstretched toward heaven.
I know the place well.
I have prayed there often.
But tonight will be different.
Tonight, heaven will be silent.
Tonight, blood will touch the ground.
Tonight, the last Adam will undo the fall of the first.
We pass through the valley, shadows weaving like spectres around our feet.
The garden draws near.
I can hear My own heartbeat pounding against the night.
The road narrows.
The night thickens.
The final hour has come.
And I walk into it—willingly.

A rustle by a distant tree draws My attention. I see him, gnarled and bent, laughter shining in his eyes. I say nothing, tonight does not belong to him. He retreats.
We step beneath the ancient trees, their shadows wrapping around us like a shroud.
I pause.
The others gather close, their faces drawn and uncertain.
I feel their weariness — the long days, the heavy nights, the unseen battle already draining them.
They do not know how quickly their strength will fail.
But I love them still.
"Sit here while I go over there to pray," I say, My voice low, steady.
And still the trees whisper.
And still the cup waits.
I rise from the place of vision, My face wet with sweat and grief.
The others wait at the garden's edge, restless, uncertain.
But now, the path narrows further.
I must go deeper.
I call them—
"Kephas. Yaakov. Yochanan."
Their names fall heavy into the night air.
The three who have seen My glory atop the mountain.
The three who now must glimpse My agony at its lowest valley.
They follow without question.
Their footsteps crunch on the dry earth behind Me, each step heavier than the last.
Even they, bold and loyal, feel the weight.
The olive trees lean in, solemn witnesses to the unfolding mystery.

We press further into the grove, where the shadows grow thicker, and even the stars seem to dim.
Here, the world feels thinner, stretched tight between heaven and earth.
Here, flesh and spirit wrestle unseen.
I stop beneath a gnarled olive tree, its roots twisted like old wounds.
I turn to them, My voice low, trembling not with fear, but with the burden of what is to come.
"My soul is overwhelmed with sorrow to the point of death," I whisper.
"Stay here...and watch with Me."
Their eyes search Mine—confused, sorrowful, helpless.
They want to speak.
They do not know what to say.
They only nod.
I step forward to where the Spirit leads.
There I kneel.
Something feels so different.
"Av, Abba. Father," I cry. "Why do You feel so far from Me?"
The weight presses deeper.
It is not the pain of flesh alone that bends Me low—it is the stench of sin, gathering thick as smoke, rising from every corner of humanity, settling onto My shoulders.
I, who have never known the stain of rebellion, feel the crushing filth of every betrayal, every lie, every act of cruelty, coiling around My spirit like chains. Weight so heavy, I feel it pushing me to the ground.
My divinity recoils in revulsion.
For God cannot look upon sin without judgment.
Yet now I am wrapped in it.
I choke on the bitterness.

Still—I reach for the Father.
Still—I cling.
But the heavens are silent.
The divine within Me aches to cast it off—to unleash a single word and sweep the world clean. To let justice roll down like a flood and drown rebellion in holy fire.
But the flesh— the flesh weeps.
I feel the weightiness of judgement. The impending doom.
The flesh trembles.
the flesh must drink the cup.
Not for angels.
Not for the righteous.
But for the lost.
For the broken.
For mankind.
For the ones who even now sharpen their swords and weave their whips.
The war rages within Me.
The Lion roars to defend.
The Lamb bows to be slain.
The sweat on My brow beads crimson, blood forced through torn vessels by the agony of choice already made.
But the heavens are silent.
And the silence is louder than the crowds that will soon mock.
Yet still, I speak it aloud—because the flesh must surrender.
"Father... if it is possible, let this cup pass from Me..."
The human cry—the frailty of the Son of Man.
A pause.
The whole of eternity hangs in the balance.
The night around Me seems to peel back.
I am transported — not home, not into comfort — but to a beginning that was meant to be forever.

Before Me, the garden blooms — Eden, untouched, unbroken.
I see the first man, Adam, formed from dust, kissed into life by the breath of God.
His eyes open wide, filled with wonder. No shame. No fear.
Only glory reflecting back to Heaven.
He walks with the Father, hand in hand, voice to voice.
The world hums in tune with his joy.
Creation folds into the moment to hear their laughter.
But then — a whisper.
Not the whisper of the Spirit, but a thin, sly hissing.
Another voice winds its way into the garden.
The accuser.
The liar.
The thief of trust.
The first test.
Adam's gaze falters.
Adamah's hand trembles.
And the fruit is taken — not with force, but with agreement.
A breach opens.
A gash in the fabric of what was whole.
The air itself recoils.
The ground grows thorns.
The heart of man fractures.
I see Adam's face — not bold now but bowed in shame.
The image once blazing with our likeness dims, cracked by rebellion.
He hides among the trees, clothed in leaves that cannot cover what is lost.
And I feel it.
The ache of separation.
The cavern between God and His beloved.

I fall forward onto the ground of Gethsemane, My hands digging into the earth.
This was not how it was meant to be.
But this — this is why I am here.
I turn back toward the olive trees where I left them —
Kephas, Ya'akov, and Yochanan — the ones closest to My heart.
Their forms are slumped in sleep, heavy with sorrow.
My heart aches, not in anger, but in tenderness.
"Could you not watch with Me one hour?"
I whisper it, not with reproach, but with the ache of love unmet by frail humanity.
I kneel beside them briefly, brushing the dust from My hands, gathering the strength given through surrender.
The hour has come.
The betrayer is near.
And I must meet him — not with sword or shield — but with the full, blazing mercy of a love that will not turn away.
I choose the Cross.
I choose them.
I rise—weary, broken, resolute.
The Spirit moves again.
The vision shifts.
I see altars rising from dust and stone —
Hevel's offering, smoking sweet toward Heaven.
Noach, bowing on the new earth after the flood.
Avraham, knife raised in trembling obedience over Yitzchak until the ram was provided.
The blood of lambs, goats, bulls staining the ground year after year.
A river of sacrifices that could never fully cleanse, only cover.

The Law, holy and pure, descending like thunder on Sinai.
Torah etched by the finger of God Himself —
Words that reveal, restrain, convict —
But cannot transform the heart of stone.
I gave them choice.
Prophets crying in the wilderness.
Priests weary from endless offerings.
Kings rising and falling, some after God's heart, others after their own lust.
Generation after generation.
Promise after promise.
Sin after sin.
Hope flickering like a dying lamp.
I stand, look towards the sleeping three.
Confusion – but not confused
Battling with Myself.
Can I do this? Separation, I mean. This is at the heart of My struggle.
The earth seems to pulse beneath My feet, trembling at what it knows is coming. Stones bite into My knees as I fall to the ground. My breath catches, ragged.
"Abba..." My voice breaks the silence. "All things are possible for You. Take this cup from Me."
I rise
I step a little further.
The ground pulls at My knees.
I fall again into prayer, the earth cold against My skin.
Face to the soil that soon will drink My blood.
The agony deepens. The weight presses. Blood bursts from My capillaries, mingling with My sweat, staining the ground red. It seeps into the soil, a silent covenant.

Hands clutching the dust from which man was formed.
Breathless sobs tearing from My lips.
Words that cannot be spoken.
Sorrow so deep.
"Abba, if it is possible—let this cup pass from Me."
The words rip through the darkness.
They are not weakness.
They are surrender.
"Yet not My will, but Yours be done."
The heavens hold their breath.
And the garden keeps its silence.
Behind Me, I hear their slow breathing—already heavy with sleep.
Even here, the spirit is willing, but the flesh is weak.
Still, I love them.
Still, I press deeper into the will of the Father.
The hour draws near.
And the garden waits to be disturbed.
The Spirit speaks, not with words, but with a deep knowing:
There is no other way.
Not through sacrifices.
Not through law.
Not through kings.
Not through prophets.
Only through blood.
Only through a Son.
Only through Me.
I weep — not from fear of death — but from the weight of it all.
The shame.
The betrayal.
The loneliness.
The abandonment.

The wrath.
The curse.
I know The Father will withdraw from me. I already feel the
chasm widening.
All of it must be borne.
All of it must be carried.
All of it must be nailed into wood by My own pierced hands.
The cup is pressed into My palms.
It smells of bitterness.
It reeks of judgment.
It trembles with the fury of justice and the agony of mercy
intertwined.
I feel the weight of it,
Sin.
I have been here these 33 years, still I shun it.
Hate to see it.
But I must wrap Myself in it.
Knowing to do this means total separation.
Like pulling skin from flesh. Deeper still is My pain.
The shadows shift.
The night folds tighter around Me, but then—
A tremor in the air.
A crack, like the shattering of glass across unseen realms.
The veil between heaven and earth strains, buckles—and for
a moment, splits.
Light.
Not the soft, golden light of morning.
No—this is the light of eternity. Blinding. Fierce. It falls
around Me in torrents, brighter than ten thousand suns, yet
it does not burn. It *reveals*.

The garden, for an instant, is not a garden but a throne room.
Olive trees bend low as if in reverence. Rocks split silently
under the weight of glory unseen.
Angels descend, flashing like living fire.
Some kneel. Some stand, hands over hearts, swords
pointed downward in mourning respect. Others weep—
bright streams of sorrow falling to the ground like molten
gold.
I remain on My knees.
Face pressed to the dust, sweat mingling with blood that
leaks from My brow.
I see them—but My focus is on the Father.
Still the cup stands before Me.
Still the agony twists within.
Above Me, the hosts shift—the same host that sang at
Bethlehem now stands battle-ready. Gavri'el among them,
his face like lightning, his blade gleaming with judgment
held back.
"Even now, command us and we will defeat the enemy, here
and now!"
Mikha'el waits, hands clenched into fists of fury, aching for
the command to defend the Son.
But none comes.
They stand still as guards.
No sword is drawn.
No hand intervenes.
Because the command is not "Rescue."
It is "Witness."
I pray again, hoarse, broken.
"Father, if it is possible...let this cup pass from Me.
Nevertheless—not My will, but Yours be done."
Another flash—the memory of the mountain, the
transfiguration.

Mosheh and Eliyahu standing at My side, faces radiant, speaking of this very hour.
The hour when all would be fulfilled.
The glory of that day hovers near now—yet I am clothed in blood and earth, not shining garments.
The glory presses in, aching to burst forth again—but I hold it back.
For if it broke through now, if I clothed Myself again in light, no hand could touch Me, no whip could tear Me, no nail could pierce Me.
But the cup must be drunk in full.
And so, I remain—veiled.
Mortal.
Bleeding.
Silent.
A final surge of light erupts among the trees—angels sweeping outward, their cries like distant thunder.
Then—suddenly—stillness.
The rift closes.
The stars blink cold again.
The garden is once more just a garden.
And I am once more just a man, kneeling in dust, body trembling, heart surrendered.
My agony has begun.
But I lift it to My lips.
"Not My will, but Yours be done."
Heaven does not thunder an answer.
The Father does not pull Me back.
The angels hold their breath.
Creation itself tilts, waiting for the drink.
I drink.

And the garden, once a place of perfect fellowship and later
of betrayal, becomes now a place of surrender.
A new Eden.
Where the Son stands faithful where the first man fell.
Where love wins where rebellion once ruled.
I step deeper into the darkness, alone.

Heaven opens. Angels ascend and descend. They are all
around Me, comforting Me. Giving Me food to eat and drink
to drink. Not earthly but heavenly. I feel strength returning.
A renewal. An awakening.

This was the heavenly battle.

The earthly battle is knocking at My door. It will be hard,
difficult, but this stance will see Me through it.

I rise from the ground, knees and hands stained with dust
and blood and tears.
The garden watches.
The trees tremble.
They seem to bend closer.
The night splits — not yet with light, but with resolve.
Even the stars above dim, veiling their faces.
I walk back toward My friends, their cloaks pulled tight, their
breathing slow. I crouch next to them.
"Wake up now, it is time"
The road to the cross is set.
The heel of the Son will be bruised.
But the serpent's head —
It will be crushed.
I step forward.
Toward betrayal.

Toward trial.
Toward scourging.
Toward thorns.
Toward nails.
Toward death.
And beyond death — to glory.
I wipe My face, the salty sting of blood and sweat blurring My
vision. The garden sways around Me — silent witnesses to
the vow sealed in heaven's court.

A flicker of torchlight dances among the olive trees.
Footsteps—loud, hurried, full of malice—grow nearer.
The hour has come.
And still—I stand.
Heaven watches.
Earth holds its breath.
The Son surrenders.

The footsteps approach, heavy and clumsy—the sound of
betrayal borne on human feet.
The hour has come.
The Son of Man is betrayed into the hands of sinners.
I rise slowly, strength flooding back into battered flesh—not
the strength of muscle, but of mission.
Angels stand still, breathless.
Creation pauses.
And I—
I am ready.
The flicker of torchlight grows nearer.
Voices—sharp, urgent, filled with false courage—slice
through the night air.
The clatter of swords, the stomp of sandaled feet, the crack

of branches pushed aside.
They come.
Led by one of My own.
The eleven, jump to their feet. Every bit of weariness flees;
replaced by confusion and fear!
Yehudah Ish-Keriyot walks ahead of them, his face half-lit
by the flames he carries.
The silver from his betrayal weighs heavy in his pouch,
though heavier still is the darkness pressing against his soul.
He comes close, eyes darting, breath quickening.
But his steps do not falter.
Not yet.
He calls out, his voice too loud, too eager.
"Rabbi!"
The title hangs mockingly between us.
I do not move away.
I do not rebuke.
I do not resist.
He leans in, the kiss burning colder than any wound that will
follow.
A sign—simple, brutal, final.
One last false embrace.
"Yehudah Ish-Keriyot ," I whisper, "do you betray the Son of
Man with a kiss?"
The soldiers surge forward.
Metal flashes.
Rough hands grab for Me.
The disciples, torn between terror and loyalty.
Kephas lunges forward, the short blade flashing in the
torchlight.
A shout—
A cry—
And the ear of the high priest's servant falls to the ground.

Chaos erupts.
Weapons drawn.
Shouts filling the garden.
Fear crackling in the air like fire.
But I raise My hand—not in violence, but in mercy.
"Enough!" I command.
I stoop, touching the severed ear—bloodied, trembling—
and restore it whole.
Even now, My final miracles are mercy.
I turn to the soldiers, their hands still trembling on their
swords. Fear gripping their heart.
"You have come out with swords and clubs as if I were a
robber," I say, voice steady as the earth itself.
"Every day I was with you in the temple courts, and you did
not lay a hand on Me.
But this is your hour—and the power of darkness."
Lucifer draws near; eyes twinkling, corners of his mouth
twitched.
Then I hear it.
Laughter, cold, mocking.
Mikha'el takes a step forward. The laughter stops.
The disciples falter—caught in the whirlpool of fear and
confusion.
Their courage, so bold moments ago, shatters like brittle
clay.
One by one, they flee—vanishing into the folds of the trees,
into the folds of the night.
I stand alone.
The ropes are tied tight around My wrists, rough against the
skin that will soon bear nails.
They pull Me forward.
I do not resist.

The garden, so often filled with My prayers, now echoes with
the sound of betrayal.
The olive trees sway silently.
The stars dim behind gathering clouds.
And thus, the Lamb is led away.
Into darkness.
Into judgment.
Into sacrifice.
But not into defeat.
Never into defeat.

Chapter 12: Death & Burial

The ropes cut into My wrists.
Dust rises with every dragged step.
Torches hiss and gutter against the pressing darkness.
The mob surrounds Me—priests, soldiers, temple guards—
faces twisted in suspicion, triumph, fear.
They jostle Me forward, down the winding streets toward the
house of the high priest.

The city sleeps, but not the leaders.
No, tonight they are awake.
Tonight they taste what they think is victory.

I am pushed through the courtyard gate into the stone-
walled compound.
The chill clings to the stones, heavy with old prayers and
fresher conspiracies.

Inside, they gather.
The Sanhedrin—men draped in fine robes, voices sharp as
knives.
Qayyafah, the high priest, sits in the centre, his eyes
glittering beneath his heavy brow.

They waste no time.
Preprepared, false witnesses are paraded before Me —
fumbling, contradicting, stammering.
Fear grips. Confusion hisses.
Stories stitched together by fear, frayed by greed.
Like Balaam of old — summoned to curse, but unable to
speak what was not given.

Their mouths move, but the weight of truth tangles their
tongues.
They try to strike, but every word crumbles in midair.
No accusation finds anchor. No lie can root in soil soaked
with truth.
They seek something, anything, that will condemn Me.
But even lies struggle to find footing against truth.

I stand silent.

The law they claim to uphold demands two witnesses
agreeing.
None can be found.
Their words collapse under their own weight.
Frustration gnaws at them.

Qayyafah rises — robes swirling, anger barely concealed.
He is no longer seated in judgment. Now he circles,
prowling.
The room stills beneath his authority — or the fear of it.
He steps forward, close enough to smell — not just the
incense of the temple,
but the sweat of effort, of control slipping through his
fingers.
He cannot hold back the trembling of his hands, so he hides
them in the sleeves of power.

"Have You no answer to these charges?" he demands —
his voice rising to mask the cracks beneath it.
Eyes turn to Me — some pleading, some gloating, some
uncertain.
Still, I say nothing.

I will not defend what needs no defence.
Truth does not flinch under accusation.

He draws himself taller — shoulders squared; head lifted
like a high place.
He does not see that he stands on sinking ground.
The trap is set. The moment they've engineered now hangs
before them like a blade.
And he speaks the words — the ancient demand, the sacred
provocation:

"I put You under oath by the living God:
Tell us if You are the Messiah,
the Son of God."

Time stills.
Silence deepens — not of absence, but of weight.
He has spoken more than he knows.
Invoked the Name.
Opened the door.

Then I speak—clear, unshaken.

"You have said it.
And I tell you: from now on, you will see the Son of Man
seated at the right hand of Power, and coming on the clouds
of heaven."

The court erupts.

Qayyafah tears his robes—an act of feigned outrage.

"Blasphemy!" he cries. "What further need do we have of
witnesses? You have heard it yourselves!"

They shout for My death.

Spit flies from angry mouths.
Fists strike My face.
Mockery drips from their tongues.

"Prophesy to us, Messiah! Who hit You?"

They blindfold Me and strike again.

And outside—
In the courtyard—
Another battle rages.

Kephas.
Brave, stubborn, broken-hearted Kephas.

He lingers in the shadows, his spirit torn between love and fear.

A servant girl approaches, her lamp casting trembling light.

"You also were with Yehoshua of Galilee," she says.

Fear seizes him.

"I don't know what you're talking about," he snaps, backing into the deeper shadows.

Another servant—a man this time—points at him.

"This fellow was with Him!"

Again, denial spills from Kephas's lips.

"I don't know the man!"

A third voice joins—accusing, insistent.

"Surely you're one of them—your accent betrays you!"

And Kephas, heart hammering, curses and swears.

"I do not know the man!"

The words leave his mouth just as the rooster crows.

Piercing.
Final.

And I, inside, amid bruises and blows—
I turn.
Our eyes meet across the courtyard, across the wreckage of
good intentions.
My gaze does not condemn.
It aches.

Kephas staggers back.
Tears erupt, flowing uncontrollably, blinding him as he runs
stumbling through the darkness.

The guards seize Me, bind Me tighter.
Their rough laughter follows Me as they drag Me toward the
holding cell, where the night will bleed into mockery, into
pain, into injustice clothed in ritual.

The false trial grinds on.
The priests scheme how to present Me to Rome.
They cannot execute without Caesar's permission.

But while they deliberate—

Another story unfolds in the hidden corners of the city.

Yehudah Ish-Keriyot.

Stumbles through the alleys, silver clinking in his fist, each
coin a brand against his skin.

"He should have escaped."
"Why didn't he walk through the guards?"
"He has done that very thing so many times before."

Thoughts cascading through his mind.

The streets seem to shift beneath his feet, narrowing, twisting, mocking him.

The temple looms ahead — cold, silent, unmoved by his cries.

He bursts through the gates, the silver flashing in the low torchlight.
"I have betrayed innocent blood!" he shouts, voice cracking with terror.
"You need to let Him go!"

The priests turn, their faces already hardened, their eyes glittering with disdain.
"What is that to us?" they say. "See to it yourself."

Yehudah staggers forward, shoving the thirty pieces toward them, pleading —
his eyes wide, unfocused, as though searching for a door that no longer exists.
But they recoil, robes pulled back, as if the silver itself hisses with guilt.
It clatters to the stones — a hollow, terrible sound that echoes across the temple courts.
Each coin a nail.
Each echo a judgment.

Coins so precious before now burn in his palms.
He shakes, lips cracked, voice raw.
"I have sinned," he cries. "I have betrayed innocent blood!"
But no answer comes.

"You came to us," they say —
their voices now one, as if the Sanhedrin itself has become a single, cold mouth.
"It is on you."

They turn their backs.
Yehudah is confused. His breath quickens.
The temple spins around him.
Guards usher him out — not with force, but with indifference.

He steps into the cold, dark night — even the moon seems lost.

Then, silence.

A silence thick with accusation, with despair.

Confusion swirls like the night air — cold, heavy, without direction.

Desolate.

And then the voices begin.

Not shouted. Whispered.
Coiling. Creeping. Cutting.

"You are cursed."
"There is no more grace for you."
"You watched Him surrender."
"You kissed Him, knowing. Knowing."

The voice of the Accuser slithers in the silence coiling around him, squeezing the breath from his lungs— not from outside, but from within.
It knows his thoughts. His fears. His regret.
It speaks with many tongues:
his own voice,
the memory of the priests,
the twisting echo of the crowd,
the cold hiss of something darker.

"You were a friend."
"You sold love for a price."
"You thought He would run, didn't you?"
"You thought He would pass through the crowd again,
disappear like before."
"You didn't think He would stay still."

Yehudah falls to his knees, clawing at the stones, sobbing.
His breath comes in short bursts.
His sobs — not loud, not dramatic — but like a man coming
apart in slow motion.
His shoulders tremble.
His lips move but form no words.
Only pleas without sound.

"You are cursed."
"You are filth."
"You are the Betrayer — capital letter, etched in eternity."
"They will never forgive you. Not them. Not Him."
"You saw His face... you saw it when they struck Him."
"And He still looked at you with love."
"Even then."

That breaks him.
He claws at his tunic.
At his chest.
As if he could tear the guilt out of his flesh.
As if he could bleed clean.
But nothing comes out.
Just pain.

"They will never accept you."
"Even the others. Especially them."
"You broke the circle. You shattered the table."

"You are no longer disciple. You are disease."
"Go. Finish it."

The stones beneath him feel like graves.
The thought of the silver — those thirty coins — rattle in his
brain, no longer valuable, no longer currency.
Just judgment.

And still the voice whispers — not louder, but closer.
"Even Heaven won't take you now."
"You are a story they will never forget... but always despise."
"You opened the door. Now walk through it."

He feels hands clawing at his robes, his neck. He turns.
No one there.

His heart hammers at the chest wall. Tears fall like rain.

Yehudah rises. Slowly.
Like a man with no hope.
Hope is a sound long gone from his ears.
And as he walks, he does not hear My voice —
Not because I do not speak...
But because shame has deafened him.

I feel him even now — the twisting of his soul, the anguish
that gnaws him alive.
My heart breaks for him.

"Oh Yehudah..."
"If you had only waited a little longer."
"Mercy was coming for you too."

But he does not wait.

The noose tightens.
The branch creaks.

And Yehudah Ish-Keriyot falls — swallowed by darkness he
was never meant to know.

The field drinks his blood.
The earth bears silent witness.

And the night moves on.

The ropes bite deeper into My wrists as they pull Me through
the streets, toward the fortress of Antonia.
The city stirs slowly — vendors lifting shutters, women
sweeping dust from thresholds, children blinking at the first
grey light.
They do not know what this day holds.
Not yet.

Jerusalem breathes unaware.
Eternity pauses.
And hell leans forward.

We reach the Roman gates.
Rough iron. Cold hands.
The guards open them with indifference —
numb to suffering, trained by years of crucifixions and
blood-soaked sentences.
This is just another prisoner to them.
Just another dawn with chains and orders.

But not this time.

Inside, Pilate waits — pale, restless.
A man of rank, yet enslaved by fear.
He hides it behind Roman decorum, behind gestures of law
and reason, but I see it —
the tremor in his thoughts, the weight in his stare.
He has heard of Me.
And that is what unsettles him.

Behind him, scrolls of edicts. Seals of Caesar.
The pressure of empire chokes out his conscience.

The dawn breaks pale over Jerusalem.
But the real darkness —
the one no sun can pierce —
has only just begun.

Pilate studies Me — eyes flicking from My face to the priests,
to the crowd forming beyond the gates.
He senses the danger — not from Me, but from them.

He hears "Galilee" mentioned.
And like a drowning man spotting driftwood, he seizes the
word.

"Is He a Galilean?" he asks.

They nod.

Relief flickers across his features. A way to shift the burden.

Then send Him to Herod —
Let that fox gnaw at the edges of this.

Herod is in Jerusalem for the feast —
the same Herod who silenced Yochanan,
who heard My name and trembled behind his walls.

The soldiers drag Me onward — across paving stones veined
with blood and wine.
Through courtyards filled with servants too tired to care.
To a residence of marble and excess — where Herod
reclines behind embroidered curtains and performs cruelty
like theatre.

He wants a miracle.
He will get silence.

He greets Me not as a judge, but as a spectator — curious, craving a show.
He has long wished to see Me, to witness power. A sign. A spectacle.
But beneath the smile, I see his fear — a flicker of guilt for the blood of Yochanan the Baptist.
So he studies Me. Eyes digging into Mine, searching for signs of condemnation.
He fires off questions — probing, mocking, hoping.
I say nothing.
A small breath of relief escapes him.
Then he presses harder, demands signs and wonders.
Still, I do not speak.
His court begins to laugh — not out of joy, but out of fear dressed as amusement.
They drape a robe on My shoulders — gaudy, bright, a parody of kingship.
Mockery thickens.
But I remain silent.

"I tire of this game," he says "Take him back to Pilate"

The soldiers shove Me back toward Pilate, bruised but unbent.

Two rulers.

Two thrones.

And not a spine between them.

Herod and Pilate, once enemies, become friends that day — bound by shared cowardice.

I am returned to Pilate's judgment seat.

He looks wearier now.

More cornered.

The crowd swells beyond the courtyard, their voices rising like the tide.
Priests and elders weave among them, feeding the frenzy, twisting the hearts of men.

Pilate's wife appears briefly at his side, her face drawn with fear.
She leans in, whispering urgent words.

"Have nothing to do with that righteous man," she pleads.
"I have suffered terribly in a dream because of Him."

I see the tremor in Pilate's hands.
The battle within him.
But fear wins.

It always does.

He turns back to the crowd, desperate for a way out.
"You have a custom that I release one prisoner to you at Passover. Whom do you want me to release to you? Bar-Abba — or Yehoshua called Messiah?"

The name is flung like a challenge.

Bar-Abba — a murderer, a rebel — a man of blood.

The crowd hesitates... but only for a heartbeat.

The priests surge forward, hissing, shouting.

"Bar-Abba! Release Bar-Abba!"

Pilate blinks, stunned.

"What then shall I do with Yehoshua, who is called Messiah?"

The cry rises—louder now, more savage.

"Crucify Him!"

Pilate hesitates again.
"Why? What evil has He done?"

But reason is drowned by rage.
"Crucify! Crucify!"

Pilate's shoulders sag.
He calls for water.
He washes his hands in front of them all — a hollow ritual,
meant to cleanse guilt that water cannot touch.

"I am innocent of this man's blood," he declares.
"See to it yourselves."

The mob roars approval.

The ropes bite tighter into My wrists.

Pilate nods to the centurion.

The order is given.

And hell is unleashed.

They strip Me — tearing away the robe, the tunic — leaving
My body totally exposed to the cold morning air.

The weight of shame I must bear. I stand resolute, taller
somehow.

Laughter bubbles from the soldiers' throats. I see angels,
swords drawn. But I give no order, for this I came.

One brings the scourge — a Roman flagrum — leather
thongs studded with bone and iron.

They bind My hands high against the whipping post, pulling
My arms taut, straining the muscles, exposing every inch of
flesh.

The first lash falls.

It rips through skin, tearing it open.

Pain explodes — white-hot, searing — racing along My spine.

I glance toward the angel. He looks; I look away.

A second blow.
Then a third.
Then a fourth.

Each strike digs deeper, furrowing My flesh into raw, bleeding ribbons.
The bones beneath begin to show.

The soldiers laugh — a sick rhythm to their cruelty.

I forgive them.

I do not cry out.

For this I wrapped myself in flesh!

I taste blood at the back of My throat, the salt of My own sweat running into My eyes.

The world narrows to this: pain, breath, surrender.

I cling to the Father — though heaven feels distant, silent.

Each lash sings a song of mockery:

"For pride, a stripe."
"For hatred, a blow."
"For rebellion, a tear in the flesh."

I bear it all.

Not for the righteous — but for the broken.

Not for the strong — but for the desperate.

Not because they deserve it — but because they are loved.

Tenth

Eleventh

Flesh gives way.
My back tears open — stripe upon stripe, until the skin is no
longer skin, but a map of pain and purpose.

Blood runs freely — from shoulders to feet, soaking the
stones.
I hear the count.
I remember Gethsemane. The cup of bitterness that I drank.
The strength received for this journey. I pull Myself up.

I've stopped counting the blows.

My face —
once kissed by a mother, once smiled upon by children —
is now a ruin.
Swollen. Split.
A stripe blooms across My cheek, bone presses beneath
bruised flesh.
My nose bleeds. My eye swells barely able to open.
They do not know they are fulfilling the prophet's words:

"Just as many were astonished at you,
So, His visage was marred more than any man,
And His form more than the sons of men."

They do not understand this is the cost of healing.

They strike again.

And I do not resist.

Because love does not pull away.

And still —
by these stripes, they will be healed.

Suddenly the scourging ends — not with mercy, but with exhaustion.

They stop before death — just before.
Because death would be too kind.

They unbind My wrists, and I collapse onto hands and knees, blood pooling beneath Me. Black flesh hanging, crumpled. Some lying on the ground – dead.

But it is not finished.

Not yet.

They press a crown into My scalp — thorns long and wicked, piercing into bone.
Rivulets of blood snake down My face, stinging My eyes.

The seal – not of wax.

They drape a tattered purple robe over My shredded back, the cloth clinging to open wounds, material into flesh – touching bone.

A reed is shoved into My hand — a mock sceptre.

They kneel before Me in mocking obeisance.

"Hail, King of the Jews!" they sneer.

Fists strike My face. Blood spurts from an open wound at the corner of My cheek.

I feel dizzy. Angels are near – swords drawn; one holds Me up. I do not fall.
The reed is torn from My hand and slammed against My

crowned head.
Spit flies from their mouths — thick, hot, degrading.

Stinging open flesh.

I whisper a silent prayer – am strengthened.

Still more to come.

They strip the robe away again, reopening every wound,
each fibre clinging to raw flesh.

I sway — barely able to stand — My breath shallow, ragged.

Pilate appears again, motioning toward Me.

"Behold the man," he says, almost whispering.

He means it as mockery.
But even in this, truth leaks through.

Behold the Man.

The second Adam.

The Lamb of God.

Standing bloodied and broken — yet undefeated.

The judgment is final now.

I am led away like a lamb to the slaughter.

The crossbeam of death laid across My torn shoulders.

It bites deep into fresh wounds.

Splinters dig into raw muscle.

Each step forward feels impossible.

The mob lines the streets — shouting, laughing, weeping.

Women beat their breasts in mourning.

I stagger forward, the world tilting with each step.

"Look at him, where's his power now?" they jeered

He opened blind eyes — can't even save himself" someone spat.

Words, slander, humiliation.

I see her, Miryam, My mother. Her eyes wet, open tears down her face. The sword that will soon pierce My side, has already pierced hers.

There are others, some I see some I sense.

I hear the prophet speaking of Me.

"He has no form or comeliness;
And when we see Him,
There is no beauty that we should desire Him.
He is despised and rejected by men,
A Man of sorrows and acquainted with grief.
And we hid, as it were, *our* faces from Him;
He was despised, and we did not esteem Him."

My mind switches to the searing pain. To the absence of The Father. But I hear heaven willing me on. Angels walk with me. I slow My pace.

The weight of the beam crushes Me down, grinding My face into the dust of the street.

Soldiers curse and kick.

One seizes a man from the crowd — Shimon of Cyrene — forcing him to lift the beam.

He hesitates — afraid, unwilling — but obeys under the glint of Roman steel.

He shoulders the cross.

I shoulder the sin.

Side by side, we walk the road of sorrows.

Via Dolorosa.

The city walls loom ahead.

Beyond them — the Place of the Skull.

Golgotha.

Death gathers on the horizon like a storm.

I lift My eyes once more to the heavens.

They are silent.

But I am not alone.

The Spirit burns within Me — a fire no scourge, no thorn, no nail can extinguish.

I press on.

For them.

For the joy set before Me.

For the healing of the world.

The hill rises before Me — barren, broken, a skull grinning at the sky.

Golgotha.

The soldiers waste no time.

They tear away My garments — rough hands ripping cloth from blood-crusted flesh — exposing Me to the jeering crowd.

Even the last shred of human dignity is stripped away.

Naked, bleeding, trembling — yet unbroken — I am thrown onto the crossbeam.

The wood bites into torn shoulders.

I hear the clink of iron.

I see the hammer lifted high.

The first nail punches through flesh and bone, anchoring My right hand to the beam.
Pain explodes — not as a sharp spike, but a roaring flood, consuming every nerve.

I cry out – involuntarily.

Another nail — My left hand — stretched, pinned.

I do not cry – I grit my teeth.

My legs are drawn up, twisted against the wood.

The final nail drives through My feet — brutal, final.

The crossbeam is hoisted, dropped into place with a jolt that rips through My entire body.

Every breath from now on will be a battle.

The weight of My body drags downward — tearing at torn shoulders, pulling against nails driven through bone and sinew.

The wooden beam grinds against open wounds.

My chest constricts — every inhale a war.

To breathe, I must force Myself upward —
pressing against the nails driven through My feet,
feeling flesh tear further with every desperate push.

The agony is blinding — white-hot — racing through My
limbs like fire.

Every gasp demands a choice.

To live one heartbeat longer...
To speak one more word...
To endure one more moment of crushing pain.

The muscles cramp, seizing violently.

Blood loss drains strength with every droplet.

The nerves scream.

The lungs burn.

The heart stutters under the weight of suffering.

And still — I cling to life.

Still — I choose to breathe.

Still — I choose the Cross.

Not because the nails hold Me.
Not because the wood binds Me.
But because love compels Me.

Love for them.

Love for you.

Love even for those who now mock Me from below.

Every breath is a sacrifice.

Every heartbeat is a vow.

Every gasp is a love song — sung in agony — for a world that does not yet understand.

Through the pain, I see them, feel their presence.

Angels – swords drawn.

Above My head, a sign is nailed:

"Yehoshua of Nazareth, King of the Jews."

Written in Hebrew, Latin, and Greek — the languages of covenant, conquest, and culture.

They do not know how true it is.

The crowd gathers — priests, scribes, soldiers, passers-by.

They shout, mock, spit.

"He saved others; He cannot save Himself!"
"If You are the Son of God, come down from the cross!"

Their words stab deeper than the nails.

But I remain.

For love.

For them.

For the ones who hate Me.

There are some who weep openly.

Many who were healed.

The seventy.

My earthly family, some hide in the shadows. Some will Me to see them.

The voices blur into a single, throbbing roar — hatred, sorrow, confusion, hope — all woven together beneath the darkened sky.

I search their faces through the haze of blood and dust.

Some weep, hands over mouths, hearts breaking.
Some turn away, unable to bear the sight.
Some glare with hollow eyes, deaf to mercy.

I see the ones I taught, the ones I touched — the lepers made whole, the blind given sight, the children cradled in My arms.

I feel their prayers rising — fragile, desperate, wordless.

But the tide of mockery swells again, drowning their whispered love.

And beside Me —
pain not My own.
Two others groan under the weight of death. Crucified beside Me — criminals, rebels.

One joins the mockers.

"Are You not the Messiah? Save Yourself and us!" he sneers.

But the other — broken, gasping — turns his bloodied face toward Me.

"Yehoshua... remember me when You come into Your kingdom."

I lift My gaze, tasting blood, fighting for breath.

"Amen, I tell you: today you will be with Me in Paradise."

Hope blooms even here — on a hill of death.

Below Me, soldiers gamble for My clothing, tossing dice as if My suffering were sport.

Fulfilling scripture

"They divide My garments among them and cast lots for My clothing."

I lift My eyes further — searching the crowd.

There.

Miryam — My mother — her heart shattered, face pale, barely able to stand.

Hands support her as she stands beneath the cross.

Beside her, Yochanan — the beloved disciple, trembling but steadfast.

I gather strength, forcing the words through cracked lips.

"Woman, behold your son."

Miryam's eyes overflow.

"Yochanan, behold your mother."

And so, even now, in the midst of death, I build family.

Hours pass.

The sun blazes above, but a deeper darkness begins to gather.

At the sixth hour, the sky trembles.

The light fails.

A heavy, unnatural night falls across the land.

The earth itself recoils.

I feel it — the weight of every curse, every broken covenant, every sin laid upon Me.

The Father's presence — once so near — draws back.

Not in anger.

In judgment.

The full penalty must fall.

And for the first time since before time began —
I am alone.

A cry tears from My soul — raw, guttural, ripping the heavens:

"Eli, Eli, lama azavtani?" (אֵלִי אֵלִי לְמָה עֲזַבְתָּנִי)
"My God, My God, why have You forsaken Me?"

The bystanders murmur, misunderstanding.

"He calls for Eliyahu."

But no help comes.

No rescue.

Only the silence of judgment.

The Lamb bears it alone.

I thirst.

A soldier lifts a sponge soaked in sour wine — bitter, burning — pressing it to My cracked lips.

I taste it — the vinegar of suffering.

I lift My gaze one last time.

The end draws near.

The victory is at hand.

I summon all that remains of life within Me, drawing a final breath deep into labouring lungs.

And I cry out — not in defeat, but in triumph:

"It is finished!"

The moment the words leave My lips — the world convulses.

The earth shudders violently — a groaning deeper than sound, older than stone.

Rocks split apart.

Graves burst open — the righteous dead stirred from their long sleep, awakening in the shudder of redemption.

In the Temple — high upon Mount Moriah —
the veil guarding the Most Holy Place — thick, heavy, ancient —
is torn apart from top to bottom.

Not by human hands.

Not from earth upward.

But from Heaven downward.

The barrier between God and man is shattered.

The mercy seat is unveiled.

The way home is opened.

The Roman centurion standing at My feet stares upward,
eyes wide with awe, as dust and darkness swirl around him.

"Truly this man was the Son of God."

The weight of sin, shame, wrath — all of it —
pours itself into Me like a flood.
And then — passes through.

The cup is emptied.

The debt is paid.

I surrender.

Not defeated.

Victorious.

I bow My head.

I release My spirit.

And I die.

The earth moans underfoot.

The mountains tremble.

The sky weeps dark tears.

The angels — unseen to mortal eyes — fall silent.

For the Lamb has been slain.

But death will not hold its prize.

The grave will not close its mouth.

The stone will not stay sealed.

This —
this is not the end.

It is only the door opening.

The world tilts and staggers beneath the weight of My death.
The darkness lingers — heavy, suffocating — even as the
crowds drift away, unsettled by the trembling earth and the
torn heavens.

The soldiers remain.

They approach the crosses with grim efficiency, breaking the
legs of the thieves to hasten death.

They come to Me — but I am already gone.

Still, one of them — rough, careless — thrusts a spear into
My side.

Blood and water flow out — the final witness of a heart
broken; a temple torn down.

I feel it — even now — from beyond the veil of breath.

The fulfilment.
The finality.
The beginning of something new.

As evening falls, two men come forward — bold now, where
once they hid in fear.

Yosef of Arimathea — a wealthy man, a secret disciple.
And Nikódēmos — the teacher of Israel who once sought Me
by night.

They come to Pilate, requesting My body.

Pilate, surprised that I am already dead, verifies it through the centurion.

Permission is granted.

They approach the cross — careful, reverent, trembling.

They lower Me down — arms heavy, bloodied, limp.

Hands that once healed the sick, lifted the broken, raised the dead — now lifeless in their arms.

They work quickly — Sabbath draws near.

Tender hands cleanse the blood and dust from My battered body.

Nikódēmos brings spices — myrrh and aloes — a king's burial.

Yosef offers his own tomb — new, unused — hewn into solid rock.

They wrap Me in linen, layer upon layer — winding sheet over torn flesh, over the silence of death.

They place Me in the tomb, cold and still.

The stone is rolled across the entrance — heavy, final.

The sound echoes like thunder in the hollow space.

The tomb is sealed.

Soldiers are posted.

The priests remember My words:
"After three days, I will rise again."

They fear what they do not understand.

They secure the tomb — as if mortal hands and stones could hold the Author of life.

Inside the darkness, My body rests.

Motionless.

Silent.

But My spirit — My spirit is not still.

I descend.

Not fallen but sent.

Not defeated, but victorious.

Through the veil of death, I move — through the shadows and cold silence of the grave.

The realm of the dead stretches before Me — vast, hollow, trembling.

Chains clatter in the darkness.

Doors creak on rusted hinges.

The air is thick with despair — ancient, choking.

The souls of the dead stir — some weeping, some raging, some long silent in their sorrow.

I walk among them — the Living One in the land of the dead.

The gates of Sheol loom ahead — massive, ancient, fortified.

Their bars have held kings and slaves alike.

No man has broken them.

Until now.

Demons recoil at My presence.

Their shrieks echo in the blackness.

The prince of darkness — the ancient serpent — draws back, his face twisted in horror.

He thought the cross was victory.

He thought death would hold Me.

He was wrong.

I lift My voice — a voice that once called stars into being — and it thunders through the depths:

"Lift up your heads, O you gates! And be lifted up, you everlasting doors! And the King of glory shall come in."

The very stones tremble.

The chains snap like twigs.

The gates shatter — splintering outward with a sound like a thousand storms.

Light floods the darkness.

Brilliant.

Pure.

Unstoppable.

The righteous dead lift their heads — faces wide with wonder, eyes burning with hope.

Adam and Chavah — their shame long carried — see Me and weep with joy.

Avraham, the friend of God, smiles through his tears.

Mosheh lifts his staff high.

David throws back his head and laughs, the sound of a freed king.

The prophets, the martyrs, the faithful — they gather, a great cloud of witnesses.

They know Me.

They have waited for this day.

They have hoped against hope.

And now — Hope stands among them.

I reach out My hand.

"Come," I say.

"Come forth. The price is paid. The way is open. Death has no hold on you any longer."

They rise — their chains falling away — hearts blazing with new life.

I lead them out — a procession of glory — a river of light bursting through the broken gates of death.

The enemy howls — a cry of rage and defeat — but it cannot touch Me.

I have conquered.

I have triumphed.

I have fulfilled all that was written.

I rise, leading captivity captive.

I ascend through the broken realms.

The earth stirs above — stones shifting, graves trembling.

Those who were dead will walk again, signs of the power
unleashed this day.

The grave is broken.

The curse is reversed.

The gates are shattered.

The King is coming.

But first —
the stone must be rolled away.

The morning must dawn.

The world must behold —
an empty tomb.

Chapter 13: Resurrection

Silence.

Heavy, deep — the silence of the grave.

Darkness wraps around Me, thick as a burial shroud.

Yet even here, even now — life stirs.

The Spirit hovers.

The breath of the Father moves across the void once more.

Then —
light.

Brilliant, searing, living light — flooding the tomb from within, not from without.

I feel it first — a pulse — deeper than heartbeat, older than flesh.

The voice of The Ruach HaKodesh:

"Rise, My Son."

Obedience surges through Me — joyful, unstoppable.

Spirit and body reunite.

Breath rushes into lungs collapsed by death.

Eyes flutter open — not dim but blazing.

Muscles knit.
Torn flesh heals.

The heart begins to beat — not with mortal weakness, but with immortal strength.

The shroud falls away like mist before the morning sun.

I sit up —
the grave clothes clinging loosely, unable to hold Me; It falls away. Replaced by shining white garments – not knit by mortal hands.

The stone still stands before the entrance — but it is no barrier.

The earth groans again — and the stone trembles.

Outside, soldiers sleep, stunned into stupor.

Above, the heavens blaze — angels descending swift and fierce.

They roll the stone away — not to let Me out, but to let the world look in.

The tomb is empty.

I step forward — radiant, unseen.

Alive.

In the garden outside the tomb, the first witness approach.

Miryam of Magdala — faithful, fierce, weeping.

She comes with spices — the tender offerings of love to a corpse she will not find.

She finds the stone rolled away.

The tomb gaping open.

Terror and wonder war in her heart.

She stoops. kneels by the entrance, sobbing.

"Where have they taken my Lord?" she weeps. "I do not know where they have laid Him."

Two angels sit within the tomb — at the head and foot of where My body had lain — but her grief blinds her to glory.

"Woman, why are you weeping?" they ask.

She turns — sensing another behind her.

She sees Me — but in her sorrow, in her tears, she does not recognise Me.

She thinks I am the gardener.

"Woman," I say gently, "why are you weeping? Whom are you seeking?"

She chokes out, "Sir, if you have carried Him away, tell me where you have laid Him, and I will take Him away."

I smile — tender, powerful.

One word.

One name.

"Miryam."

Her breath catches.

Her eyes widen.

Her heart knows before her mind does.

She falls at My feet, clutching the hem of My robe.

"Rabboni!" she cries — My Teacher! My Master!

Joy floods her soul.

Hope reborn in an instant.

I bend close, My voice full of life beyond life.

"Do not cling to Me, Miryam. For I have not yet ascended to My Father. But go — go to My brothers and tell them: 'I am ascending to My Father and your Father, to My God and your God.'"

She nods — sobbing, laughing — her heart lighter than wings.

She runs — runs faster than fear, faster than sorrow — the first herald of resurrection.
The ground blurs beneath her feet. The wind catches her shawl. Her heart beats faster than her sandals strike the path. Her tears haven't stopped, but flows, uncontrollable but now they run for joy, not despair. She can still hear My voice in her ears—*Miryam.* No one says her name like that. Not before. Not since.

They won't believe me.
But I must tell them.

The house is dim when she arrives. The others are still sleeping or pretending to. Kephas stirs. Yochanan sits up, bleary-eyed.

She bursts through the door, breathless. "He's—He's not there."

They rise quickly, confusion rising like steam.

"What!?"

"The tomb—He's gone. But it wasn't stolen. I saw Him. I spoke with Him. He called me by name. He's alive."

Kephas stares.
He doesn't speak. His jaw clenches.

Yochanan runs.

They all rise, uncertain whether to doubt or hope.

I rise higher, the earth falling away beneath Me.

The realms' part — heaven bending low to receive the victorious Son.

The Temple not made with human hands shines before Me — the Heavenly Sanctuary.

I enter — robed now in light, crowned with glory.

Heaven is silent as I enter.
The veil in the Temple has torn on Earth, but here—here in the true tabernacle—I step beyond the veil not as sacrifice only, but as priest.

I enter—not with shouts of conquest, but with blood in My hands.

The altar awaits.

"Father, I have fulfilled My purpose."

"See— I carry the blood —not of bulls or goats, but My own. Poured out, willingly. Spilled, yet sovereign. The blood of the covenant. The blood that speaks better things than the blood of Hevel. The blood that redeems. That restores. That finishes what was begun before time."

I step forward.

I approach the Mercy Seat — the true one, of which the earthly ark was only a shadow.

I carry the offering.

Perfect.

Sinless.

Poured out.

I sprinkle it on the altar — once, for all.

It cries not for vengeance, but for mercy.

All of Heaven watches in stillness.

The Father looks—not at My wounds, but through them. He sees the obedience. The agony. The love. And He is satisfied.

A voice, like thunder and stillness all at once, fills the expanse:

"It is accepted."

And all creation sings.

The work is finished.

The covenant is sealed.

Redemption is accomplished.

The contract fulfilled.
The gates will never be closed again.

But My mission is not yet done.

I will return.

I will show Myself to them.

I will heal their wounds.

I will rekindle their hope.

I will send them out — burning with the fire of the Spirit — into a world desperate for light.

I return again to earth,

Just as the sun begins its slow descent beyond the hills of Jerusalem.

The city hums behind Me — restless, broken, blind to what has already happened.

Two men walk the dusty road toward a village called Emmaus — their heads bowed, their steps slow, their hearts heavy with sorrow.

Their faces are familiar — Kleópas and Shimon — disciples, two of the seventy, seekers, lovers of truth.

They speak in low voices, burdened by confusion, by crushed hopes.

"We had hoped..." they murmur.

Hope — past tense.

The weight of it hangs between them like a funeral shroud.

I draw near — quiet, ordinary, unrecognised.

I match their pace.

They glance at Me, offering tired nods, assuming Me a traveller like themselves.

"What are you discussing as you walk along?" I ask, though I know their hearts already.

They stop, faces full of pain.

Kleópas answers, surprise and sorrow sharpening his voice.

"Are you the only visitor to Jerusalem who does not know the things that have happened there in these days?"

I smile gently.

"What things?"

They pour it out — the story, the heartbreak, the deep ache of disappointed dreams.

"Yehoshua of Nazareth," they say — My own name, still tender on their lips — "a prophet, mighty in deed and word before God and all the people..."

They speak of My trial.

My crucifixion.

Their shattered hopes.

"We had hoped that He was the one to redeem Israel."

Hope — past tense again.

And now, confusion — women speaking of empty tombs, visions of angels, rumours of life.

But they do not dare believe it.

Not fully.

Not yet.

Their hearts cling still to death.

I let the silence settle a moment.

Then I speak — My voice steady, filled with the pulse of eternity.

"O foolish ones, and slow of heart to believe all that the prophets have spoken! Was it not necessary that the Messiah should suffer these things and enter into His glory?"

Their eyes widen — not with recognition, but with hunger.

They listen — souls starved for understanding.

And so, I open the Scriptures to them — weaving the tapestry of redemption from the first word to the last.

From Mosheh to the Prophets, I reveal the hidden story.

The Seed promised in Eden.
The Lamb provided on Moriah.
The Deliverer foreshadowed in Yosef.
The Blood painted on the doorposts of Egypt.
The High Priest entering the Holy of Holies.
The Suffering Servant despised and rejected.
The King riding on a donkey, pierced yet victorious.

Thread by thread, I weave the pattern before their eyes.

Their hearts ignite — slow embers flaring into flame.

Hope — present tense.

Hope — living.

Hope — breathing.

The village rises ahead — Emmaus — its small houses crouched against the dying light.

I make as if to walk further, but they urge Me strongly:

"Stay with us, for it is toward evening and the day is far spent."

I accept.

I enter their home — low-roofed, humble — filled with the scent of baked bread and old wood.

We sit at the table.

I take the bread in My hands.

Hands once pierced — still marked, yet whole.

I lift My eyes.

I bless the bread.

And as I break it — their eyes are opened.

They see Me — truly see Me.

Not merely a prophet.

Not merely a memory.

But the Living One.

The Risen King.

Their mouths fall open in awe, hearts pounding with sudden, overwhelming joy.

Before a word can be spoken — I vanish from their sight.

But their hearts — oh, their hearts — burn within them still.

They leap up — running back toward Jerusalem — feet flying faster than fear, faster than sorrow.

And I walk ahead — unseen — into the Upper Room where trembling hearts wait behind locked doors.

Soon they too will see.

Soon they too will believe.

Soon the world itself will burn with this unquenchable fire.

The room is shuttered tight.

Doors barred.

Breath held.

Fear thick in the air like smoke.

The Eleven — and those with them — huddle in shadows, hearts hammering with every footstep beyond the door.

They have heard whispers.

Miryam's breathless report.

Kleópas and his companion rushing in with burning eyes.

But still they hide.

Still, they tremble.

Still, they wonder — could it be true?

I come to them.

Not through the door.

Not with knocking or clamour.

I stand among them — suddenly, simply — as real as the wood beneath their feet, as certain as the beating of their hearts.

They startle — gasping, stumbling backward — fear etched deep on every face.

They think Me a spirit — a shade — a ghost summoned by grief.

I lift My hands — scarred, yet whole — and speak, My voice steady, rich with love.

"Shalom"
"Peace be upon you."

The words settle like dew on scorched earth.

Still, they hesitate.

Still, they struggle to believe.

"Why are you troubled?" I ask gently. "And why do doubts arise in your hearts? Look at My hands and My feet — it is I Myself! Touch Me and see; a spirit does not have flesh and bones as you see that I have."

They draw closer — trembling, wide-eyed — reaching out cautious fingers.

They touch the wounds — rough scars over soft skin.

Their breath catches.

Tears well.

Laughter bubbles up — disbelieving, giddy, like children waking from a nightmare.

Still, they marvel.

Still, they cannot fully comprehend.

I smile.

"Have you anything here to eat?"

They rush to offer broiled fish — the simplest meal, the simplest proof.

I take it.

I eat before them — living, breathing, risen.

Their joy fills the room, pressing against the walls until it bursts outward in laughter, tears, embraces.

Hope — no longer past tense.

Hope — alive.

But one is missing.

Toma — called the Twin — was not with them.

He heard the stories later, wild with light and breath and wounds.

And when they tell him, his face hardens, grief twisting into stubbornness.

"Unless I see in His hands the mark of the nails," he says, *"and place my finger into the holes, and place my hand into His side, I will never believe."*

Grief blinds.

Grief hardens.

Grief clenches fists against hope.
One thing he needed more than words: proof.

Eight days later — the doors once again locked — they gather.

Toma with them this time.

And once again, I come.

Sudden.

Silent.

Present.

"Shalom"

I turn to Toma — My gaze piercing through all the walls he has built.

Tenderness fills Me — not anger.

He needs what he asks for.

And I am willing.

I lift My hands — palms outward — the wounds plain.

"Put your finger here," I say, stepping closer.

"See My hands.
Reach out your hand and put it into My side.
Do not disbelieve — but believe."

Toma's face crumples.

The defiance melts away, stripped by love too pure to resist.

He falls to his knees — tears streaming down his face.

"My Lord and my God."

The confession echoes through the room, shaking the walls of grief and doubt.

I reach for him — lifting him gently.

"You have believed because you have seen Me," I say softly. "Blessed are those who have not seen — and yet have believed."

The blessing flies outward — a seed carried on the wind of coming centuries.

To you, little flock.

To those not yet born.

To those who will trust without touching, love without seeing.

Blessed.

Blessed forever.

And still, My time among them is not yet complete.

There are more hearts to mend.

More fires to kindle.

More love to pour out.

Soon — breakfast by the sea.

Soon — words of forgiveness.

Soon — a commission that will turn the world upside down.

But for now —
I am here.

Alive.

With them.

And the darkness has no hold on us anymore.

I return to the house where I once laughed and laboured.
Where wood dust lingered in the air and love soaked into every surface.
The walls have not changed. But the atmosphere has.

Grief has moved in.
It sits in the corners like a quiet guest no one can send away.

I walk the path I've walked a thousand times — barefoot as I once was — and press My hand lightly against the gate.
The olive tree beside the doorway still leans slightly to one

side, still groaning when the wind shifts.
Inside, I hear voices — hushed, uncertain, heavy with memory.

Miryam speaks first.
She always does when the room is too still.
Her voice wraps around their silence like a blanket.
But there's sorrow in it now — the kind that doesn't reach the eyes.

I enter without knocking.

Yosi is the first to notice — he stands abruptly, knocking over the clay cup in his hand.
It shatters. No one flinches.
They are all staring at Me.

Miryam rises slowly, her eyes already filling.
She does not run. She does not scream.
She brings her hand to her mouth, fingers trembling.
And in a whisper so deep the floor seems to breathe with it, she says:
"Yehoshua?"

I nod once.

She falls into My arms.

Her sobs are wordless — like the sound of oceans returning to their shore.
I hold her like I did the night Yosef died — when she wept so hard, she shook.
This time, she weeps with a joy that cannot find its shape.

"But how?" she says between sobs

The others do not move.
Shimon's hand is half-raised, as if he doesn't trust his own

sight.
Shlomit presses herself into the wall.
Yehuda mouths something — a prayer? A curse? I cannot tell.

Yakov stands back — arms folded, jaw tight.
His eyes burn, not with hatred, but with the fire of a man whose world is being undone.
He wants to believe.
But belief will cost him everything.

Miryam, the younger, edges forward, slowly unsure.

"Touch Me," I say, My voice low. "See for yourselves."

I extend My hands — palms torn open, still bearing the marks.
The room stills.

Yosi steps forward, joining Miryam the younger.
His fingers tremble as they reach for Mine.
He touches the scar — and gasps as if it burns.

Miryam the younger holds me tight, tears flowing.

"It's real," Yosi whispers.

Then the rush begins.

Shimon clutches Me around the waist, sobbing.
Shlomit moves closer, tentative, then clings to My robe.
Even Yehuda, who once questioned everything, falls to his knees and grips My feet.

But Yakov remains still.

I turn to him — not with demand, but with invitation.
He does not lower his gaze.

"You died," he says, barely audible.

"I did."

He swallows hard.
"And now?"

"I live."

A silence passes between us that only brothers can know.
A silence built on years of shared chores, shared questions, shared blood.
A silence forged in the gap between *knowing* and *believing.*

Questions fly

"But how" mum asks again.

Before I could answer, "Why are you here"

"Are you a spirit?"

"No, can you not feel My breath? I am alive, death is defeated"

"You could have stopped it," Yakov says, but there is no accusation in his voice. Only ache.

"Yes."

"Why didn't you?"

"Because love doesn't run from pain, Yakov. It redeems it. I came to fulfil the law"

He looks down.
His shoulders rise and fall.
Then he whispers — so softly only I can hear it —
"Forgive me."

I step forward, place My hand on his shoulder.
"I already have."

He breaks then — not like a child, but like a man who's carried a burden far too long.

Miryam pulls him close. She weeps again, but this time so does he.

We sit together — not as a king among peasants, not as the divine towering over the fragile —
but as a family. As we used to.

Bread is brought.
Fish, figs, olives.
They eat slowly, still watching Me between bites — afraid I might vanish.

Yosi says little.

Miryam the younger watches intently.
Shimon talks too much.
Shlomit leans her head against My arm, just as she used to.

And Yakov?
He watches — but not with scepticism anymore.
With awe.

No one rises to help their mother. But she doesn't mind. Her pierced side, figuratively, healing.

Silence settles again — not awkward, but full.

"It is hard for you. You know Me as brother, son. We grew together, but you know only My flesh."

I look around at their faces.

They have known My kindness. My laughter. My stories. My strength.
Now they must know the rest.

"I Am," I say quietly.

"The One who walked with Adam in the cool of the garden.
The voice in the fire.
The Rock in the wilderness.
The Lamb at Passover.
The arm of salvation stretched out from Heaven."

Their eyes do not leave Me.

"I am the Word made flesh.
The Son of the Living God.
The Firstborn from among the dead.
The door you have not yet walked through — but soon will."

I reach for Miryam's hand. "And still — I am your Son."

I turn to Yakov. "And your Brother."

I glance to the others — "And your Lord."

Silence.

I answer the unspoken questions.

"It was necessary — for God to become man. To stand in Adam's place. To carry what no other could.

To crush the serpent's head and yes, My heel was bruised.

To defeat death and the grave."

I walk them through the Torah, the Nevi'im, the Ketuvim.
Scriptures that I had breathed into prophets of old.

No one speaks.
But something shifts in the air — like an old curtain pulled back to reveal light they've only dreamed of.

They take it in. Slowly, understanding begins to dawn.

Later, as the light fades and the room dims, I stand.

They rise with Me, unsure what to do.

"There is more to come," I say.
"But for now — peace be with you."

I touch each one gently — a hand on the head, a thumb
across a brow.
They do not understand what I give them.
Not yet.

But they will.

Yakov will rise to lead — a foundational stone in the early
Church.
Yehuda will write words that echo through the generations.
Yosi and Shimon, mighty men of valour, will carry the Word
wherever they go.
Even Miryam the younger and Shlomit will take fire into every
place they walk.
They will remember this night —
when the dead Son came home,
and the Kingdom began in a kitchen full of crumbs and
tears.

I leave as I came — quietly, without fanfare.
But heaven knows.
Heaven sings.

The morning air is cool over the waters of Kinneret.

Mist drifts low along the surface, veiling the distant hills.

The disciples are there — familiar faces — weary and
restless, returned to nets and boats, unsure of how to wait,
unsure of what resurrection means for fishermen.

Kephas, always restless, always first to leap, had said, "I am
going fishing."

The others had followed.

All night they laboured — casting, drawing, casting again — and caught nothing.

Their nets, like their hearts, came up empty.

I stand on the shore, watching them.

The rising sun at My back casts long shadows on the sand.

They do not recognise Me yet.

Their eyes, like their hearts, are still clouded.

I raise My voice across the water:

"Children, have you any food?"

They answer with a simple, dejected "No."

I call again:

"Cast the net on the right side of the boat, and you will find some."

They hesitate — a flicker of memory stirring — then obey.

The net sinks deep — and suddenly strains under the weight of fish.

A catch too great for human strength alone.

Their eyes widen.

Yochanan gasps, his heart leaping ahead of his mind.

"It is the Master!" he cries.

Kephas does not hesitate.

He throws himself into the sea — the water crashing around him — swimming, stumbling, half-running toward shore.

The others follow, dragging the bulging net.
153 large fish.
Not 150. Not "about a hundred."
They count them — as if something holy is hidden in the number.
It is not just a catch.
It is a sign.
The fullness of the harvest. The nations. The redeemed.
And still — the net does not tear.

A fire burns low on the beach — coals glowing, the smell of bread and roasting fish filling the air.

I gesture them closer.

"Bring some of the fish you have just caught," I say.

They move slowly, reverently, still half-afraid, half-overjoyed.

Kephas stands dripping before Me — shivering not from cold, but from awe.

I break the bread, passing it to them.

I serve the fish.

The meal is simple — earthy, holy.

The first meal after death.

The first communion of the new creation.

They eat in silence, marvelling.

None dare ask, "Who are You?" — for they know.

They know.

When the meal is finished, I turn to Kephas.

The fire crackles between us.

The others fall silent, sensing the moment.

I look into Kephas's eyes — windows clouded by shame, by failure.

He looks down.

I speak — gently, but with a weight that presses the air around us:

"Shimon, son of Yonah, do you love Me more than these?"

He lifts his eyes — pain and hope warring within him.

"Yes, Master," he whispers. "You know that I love You."

I nod.

"Feed My lambs."

I ask again:

"Shimon, son of Yonah, do you love Me?"

His heart trembles.

"Yes, Master. You know that I love You."

"Tend My sheep."

A third time — mirroring the three denials, not to shame, but to heal:

"Shimon, son of Yonah, do you love Me?"

Tears brim in his eyes.

Grief rises — but it is grief that cleanses, not condemns.

"Master," he chokes, "You know all things. You know that I love You."

I reach across the fire — steady, sure.

"Feed My sheep."

The chains fall from his soul.

The sting of denial is undone.

The mantle of leadership is restored.

Love, not strength, will be his weapon now.

Mercy not might.

I lean closer — My voice low, filled with a solemn joy.

" Most assuredly, I say to you, when you were younger, you girded yourself and walked where you wished; but when you are old, you will stretch out your hands, and another will gird you and carry you where you do not wish."

He understands.

Not the details, not yet.

But the path.

The cross.

The crown.

Then I speak the words that will echo in his spirit all his days:

"Follow Me."

The sea laps gently at the shore.

The fire crackles.

The morning brightens.

And Kephas rises — forgiven, called, beloved.

But there is one more moment yet to come.

One more charge.

One more mountain to climb.

Our pace slows. They don't yet know what this ascent will mean — but I do.

The mountain rises before us — strong, steady — a silent witness to eternity bending low.

I lead them there — the Eleven, still stunned by wonder, still carrying the scars and the glory of what has passed.

Some walk boldly.

Some hesitate, doubt flickering still in their hearts.

I welcome both.

Faith and fear alike are drawn to Me.

We gather on the slopes, the wind carrying the scent of earth and sky.

The sun blazes overhead, brilliant, relentless, alive.

I stand before them — no longer veiled in weakness, no longer bound by sorrow.

Alive.

Radiant.

Victorious.

The Lamb who was slain.

The King who reigns.

The bridge between heaven and earth.

They fall before Me — some with faces pressed to the ground, some lifting trembling hands.

Worship and wonder mingling.

I look at them — My brothers, My friends, My sent ones.

The ones who will carry light into the deepest shadows.

The ones who will bleed and sing and die and rise.

The ones for whom I died — and the ones through whom I will live.

I lift My voice — steady, commanding, full of unshakable love:

"All authority in heaven and on earth has been given to Me."

Not some.

All.

Given by the Father to the Son.

Not taken by force.

Given in love.

Earned in obedience.

Sealed in blood.

"Go therefore..."

I speak it into their hearts — a seed that will bloom in deserts and prisons, across oceans and empires.

"Go and make disciples of all nations..."

Not only Israel.

Not only the faithful remnant.

But the nations.

The Gentiles.

The exiled, the forgotten, the broken.

"Baptising them in My Name — the Name of the Father, the
Son, and the Ruach HaKodesh — for We are One."
A Name greater than kings.
A Name deeper than generations.
A Name that breaks chains and raises the dead.

Yehoshua.

It is through My Name that entrance is granted to the Father
—

Through My Name that you heal the sick, feed the hungry,
cleanse the leper, cast out demons, and raise the dead!

"Teaching them to observe all that I have commanded you."
Not a dry recitation.
Not a hollow tradition.
A living Word.

Written on living hearts.

They listen — drinking it in — the fire kindling behind their
eyes.

They do not yet know the cost.

But they know enough.

They know Me.

I continue.

Smiles

Wet eyes

Understanding flickering.

One day whilst teaching I see shadows in the distance.
I am not distracted. I continue.

They think I do not see them.
But I do.

Cloaked men in layered robes — chief priests, scribes, elders — slipping through alleys long after the crowds have scattered. Their steps are fast, low to the ground, hearts pounding with something they won't name.

Not belief.
Not yet.
But fear.

I feel it like a tremor underfoot.

They stand just beyond the olive trees, beneath the cover of dusk.
Watching.
Listening.
Weighing every word like it might accuse them. Or free them.

I speak louder. Not for them — but for the truth.
Still, they flinch.

I speak of the Kingdom. Of the harvest. Of the mercy that waits even now at their gates.

Their eyes narrow.

They shift their weight.

They recognise My voice —
not just from the temple courts or Galilean hills,
but from the scrolls they know by heart.

And still... they stay hidden.

They thought the tomb would end Me.
Thought the stone, the seal, the silence would hold.
But even now, their hands shake.

They speak in hushed tones, just beyond the edge of the
grove.
Afraid to come closer.
Too proud to turn away.

They do not watch me alone, but their eyes flicker sideways
— to the ones at My feet.
Fishermen. Tax collectors. Women once nameless.
They watch not just what I say, but who dares to believe it.

One locks eyes with Me for a moment.
Brief. But enough.

I see the tremble in his jaw.
The war inside him.

They retreat like smoke, swallowed by stone corridors and
political silence.
But I know this:

They have seen.
They have heard.
And they will not forget.

They will not admit it — not now.
But in the silence of their own breath, they will remember
this moment.

And wonder if perhaps...
the stone did not win after all.

Behind them, My disciples remain — not in robes of power,
but in garments of hope.
Their hearts burn, though they do not yet understand the
fullness of the fire.
And so, I give them the promise that will anchor them when
the nights grow long, when prisons close around them,
when swords and flames rise against them.

A promise stronger than stone, surer than the rising sun:

*"And behold, I am with you always, even to the end of the
age."*

The words settle over them like a mantle.

A shield.

A song.

The Spirit stirs — the first whisper of the rushing wind yet to
come.

I smile — joy blazing in My heart.

They will go.

They will fall and rise and fall again.

They will heal and teach and suffer and dance.

They will set the world ablaze with a fire no empire can
quench.

I turn My face toward the heavens.

The time draws near.

Soon the Spirit will descend.

Soon tongues of fire will crown trembling brows.

Soon the gates of the Kingdom will swing wide.

But for now —
for this moment —
I remain with them.

Their Teacher.

Their Son.

Their Brother.

Their King.

Their God.

The mountain holds its breath.

The earth tilts toward redemption.

And I —
I Am with them.

Always.

Even to the end.

Chapter 14: Home

The time draws near.

I feel it in the hush of the air, in the trembling of the olive leaves, in the way the light leans longer on the hillsides. The earth itself seems to wait, breathless, for something it cannot name.

I gather them — those I have loved until the end.
Not many.
Only a handful.
But from these few, the whole world will change.

We walk the familiar paths — out through Jerusalem's gate, past the gardens heavy with spring growth, up the slope of the Mount of Olives.
The city behind us glows in the sinking light — domes and stones catching fire from the setting sun.

The Eleven walk close, heads bowed, steps unsure.

They still do not see it all.
But they will.
Soon.

We stop halfway up the mount.
The grass bends in the evening breeze.
The stones are warm from the day's heat.
I look at them — every face etched into My heart.

Kephas, impulsive and broken yet bold.
Yochanan, the beloved, heart already ablaze.
Yaakov, Andrai, Philippos, and the others — some still bearing the dust of doubt, some the scent of hope.

They gather near, waiting.

The sun dips lower.

I smile — feeling their ache, their worry, their fear of what they cannot yet understand.
I too feel the pull of compassion.
I love them more fiercely than words can hold.

But I must go — so that He, the Ruach Hakodesh, can come.
Not as I came — clothed in flesh — but clothed in fire, in power, in presence.

The time is upon us.

Forty days have ended — forty days as a bridge between what was and what is to come.

A sacred hinge.

A time thick with divine preparation.

I lift My hands.

The words come not as command but as blessing — ancient, deep, woven into the fabric of creation itself.

"All authority in heaven and on earth has been given to Me.
Go therefore and make disciples of all nations, baptising them in the name of the Father, and of the Son, and of the Ruach HaKodesh.
Teach them to observe all that I have commanded you.
And behold — I am with you always, even to the end of the age."

Their faces lift toward Me, some with tears already welling.
I see the war in their hearts — the ache to cling, the call to go.

I step closer, touching each brow lightly with My hand —
sealing them with the blessing not of earth, but of Heaven.

"Wait in Jerusalem," I tell them, "Until you are clothed with
power from on high."

They do not understand the fullness of it yet.
But they will.

Soon.

I take a breath —
not because I need it, but because the moment is full, rich,
sacred.

I look once more at the city — the place of betrayal, the
place of redemption.
And beyond it, in the Spirit, I see every city, every village,
every heart that will soon awaken.

The time has come.

The veil between dimensions shimmers.

The earth grows thin beneath My feet.

They see it now — the way the air bends, the way the light
gathers.

I feel the pull — upward, outward, homeward.

My feet leave the soil.

Slowly.

Softly.

The grass still ripples where I stood.

Their eyes widen.

Kephas steps forward instinctively, hand half-raised as if to catch Me.
Yochanan falls to his knees.
Yaakov shields his face from the growing radiance.

I rise — not with violence, but with serenity.

The world falls away.

The wind carries the echoes of their gasps, their prayers, their worship.

I ascend—not only from earth to sky, but from completion to communion. The dust of Golgotha still clings to Me. The scent of sorrow lingers in My garments. Yet I rise—not in defeat, but in triumph. The grave is empty. Death, disarmed. Sin, silenced.

The heavens open — not torn with noise but drawn apart like a curtain revealing the greater stage.

For their sake, I ascend—so they may see, and understand. Higher than eagles, beyond the veil, past sky and stars, through realms known and unknown.

The Mount of Olives shrinks beneath Me — a stone cradled by hills, a cradle about to be rocked by fire and Spirit.

I see others now looking up trying to understand what they are seeing. I am too high for them to make me out. Light flashing too bright for their eyes.

Clouds gather — not heavy with rain, but thick with glory.

I pass through them.

Until I have vanished from their sight.

The air hums with soundless music — notes that shaped the stars now rising to meet their Composer.

Below Me, they still gaze upward —
small figures clinging to a hilltop,
hearts clinging to a Promise.

Suddenly — two angels stand among them, their garments
flashing like polished bronze.

"Men of Galilee," they say,
"why do you stand looking into the sky?
This same Yehoshua, who has been taken up from you into
heaven, will come back in the same way you have seen Him
go."

Hope floods the mount.

The disciples fall to their faces — some laughing through
tears, some trembling with wonder.

But I — I ascend higher still.

The gates of Heaven swing wide.

Now I step into what is beyond human comprehension— My
apparel changes, back into my heavenly body.
Home at last.

Though if you can truly understand...

I never left.

The veil is torn.

The heavens open.

Angels, who once wept at My descent, now rise in ranks to
greet Me. Seraphim fold their wings. Cherubim bow low. The
elders around the throne fall facedown, their crowns cast
before the radiance of My return.

The Four — the Living Ones — those who have never ceased to cry, *"Holy, holy, holy…"*
They stand — not on ground, for they know no dust — but in the eternal space around the Throne, hovering on wings that gleam with fire and eyes.

One has the face of a lion — fierce with royal might.
One like an ox — steady, strong, immovable.
One like a man — eyes wide with wonder, ever perceiving.
And one like an eagle — alight with speed and vision beyond horizons.

Their wings stretch and fold, stretch and fold — covered in eyes within and without, ever-seeing, never resting.

And then — the wheels.
The Ophanim.

They turn within themselves — vast, luminous circles.
Wheels within wheels, layered with countless eyes that pulse like stars.
They do not move as flesh moves — they shift as will moves, as glory moves.

And they see Me.

And they know Me.

The moment I cross the threshold of heaven's veil, their cry rises — not new, but deeper.

"HOLY! HOLY! HOLY is the LORD Elohim Tzeva'ot — Hosts who was, and is, and now returns as the One who lives forever and ever!"

Their voices shake eternity.

The wheels spin, glowing with fire.
The eyes within the wheels widen, reflecting My scars, My victory, My unveiled glory.
They move as one, encircling the Throne — not to guard it from Me, but to welcome Me to it.

Their worship is not ceremony. It is recognition.
They knew Me in glory.
They saw Me leave.
They watched the Lamb descend.

And now — they behold the Son returning, crowned with blood and majesty.

They bow.

The lion-face roars.
The ox-face trembles.
The man-face watches Me with awe.
The eagle soars upward in spirals of light.

And still they cry — *"Kadosh, Kadosh, Kadosh..."* *"Holy, Holy, Holy..."*
As they have always done.
But this time, they cry it not for who I was alone — but for who I have become:

The slain Lamb.
The risen King.
The firstborn from the dead.

The Throne burns with brilliance.

The Living Creatures bow lower still.

another sound rises.

Footsteps.

Thousands upon thousands.

Not the tread of angels, swift and weightless —
but the tread of those who once knew dust, pain, hope, and
hunger.

The ones I came to find.

The ones I would not leave in darkness.

I see them now — clothed not in rags, nor in sorrow, but in
garments of light woven by Heaven's own hand.

They come.

Mosheh — his staff still gleaming with the fire of Sinai, his
eyes shining with the fulfilment of every word he wrote by My
breath.
David — leaping forward, harp on his back, laughter and
worship burning on his tongue.

Samuel — my prophet who anointed him, oil still in hand.
Eliyahu — the whirlwind still in his hair, the fire still flickering
in his spirit.
Avraham — arms outstretched, as if to gather every son and
daughter into the promise now fulfilled.

Hannah who waited in the temple until her eyes saw me.

Shimon, who asked that his eyes not close until they saw
the messiah come.

Behind them — a multitude too great to count, yet I know
the number of them.

Prophets with scrolls rolled beneath their arms, priests with
linen robes unstained, widows and warriors, psalmists and
shepherds — every heart that ever yearned for Me without

seeing, every soul who clung to a coming hope in the shadow of death.

They fall before Me — not with fear, but with joy that splits the heavens.

They cast their crowns at My feet — crowns forged not of gold, but of waiting, of believing when the night was long and the dawn unseen.

They shout:

"Worthy is the Lamb who was slain,
to receive power and riches and wisdom and strength
and honour and glory and blessing!"

Their voices shake the expanse.

It is not a choir.

It is a tide.

A flood of gratitude rising to meet Me.

I see Yeshayahu — the prophet who glimpsed My glory in temple visions — now covering his face again, not in dread but in awe fulfilled.
I see Yeremiyahu — tears streaming, no longer for ruin, but for restoration.
I see Yechezkel — standing tall among the wheels he once described, now understanding the full circle of it all.

I see women —
Miryam of old, sister of Mosheh, tambourine lifted high.
Ruth, the foreigner, blood of kings in her womb.
Hannah, who lent her son to the altar, now receiving far more than she gave.

The children dance.

The elders' bow.

The warriors beat their swords into lyres.

They know Me.

They always did, though they had not yet seen My face.

They know Me now.

The roar of their worship rises to the Throne — a fragrance too rich for earthly lungs, a sound too wide for earthly ears.

I walk among them.

I touch their heads, their shoulders.

Not as a stranger.

As a brother.

As the long-awaited One.

The angels step back, singing still, but yielding the centre to those I came to redeem.

They, the rescued, become the choir.

They, the found, become the glory.

And Heaven watching sons and daughters crown their King.

The scroll, sealed from eternity, now rests in My hands. Worthy is the Lamb who was slain. I take it, not with hesitation, but as One who has already paid the price. I break the seal—not with force, but with right.

I have poured the blood upon the mercy seat—not of earth, but of the heavenlies. The contract is redeemed. Written in blood. Ratified in resurrection. Justified by love.

The law, once chiselled in stone, is now inscribed on hearts. The veil, once thick with division, is now torn by union. The curse, once heavy with judgment, is now shattered by grace.

Other angels take a step. A roar rises from the heavenly host, thunderous and pure.

"He returns!" they cry. "The Lamb! The Lion! The Son!"

I see them — Mikha'el, sword lowered in reverence;
Gavri'el, face blazing with holy fire;
multitudes beyond counting — rank upon rank, wingtip to wingtip, heart to heart — singing the Song of the Worthy Lamb.

The air shakes with it.

The universe itself bows toward its maker.

Multitudes upon multitudes sing a new song:

"Worthy is the Lamb who was slain—to receive power and wealth and wisdom and strength and honour and glory and praise!"

The gates are not closed to Me. They were never closed. But now, they open wide for the One who left and returns with scars as trophies. Heaven has seen victory in many forms— but never like this.

All heaven watches.

I lift My hands.

"The price is paid. The curse is broken. The gate is open."

The accuser is silent. The courtroom cleared. There is therefore now no condemnation for those who are in Me.

I see them—the ones marked by My name. The once-weary, now awakened. The once-shamed, now seated in honour. They are clothed in righteousness not their own. Washed. Covered. Free.

They do not yet stand here in glory, but their names are known. Engraved upon the palms of My hands. Written in the Book that cannot be erased.

The angels do not look at My scars with pity, but with awe. For each mark speaks of victory. Each wound, a key turned in the lock of death.

And the Father speaks:

"Sit at My right hand, until I make Your enemies a footstool for Your feet."

I sit at the right hand once more—not only as Word, but as the way, the door, Lamb. Wounded, risen, reigning.

The plan is not paused—it is fulfilled. The Son has returned, not only bearing the likeness of man, but bearing many sons and daughters to glory.

From Eden's breach to Calvary's hill, every shadow now finds its substance. Every sacrifice, its answer. Every silence, its Word.

I have come home.

But I do not come alone.

I carry the names of the redeemed, the echo of their prayers, the imprint of their suffering. I am their High Priest. Their Intercessor. Their Brother.

I do not forget Gethsemane, nor Golgotha, nor the garden of the resurrection. These are not just memories. They are milestones. Markers of love.

I sit. The throne is Mine.

The scroll is in My hand—the contract fulfilled; the covenant sealed. Written before time. Signed in blood. Authorised by obedience. Completed in sacrifice.

Heaven waits—but not in stillness.

Crowns are cast. Prayers rise like incense. The elders fall before the throne.

"Holy, holy, holy is the Lord God Almighty, who was and is and is to come."

The Lamb stands—alive, yet slain. Marked by mercy. Bearing the testimony of love that bled.

The Father rises from His throne.

Joy.

Power.

Glory.

Love.

The crown is placed.

Not of thorns — but of glory.

Not of mockery — but of majesty.

Crowned not with mere gold but with obedience, enthroned not with violence but with surrender

It rests upon My head —
a crown no forge has ever fired,

no smith has ever touched.
Not shaped by hammer and anvil, but by glory and
righteousness.

It gleams with gold — but not the dull yellow of earth.
This is **pure gold, transparent as glass,**
refined beyond time, heavy with weight and wonder.

Set within it are stones — not arranged for decoration, but
for meaning:

- **Sardius** and **jasper** — fiery red and translucent light.

- **Onyx,** deep and secretive, like wells that never run
  dry.

- **Emerald,** glowing green like the Garden remembered.

- **Sapphire,** as blue and endless as the pavement
  beneath the throne.

- **Topaz** and **chrysolite,** like sunlight caught mid-
  breath.

- **Beryl, amethyst, agate,** and **diamond** — each flashing
  with covenant and memory.

And others —
Stones unnamed by man,
carved from the first light of creation,
holding colours the human eye has never seen,
tones not found in earthly palettes.

They burn, not with heat, but with revelation.
Each one a song.
Each one a prophecy fulfilled.
Each one a name remembered —

a life redeemed, a tear collected, a soul engraved upon My heart.

It is a crown of kingship,
but also of priesthood,
and above all, of sacrifice.

Its band wraps around My brow like the circle of time itself
—
unbroken, eternal, perfect.

No jewel falls out of place.
No weight is too heavy.
This is not a crown I earned —
It is the crown I *became worthy to wear.*

For I bore the thorns.
Now I bear the glory.

And this crown —
this blazing, trembling, holy thing —
is only the beginning.

I walk again in the garden where Adam fell.

I hear the rivers that flowed before time had name.

I pass through halls lined with stars, among saints and angels, prophets and psalmists, all watching the unfolding of redemption with eyes full of wonder.

The veil is no more.

The Son has returned.

The scars remain.

The throne is filled.

The curse is broken.

The bridge is built.

And the story continues.

I begin to intercede.

And even as I sit, I prepare.

For one day, the heavens will split again.

And I will rise—not to return alone, but to bring them home.

But for now—I am home.

But even as heaven resounds, the earth waits — upper
rooms, trembling hearts, wind yet to come.
They will carry the flame now.
And I — I will be with them in fire, in breath, in Spirit.

Signed in blood.

Chapter 15: Echoes on the Earth

Below, earth still turns. Rome still marches. The Church begins to breathe.

I see into the future. See them gather in one place. I see fire descend. I hear languages spoken; hearts awakened. What begin in an upper room will overflow into every nation.

The throne room is filled with worship still ringing from My return. The elders bow low. The angels burn with reverence.

But now – Heaven holds its breath once more.

A holy silence spreads — one made not of stillness, but of anticipation.

I turn toward Him — the Spirit who hovered over the waters, who whispered to the prophets, who breathed life into clay and fire into men.

Ruach HaKodesh.

He stands — not as shadow, not as mist, but as glory veiled in tenderness, power wrapped in presence.

"We are ready," I say.

He nods — He has always known.

"You will go," I say gently, "not to walk beside them as I did, but to dwell within them."

He burns brighter — ready for a different purpose.

"As we agreed, you will remind them of all I have spoken. You will point them to the Father, through the finished work of the Son. You will be the wind they feel but cannot grasp, the fire they carry but cannot contain."

The Father speaks — thunderous, steady, loving:

"Go. Mark them. Fill them.
Seal them for the day to come."

Ruach nods in perfect unity.

The plan has always been threefold.

Creation. Redemption. Indwelling.

The time is now for the fire to fall.

The Spirit moves.

An echo of Himself goes forth — yet He remains, fully present.

They wait — just as I told them.

In the city where I was pierced. In the upper room where fear once whispered louder than faith. Doors locked. Lamps dimmed. Eyes searching the air for something they've never seen but now desperately hope for.

They do not know how close Ruach is. What form He would take. They do not understand but they obey.

They pray — not with eloquence, but with ache.

They miss My physical presence.
Kephas's voice is hoarse. Yochanan's lips tremble.
Miryam is there too. She speaks little, but I feel the weight of her knowing.
She is torn — aching for the Son she lost yet rejoicing in the Messiah I Am. Knowing the part that she and Yosef played in shaping and protecting My earthly form.

Her hands rest folded over her heart.
She remembers the promises whispered to her before
Bethlehem ever heard My cry. And then —
A sound.

Not a gentle breeze.
Not a whisper.

A storm within a storm — hurricane in force, tornado in
motion — and yet not a wall cracked. Only hearts. Only
heaven.

A wind — *violent, rushing,* alive.
It does not shake the walls.
It shakes *them.*

They lift their heads as the air thickens — not with dust, but
with Presence.
Their eyes widen.
Their knees buckle.

They bow low.

Flames descend.

They fight fear before recognition comes.

Real.
Not symbolic.
Tongues of fire, separating, hovering, resting.
One for each.
None excluded.
Not even the quiet ones in the back.
Not even the doubters who still aren't sure if they belong
here.

Ruach enters.

Their lungs expand with language they've never learned.
Their lips release glory in dialects they've never heard.
Persian. Latin. Libyan. Aramaic. Egyptian. Greek. Unknown, heavenly and unstoppable. Each one a song. Each one a sword. Each one a spark.

Outside, the city stirs.

The Spirit shifts, and they follow — feet leaving the upper room, hearts burning, into the open courtyard below.

Pilgrims from every nation draw near, first with curiosity, then with confusion. Then awe.
They hear the sound.
They hear *their* languages — spoken by Galilean fishermen and tax collectors.
They hear the Gospel — not in translation, but in *revelation*.

Kephas stands.

Once the denier. Now the preacher.

I see him — his jaw set, his eyes burning. The man who once wept bitterly now stands with a roar in his chest. He lifts his voice. And My Spirit rides every word like fire on the wind.

"This is what was spoken by the prophet Yoel," he declares.

"And it shall come to pass afterward
That I will pour out My Spirit on all flesh;
Your sons and your daughters shall prophesy,
Your old men shall dream dreams,
Your young men shall see visions.
And also on *My* menservants and on *My* maidservants
I will pour out My Spirit in those days."

They listen.

Thousands.

And I see it — the moment hearts crack open.

No longer theory.
No longer parables.
Now, power.

They cry out —
"What must we do to be saved?"

He tells them.
They believe.
They are cut to the heart.

And that day — *three thousand* are reborn.

I smile.

This is the Kingdom.
Not in courts. Not in cathedrals.
But in human hearts, now blazing.

They rise early — Kephas and Yochanan — their steps steady, their hearts still burning with the echo of flame. The hour of prayer draws near. The temple stands tall, unmoved by recent wonders, its gates polished but hollow.

At the gate called Beautiful — adorned with Corinthian bronze, radiant in the sun — a man is laid down. As he has been every day. Lame from birth. Over forty years of legs that never bore his weight. His hands stretch out, not in worship, but in desperation. He asks for alms — not healing. His hope is small, shaped by years of surviving, not thriving.

But they stop.

And I see it.

Kephas looks at him. Really looks. Not at the twisted legs. Not at the withered dreams. But beyond, at the man — the one I saw long before the womb ever shaped him.

"Look at us," Kephas says.

The beggar lifts his head, expecting a coin.

But he receives a kingdom.

"Silver and gold I do not have, but what I do have I give you: In the name of Yehoshua Hamashiach of Nazareth, rise up and walk."

He does not just speak the words. He reaches.

Hand to hand. Spirit to spirit.

And power flows.

His feet strengthen. Ankles stabilise. Muscles knit in an instant. Ligaments align under the force of glory. Before he even knows it, he is standing. Then walking. Then leaping.

He shouts — not in confusion, but in joy that splits the silence of the courtyard.

The temple erupts.

Crowds gather. Eyes widen. Whispers fly.

Isn't that the man? The one who begged by the gate?

They have no answers.

But the healed man clings to Kephas — like a child to a father. And I watch as a new kind of fear spreads — not of terror, but of awe.

Kephas stands again — this time not with denial in his mouth, but with fire.

"You stare at us as if by our own power or godliness we made this man walk. No. This was done in the name of Yehoshua, the Servant of the Most-High — whom you handed over and rejected... whom God raised from the dead. And by faith in His name, this man stands healed before you."

And the name spreads.

Faster than fear. Stronger than tradition.

The priests take notice.

The Sadducees stir.

The Sanhedrin trembles — for the One they tried to silence now speaks through fishermen.

But the man who once begged by the gate?

He walks freely now.

Not just into the temple...
But into destiny.

Time passes.

Not long. But long enough for opposition to rise.

The Temple stirs.

Not with worship — but with watchfulness.

Religious fear awakens.

Darkness gathers again — quieter this time, smarter.
It does not shout as it did on the day of My death.
It whispers now.
In corridors. Behind veils. Beneath robes trimmed in gold.

"What if He comes back?"
"What if the veil torn was not the end… but the beginning?"
"What if this wind and fire is not myth… but a sign?"

They speak low — but their panic bleeds into their palms.

Some saw the sky blacken.
Some felt the earth heave beneath their feet when I breathed My last.
Some stood in that court and heard the torn curtain scream.

Some saw Me ascend from a distance.

All heard My words.

And now, they hear the roar again — not from Golgotha, but from an upper room.
Tongues in languages they cannot explain.
Miracles by the hands of fishermen and tax collectors.

Blind eyes opened not by the Temple — but by the Name they tried to silence.

They now hear the disciple's words — And fear begins to fester.

"What if He is already here?"
"What if they are preparing the way for Him to return — in fire, not forgiveness?"

They do not yet understand the second coming.
But something deep in their bones begins to tremble.

"Silence the followers," they whisper.
"Silence the Name."
"Choke the fire before it spreads."

Not because they understand.
But because they are afraid.

They fear I will come back in wrath —
That I will return as they deserve.
That I will do to them what they did to Me.

But I am not returning to retaliate.
I am returning to reign.

And they cannot stop it.

But the fire has not faded.

So, they gather.

Not in prayer, but in plotting.

The same Sanhedrin that tore their robes now tightens them in secrecy.
They summon spies. They bribe informants.
They send warnings cloaked in formality — letters, scrolls, edicts.
They threaten prison, then deliver it.
They hope fear will do what cross could not.

"Cut off the head before it grows."
"Break the bones of this movement before it finds its legs."
"Make examples of the loudest. Maybe the others will scatter."

They do not see that persecution only fans the flame.
That pressure makes My Church pure.
That blood waters the roots of boldness.

They believe they are stopping Me.
But every attempt only fulfils what the prophets wrote.
Every stone they throw lands on the road that leads to glory.

But word of Me is growing.

A centurion leans against a column in Ephesus — the
bronze of his armour dulled by sun and dust.
He has seen wars. Held the line at the edge of empire.
Silenced uprisings with blood.

But this... this movement unsettles him.

Not because of swords — they carry none.
Not because of rebellion — they speak of peace.
And yet... they do not yield.

He hears the name again — not from a Judean rebel this
time, but from a merchant off the docks.
"Yehoshua," the man whispers while unloading dye and
incense. "The One who rose from the grave."

Later, a soldier in Gaul mutters it after healing in his own
home.
A servant in Rome sings it in the night while sweeping the
halls of a senator's villa.

"Who is this Yehoshua?" he asks —
Not aloud, not yet. But the question lingers like smoke after
fire.

The reports do not stop.

Prisoners changed. Families healed.
Gatherings in catacombs and courtyards.
Words spoken in languages no legion taught.
A new kind of courage — one that bleeds and does not
break.

He remembers hearing of the Nazarene —
Crucified like a criminal.
Buried like any man.
And yet...

Now He rises in conversation, in song, in warning.
The centurion does not understand.
But he cannot escape the echo.

Even Caesar's court will hear it.
Even Rome, robed in power, cannot mute a Name that will not stay buried.

But while the name spreads through empires and courts, it also burns in the hearts of the faithful — one by one, flame by flame. And now, one such flame begins to blaze.

Stephanos.
A man filled with faith and fire.

He serves with joy. He preaches with power.
Signs follow him like footprints behind a burning torch.

A faithful man, asked to serve but does much more.

They cannot argue with his wisdom.
So they lie.
They drag him before the Sanhedrin.

I see it from Heaven.

He stands where I stood.
Same stones. Same glares.
But this time, not for trial — for testimony.

He speaks.

The Spirit gives him words like rivers.

Avraham. Yosef. Mosheh. The prophets. The Holy One.
He tells the story they do not want to hear.

They gnash their teeth.
They raise fists.
They drag him outside the city.

I rest My hands on the arms of My throne. From My seat beside the Father — I rise. The stones are raised, but My eyes are on him. Faith burns brighter than fear. As earth prepares to silence him, Heaven prepares to receive him.

He sees Me.

His eyes lock on Mine, and his face shines like an angel's.

"Look," he says. "I see heaven opened, and the Son of Man standing at the right hand of God!"

They cover their ears.

They rush him.

Stone after stone.

His blood stains the road.
But his spirit soars.

"Master Yehoshua," he prays, "receive my spirit."

One more breath.

"Do not hold this sin against them."

He falls asleep.

And I catch him.

The first to follow Me in death.
The first to wear a martyr's crown.

And as his blood cries from the ground,
the fire does not fade.
It spreads.

I see My brothers now — no longer sceptics. No longer spectators.
They were slow to believe — but their roots run deep now.

Yaakov, once guarded, once watching Me from across the table with furrowed brow...
Now he leads with steady hands.
In Jerusalem, they come to him — the broken, the bold, the newly born again.
He answers with clarity, with conviction, and with compassion.
They call him *Yaakov the Just.*
His knees wear the shape of stone. His prayers shake the room.
He does not boast. He remembers.

Yehuda, the dreamer with fire in his eyes, walks the villages with scroll in hand.
He will write — short, sharp, unflinching.
A warning to the false. A charge to the faithful.
His words will not flatter, but they will cut away what does not belong.
And when they read it, they will know: he walked with the Truth.

My other brothers walk too — Yosi, Shimon — not in fame, but in faithfulness.
They will not write letters. They will not sit in council halls.
But they will build. Serve. Pray.
Quiet pillars holding up houses filled with praise.

And My sisters...

They are not named by men — but they are named by Me.
They did not stand in pulpits.
But they stood.

Miryam the younger walks among the widows,
bringing bread, bandages, whispered prayers.
She carries the memory of My hands in her own.

Shlomit, bright-eyed and bold, teaches the children in the
shadow of the temple —
telling them stories of the boy who carved toys from wood
and fed birds from His palm.
They listen.
They know.
And when they grow, they will follow Me too.

They do not follow titles.
They follow Truth.

Walk in power given by the Spirit.
They do not carry My fame.
They carry My heart.

But as My family rises, so does resistance.
While some carry My name in love — others carry swords to
silence it.

He rides hard.

Sha'ul of Tarsus — brilliant, zealous, proud. A blade honed
by law. He believes he serves God. But he does not know
Me.

He does not yet know what mercy feels like.

His eyes are sharp, but his heart is still stone.

It was he who gave the order to stone Stephanos.

The sound of it still echoes behind his eyes — yet he
silences it with purpose.
The road ahead twists through dust and heat.

Letters clutched in his hand.
Righteous vengeance in his breath.
The names of My people on his lips — not in prayer, but accusation.

And I wait for him in the light.

I do not come with sword or fire.

I come with *glory*.

A brilliance no eye can withstand.

And then —
I reveal Myself.

The light shatters the sky.

He falls.

The others stand frozen, speechless. They hear sound, but not My voice.
But Sha'ul — he hears Me.

"Sha'ul, Sha'ul, why do you persecute Me?"

He gasps. His face is buried in dust. His certainty cracks.

"Who are You, Adonai?"

"I am Yehoshua — whom you are persecuting.
But rise. Go into the city. There you will be told what you must do."

His hands grasp for something — but he sees nothing.
The one who led others by torchlight must now be led blind.

And I love him.

Even now — I love him.

Far from Damascus, I whisper.

A quiet disciple named Ananias.

He prays. He listens. He is not mighty in the world's eyes.
But his heart is soft.

I speak:

"Ananias."

"Here I am, Adonai."

"Go to the house on Straight Street. Ask for a man from
Tarsus named Sha'ul. He is praying."

I feel his heart quicken.
He knows the name. Everyone knows.

"Adonai," he says, voice shaking. "This man... he has done
great harm to Your people."

I do not rebuke him.

I simply answer with truth.

"Go. For he is My chosen instrument.
He will carry My name before Gentiles and kings and the
children of Israel.
I will show him how much he must suffer for My sake."

And Ananias goes.

Fear and obedience walking side by side.

He enters the house. He lays hands on Sha'ul's broken
frame.

"Brother Sha'ul," he says. "The Lord—Yehoshua—has sent
me..."

My Spirit enters.

The scales fall.

Sha'ul sees — truly sees — for the first time.

He weeps.

And heaven rejoices.

From this cracked vessel, I will pour revelation the earth has
never held.
He will write what angels long to understand.
He will speak of grace so deep it silences law.
He will suffer much.
He will finish well.

And the gospel —
will go to the nations.

Years will pass.
Centuries.
Ages.

But the flame will not die.

The Church will stretch across empires and languages,
rising through persecution and shadow. The fire will flicker in
catacombs, blaze in revivals, and smoulder quietly in
hidden hearts. Yet in every generation, there will be a
remnant—those who remember where it began. Those who
still wait for the light to fall fresh again.

Kephas waits in the dark.

The cell is dark.
Cold stone. Iron bands. The scent of damp earth and rust.
Kephas lies between two guards, chained at both hands,
sleep heavy on his brow — not from peace, but exhaustion.

Four squads of soldiers watch over him.
Herod has made it clear: no escape. No miracle. No second chances.
Passover ends at dawn.
They plan to execute him after the feast — to please the people.

But prayer stirs like incense in the night.
Not in the temple — but in a house.
Hidden.
Lit only by oil lamps and desperate faith.

They pray — not once, not with fancy words.
They cry out.
Miryam, mother of Yochanan Markos, opens her home.
It is full now.
Kephas's name on every lip.
Faces buried in hands.
Tears drawn from that deep place between fear and hope.

"Adonai," one whispers.
"Spare him. Not again. Not another one."
Another voice shakes — "We believe, help our unbelief."
They do not know what the Lord will do.
But still they pray.
Still they kneel.

And then —

Light.
Inside the cell.
Not moonlight — not torchlight — but glory.
It floods the prison like water crashing through stone.
The guards do not stir.
The chains do.

They fall from Kephas's wrists like dead snakes.
The angel touches him — a firm hand, not harsh.
'Get up quickly,' he says.
Kephas stumbles, half-dreaming.
The gate swings open on its own.
Iron obeys.
Walls part.
No one sees. No one stops.
They pass through the first guard post.
Then the second.
Then out into the street.

And suddenly — the angel is gone.
The wind brushes his face.
The stars look down.
And Kephas is free.

He stands there — heart pounding, sandals barely fastened,
breath visible in the cold.
"I know now," he whispers. "The Lord sent His angel and
rescued me..."

He runs — not to the hills, not into hiding.
He runs to the house of prayer.
To Miryam's door.

He knocks.
Once.
Then again.

Inside — prayers still rise.
No one hears at first.
Then Rhódē, the servant girl, hears the knock.

She runs to the door.
"Who is it?"
"It's me. Kephas."

She freezes.

That voice.
Impossible.
She doesn't open the door.
She runs back into the room, face pale, voice high.

"Kephas is at the door!"

They stop praying.

They do not shout in joy.

They argue.

"You're out of your mind."

She insists.

They shake their heads.
"It must be his angel."

But the knocking continues.

It does not sound like a ghost.

Someone opens the door.

And there he stands.

Kephas.
Breathing.
Whole.
Glowing with a freedom they barely understand.

Gasps.
Shouts.

Tears.
Laughter like lightning splitting grief in two.

He raises a hand.
They fall silent.
He tells them — briefly — what the Lord has done.

And then he leaves, quickly.
He must stay ahead of Herod's rage.
But their joy stays.
The echo of answered prayer.

Because when the chains of sin are broken, no cell can hold
a soul.
Even the jailers will believe.
Some fall to their knees.
Some take bread with those they once locked away.
Because My gospel breaks iron and heart alike.

I see them — not only those gathered in Jerusalem, not only
those in Antioch or Rome — but the ones yet unborn. The
ones who will kneel in caves. In cathedrals. In fields and
prisons and cellars and sanctuaries. The ones who will carry
My name where it is not welcome — and still speak it.

Ruach will not grow weary.
He will burn in the hearts of children and kings.
He will comfort the widow, whisper in the cell, roar in the
storm.
He will write letters on hearts — not stone.
And He will not leave.

They will try to silence Him.
With threats.
With fire.

With reason.
With blood.

But My Spirit is not chained.
He cannot be killed.
He is not an echo of Me.
He is *One* with Me.

Wherever He is —
I am.
Wherever He speaks —
the Father is known.

He will carry My words across oceans.
He will raise the lowly and humble the proud.
He will convict, comfort, correct, and call.
He will build the Church — not as an empire, but as a body.
One that bleeds. One that heals. One that remembers.

I see My disciples through the generations —
Some hidden. Some bold.
Some in pulpits. Some in gutters.
Some singing. Some silent.
Some with Bibles smuggled in darkness.
Some with no Scripture but only memory — and faith
enough to move mountains.

They are My body.

And I am not ashamed to call them My own.

The world will rage.

Lions will roar.
Thrones will fall.
Philosophers will rise, and kingdoms will burn.
But My Kingdom — My people — will endure.

They are the echo of Eden.
The outcry of the cross.
The proof that death has lost its grip.

Because the Church is not a memory.

It is a flame.
Still burning.

And the fire...

has only just begun to fall.

She is not perfect —
but she is Mine.

She stumbled at first, uncertain on her feet.
Her voice cracked when she tried to speak.
She was mocked, hunted, scattered.
But still — she rose.
Still — she sang.
Still — she carried My name like a lamp in the dark.

She has scars.
Some from the world.
Some from herself.
But she does not hide them.
They are reminders — not of failure,
but of a love that endures.

She wears no crown yet.
Her veil is torn.
Her hands are calloused.
Her feet are bruised from the road.
But her eyes —
Her eyes are fixed forward.
She walks toward the wedding still.

She has not seen Me in fullness —
not yet.
But she loves Me.
And I —
I Am preparing a place for her.
A table. A city. A day with no dusk.

And on that day,
when the trumpet sounds and the heavens split,
I will lift the veil,
wipe every tear,
and clothe her in white more radiant than dawn.

She will be ready.
And I will present her —
blameless. Beautiful. Mine.
The Bride.
The Body.
The one for whom I bled.
The one for whom I will return.

And even as she prepares, her lamp burns brighter — for
though the night deepens, the Bride knows her Bridegroom
is not far; and time bends quietly toward the last page,
where love and justice will speak one final word.

Epilogue: The Echo of the End

The earth turns. Still groaning.

My Name spreads — carried on tongues once silent, written in blood once shed, whispered by those the world tried to forget.

Time bends toward one final day. The trumpet will sound. The sky will split. I will be seen.

And every eye will see Me.

The Kingdom has begun.

But the war is not over.

I see what others do not.
The shadow lengthens again.

The serpent is bruised, yes. But not yet bound.
The grave gapes still for many.
And the hearts of men — though stirred — grow cold again.

I look now — from My throne, from eternity — and I see the nations rage.

I see the kings of the earth rise and fall, grasping at crowns that crumble in their hands.

I see pulpits flicker with fire and then grow cold.
I see prayers that rise like incense... and others that drift like ash.

I see those who use My name, My pulpit, for hidden gain— robbing the poor to fill their own tables. They have not

understood Yehudah's fall. It was not betrayal alone — it
was greed.

I see the ones who love Me — truly love Me — and the ones
who use My name to build their own empires.

I see sheep and wolves sharing the same pew.
I see wheat and tares still growing side by side.

They laugh in temples built to honour themselves —
altars shaped not by truth, but by ego.
Their sermons flatter. Their offerings boast.
They carve My name into banners,
but their hearts beat only for applause.

They bless their idols — success, control, fame —
and call them miracles.
They curse My Father in silence,
by lives that refuse His ways while claiming His promises.

They remake Me — not as the Lamb who was slain,
but as a mascot for their kingdoms.
A Saviour with no scars.
A King who demands no cross.
An image that does not bleed,
and so cannot save.

I see it now — halls robed in gold, incense rising, lips
repeating prayers they do not understand.
The veil I tore in two, they rebuild in booths:
"Do not go straight to God — come to us, for we have His
ear."
Statues are kissed. Icons crowned.
Not all in malice — but in blindness.
What began as honour has become confusion.

What was meant to point toward Me... now obscures My face.

Idolatry.

They think I do not notice. But I hear the prayers spoken to others in My place. I see hearts diverted by ritual, by pageantry, by fear disguised as reverence. They lift hands — not to the Father — but to what their hands have made.

The prophets warned them. The law carved it in stone: *"You shall not make for yourself a carved image... you shall not bow down to them nor serve them. "*Yet here they kneel — not before Me, but before memory dressed in marble.

I do not reject remembrance. But when the created is worshipped instead of the Creator, the line is crossed.

This is not honour. It is a quiet rebellion masked in devotion.

She claims to represent Me, but her heart is far away.

She sits on scarlet thrones — clothed in splendour not her own.
Adorned in purple and gold, jewels dripping from wrists that once held truth.
But her cup is full of filth.
Not wine.
Abominations.
The blood of saints.
The tears of the poor.
The silence of prophets silenced.

She rides the beast — many-headed, many-crowned —
a system born of pride, sustained by fear.
Her laughter fills temples where I am no longer named.

Where My words are twisted into chains,
and My name is sold for silver again.

She is called Babylon —
but she lives in many cities.
She wears many names.
She preaches prosperity but feeds on deception.
She calls herself a queen, but she is drunk —
not with joy, but with power.
Not with righteousness, but with the blood of My witnesses.

Her hands once raised in worship now reach for bribes.
Her voice once soft with intercession now commands the
nations to bow —
not to Me,
but to her.

And still, she says in her heart:
"I sit enthroned. I will never see mourning."

But I see her.

And I weep.

Not because she is strong,
but because so many follow her robe and not My scars.
So many drink, from her cup and not from the fountain of
life.
So many hear her lies and forget My voice.

But the hour will come.
Her fall will be swift.
Her destruction complete.

The merchants will wail.
The kings will tremble.
The heavens will rejoice.

For I will cleanse what she has defiled.
I will tear down what she has exalted.
And I will raise up a Bride — pure, radiant, unbought, unashamed.

She who sold My name for gain will burn in the fire of her own making.
But My Bride —
She will shine.

The days darken.

War drums echo again — not on hillsides, but in hearts.
And those who once walked in light... some will turn back.
Some will twist the truth into shackles.
Some will preach peace but prepare for conquest.

But I have not forgotten.

And I — I will not stay seated forever.

The books are open.
The scroll is still in My hand.
The seals will break — one by one.
The earth will reel beneath judgments it cannot explain.
The stars will fall.
The mountains will flee.
And every eye — every single eye — will see Me.

The seals are waiting.

And when they are opened — the earth will know terror like it has never known glory.

The sky will crack.
The moon will bleed.
The stars will fall like stones cast by an angry hand.

The bowls will be poured out.
The trumpets will sound.
The silence in heaven will be deafening.

The Lamb who was slain will rise — not with bruised
shoulders and bloodied feet — but with eyes like fire, a voice
like rushing waters, and a robe dipped in blood.

I will come with sword drawn.

I will tread the winepress of the wrath of El Shaddai.

I will return.
Not as the silent Lamb, but as the roaring Lion.
Not veiled in flesh, but clothed in fire.
My robe dipped in blood — not their blood, but Mine.
For I still offer mercy...
But mercy has a limit.

Time will end.

I will ride not on a colt this time —
But on a white horse, crowned, called Faithful and True.
My voice will split the sky.
And the Word — once spoken in love — will speak in finality.

And yet...

Even in wrath, I remember mercy.
Even in fire, I offer life.
Even in the end — I still long for the return of the lost.

Until that day, My Spirit remains.
My Word stands.
My people endure.

And I — I wait,
not in slumber,
but in intercession.
Watching.
Calling.
Preparing.

I came once.
I will come again.

"Behold — I am coming soon, and My reward is with Me."

And the world will not be ready.

Not in secret.
Not in whispers.
But in thunder.
In flame.
In glory.

And all flesh will see.

Some will run.
Some will bow.
Some will wail.

But no one will ignore.

I do not speak this to terrify you.

I speak it to prepare you.

Because I am coming again.

Not as the Lamb this time —
but as the Lion.

And the echo of that roar
has already begun.

Signed in blood:

The contract

Yehoshua Hamashiach